speakeasy

Karen Biery

Library of Congress Control Number: 2014953932

ISBN: 978-1-937958-78-7 - Soft Cover

ISBN: 978-1-937958-80-0 - Hard Cover

ISBN: 978-1-937958-79-4 - ebook

Red Engine Press
Bridgeville, PA
Printed in the United States of America.

To Louie for his memories

and to Ernie for the inspiration.

Other works

by Karen Biery

Chattels

believe

pieces

Acknowledgements

The "Thank You" list is always a long one for me. It's difficult to name each one in the special spotlight in which they deserve, so forgive my inadequate attempt and know that I could not have finished this project without your guidance, suggestions, and support from all of you.

First, to my treasured husband, Jeff and children—Adam, Anne, Brian and Avery, my amazing parents, Max and Evelyn Newton and precious in-laws, Bob and Laura Biery, my sisters—Vicki, Jill, Kellie and Tracy, my aunts and uncles—John and Carol, Barbara and Skip, my "in-laws"—John and Barb, Dick and Randy, Ted, and Denise, to my dear friend and confidant, Sandy Copeland and faithful life-long friend, Pat Riley—for your love, enthusiasm, belief and support. I love you all.

To my editors, be it personal or professional – Bill and Jean Esposito, Anne Cushman, Sue Stitle, Barb Biery, Hugh Earnhart, Joyce Faulkner, Pat McGrath-Avery, and Dwight Zimmerman—the two words "Thank You" are not nearly enough.

To the two men who inspired this story—Louie and Ernie—one I had the privelege of meeting, the other I came to know through association. Although both men are gone from this earth, their stories, as well as the many lives they touched, will live in my heart and these pages forever. Thank you, Louie, for your memories of the speakeasy, and thank you, Ernie, for the faithful witness of your life.

Foreword

The Volstead Act, that gave legitimacy to the Prohibition Era of the 1920s into the early 1930s, was a failure in prohibiting sobriety. What it did do was to spawn smugglers, manufacturers, and distributors to supply "bootleg" alcohol to all who desired it. The Flipperettes and other members of the Roaring 20s were going to have their alcohol from across the border in Canada, overseas from Europe or "moonshine" from the backcountry stills.

It was the speakeasy that characterized this period of American history by bringing together a stage for the birth of the blues, creative tones of jazz, the dancing of the Charleston, forgetting the horrors of World War I, and illegal booze.

On State Street, that distinctive street, was just such a place in Salem, Ohio. If walls could talk, the third floor of 378 East State Street would tell some interesting tales. In lieu of talking to walls, Biery opted to interview contemporaries who remembered that speakeasy. From those conversations she wove a historic novel that recalls the spicy life of that era.

The novel is rich in the dialogue that might have been heard on any given night on the third floor. Here also you find the teeming fabric of the patrons that attended the business behind closed doors. **speakeasy** is a careful blend of research and storytelling.

"The candles were hushed to darkness."
Hugh G. Earnhart

Professor Emeritus
Youngstown State University
Contemporary children's author
The Forgotten Pumpkin
Orange Frazer Press

speakeasy
whispered by those under its spell

A lonely man, a tired girl
A long, dim staircase that promised pearls.
Shady deals that have gone a rye
As the night's song ended in whiskey sighs.
Whispered passwords bid ado
To lives entangled by the mood
Of a clear liquid of fire and ice.
An illegal drink forms an illegal life.

A public right stolen
From the common and rich
That bound lives together by a habitual stitch.
A life bred with secrets
That is tired and worn
Until the day comes which all are forlorn.
Nothing was gained
And most was lost
Replaced by the madness that ultimately cost
Nearly all those involved
Something precious and dear ~
Their very life lost to fear.

All for a drink,
A night on the town
Left in whispers on the ground
For those passing by
To jeer and to judge
Of the pathetic lives ruled by a jug
That's filled with clear passion -
Whiskey or Shine -
Made from objects never intended to brine.
It left those afflicted
To wallow in pain
Until their last breath silenced their flame.

A decade of struggles in America's time
Birthed Bonnie & Clyde and organized crime
Left tragically abandoned
Too long to see
How tainted our history forever would be.
Greed and deceit
With invisible bounds
If crossed left life delicately found
Hanging in balance
Between living or dead
With life's last vision a Derringer dread.

For the blessed life
Ignored outside
The organized ring was spent in pride.
Blindly feign to possess its control
One drink or two, would never console.
Forever curious if this phase would pass
While wondering if this drink
Would be their last.
For who really knew if its tainted or clear
Yet are willing to sip
Ignoring the fear
For an hour of gaiety
Music, dancing and more
To escape the day's pressure
And settle its score.

The following is a list of characters by order of appearance, not importance:

Chester Willis, rumrunner

Chandra Minch, contemporary building owner

Kathy Hendricks, contemporary real estate agent

Isabell Ramett, seer

George Whiden, speakeasy trumpet player

Mickey Rollins, speakeasy bartender

The Pussycats

> **Valetta Hamilton,** lead dancer
>
> **Silvia,** secondary dancer
>
> **Bonnie, Glory, and three unnamed dancers**

Anna Lyla Timmons, speakeasy owner

Skelly Canter, mob understudy, nicknamed Slick

Hank Emmit, Lyla's half-brother, moonshine master mind, nicknamed Bean

Joey, Hank's moonshine partner, nicknamed Shorty

Johnny Pasquel, Lyla's bodyguard and speakeasy bouncer

Sarah Willis, Chester's wife

Percy, night janitor

Paul Henbit, the speakeasy doorman

Jack Little, Salem police officer

Nora, Chester and Sarah's housekeeper

Vincent Franciasco, Sabino Mob boss, nicknamed "The Stag"

Raffaldi Sabino, Vincent's second son

Vinchento Mariucci Sabino, Vincent's first born son

Felix Hanna, Lyla's attorney

Maria Rosa Mariucci-Sabino, mob boss' wife

Thelma and Ray Fluharty, Sarah Willis' friends

Brad Cotton, contemporary speakeasy partner

1

He stood immobile captivated by a thin grey line that appeared to split the sky in two. The lighter, lower level skirted the ground, taunting him with wind whispers of calm weather, in contrast to the thick charcoal-colored upper layer that smothered any thought of an easy trip, at least for this night.

Chester Willis roared the engine in his '29 Nash 400 and headed toward the Ohio River. The rain began in torrents as if a waterfall had cascaded on him. He took it as a sign that God did not approve, but he tried to justify his actions.

"I have to feed my family . . ." he whispered softly. "The mill only pays twenty-seven dollars a week. That's not enough."

His final word stuck in his throat and made him choke. *Enough . . . what is enough?* He knew justification for his actions held little merit, so he forced the thought from his mind.

The heavy sheets of rain made clear vision of the road impossible. He dodged clumps of mud and rock sliding from the steep embankment above the carved out dirt road. His car bounced and shook from every rut he didn't see or couldn't miss. He took a chance and pulled his left hand from the steering wheel to wipe the perspiration from his forehead. His palms were slimy with sweat forcing him to grip the steering wheel even tighter.

Suddenly, the impact of the falling tree slammed into the side of his car forcing it to the edge of the road. He jammed his foot on the brakes, but they seized. Debris littered the windshield as the driver's side glass shattered from the impact. The car began to tip. He lunged through the open window, desperately grabbed a heavy limb and clung to its slippery bark. His car slid down the slope leaving Chester's body suspended and exposed. Through the blinding blankets of rain, he watched his Nash tumble to a stop at the bottom of the ravine. The car's headlamps blew out in an explosive flash.

Chandra suddenly sat up in bed and gasped for breath. Her chemise was soaked. Her hair hung in damp strings over her shoulders. Colorful, close lightning flashes fragmented her restless thoughts. For a breathless moment, in silent awe she sat frozen.

Slowly she became aware of her surroundings. Her unfinished third floor apartment lay in shambles around her. A quick brush of her hand knocked the alarm clock off the bedstand and onto the floor. Impulsively, she tried to turn on her bedside lamp, to no avail. She fumbled in the darkness for her Kindle. The light from its screen was barely enough, but she found her journal and captured her dream.

Her mind relived each emotion as she re-read her scribbles. Satisfied with her words, she closed her journal. The scripted word 'speak' in her own writing made her smile. She ran her fingers over the letters. Her mind drifted to the first time she toured the building at 378 East State Street in Salem, Ohio.

With her face pressed against the dusty windows, she peered inside the empty building. Her eyes traced a flagstone walkway until she could faintly make out a white fence. The sun slid behind a cloud making it difficult to use the fading light to her advantage. She wiped the film from the window.

"Ms. Minch?"

"Yes," Chandra answered as she turned to face a real estate agent.

The agent's smile was warm and wide. "My name is Kathy Hendricks." She extended her hand.

Chandra shook it without thinking about the coating of road grime from the window on her own. "Nice to meet you. Thank you for coming."

"It's what I do." The agent made no mention of the dirt. "Let's get in here and see what you think."

Chandra pondered about the tours on the first and second floors and smiled in the dark as she remembered the first time she walked through what is now her third floor apartment.

"Now," Kathy hesitated before opening the door to the third floor. "I have to warn you. This is rough. No one has done anything up here for at least forty years. It used to be an apartment. You'll see what is left of it. Most of the partitions and suspended ceiling have been removed."

They walked into the main room. Pieces of the ceiling littered the floor. Faded wallpaper hung in strips. A claw-foot tub sat in the middle of the room. Scattered newspaper lay in party-favor fashion as torn bits of *The Salem News* stared back at Chandra.

"Wow! You weren't kidding. This floor is a wreck!"

Kathy thumbed through her folder. "Now, the previous owner replaced the roof four years ago. I know it looks bad, but it's all old damage. They also have signed a guarantee which would protect you if something unforeseen shows its ugly face."

"What about turning it into an apartment?"

"I gathered all of the information you would need to make an educated decision in that folder." She pointed to the one under Chandra's arm.

Chandra inspected the pages. Her eyes scanned the folder but her mind was too excited to retain a word.

"As you can see," Kathy continued, "this third floor spans two buildings. As it stands right now, you share this floor with your neighbor. You may choose to either divide it or purchase it from them. But, if you do, along comes all of the roof responsibility."

"I understand." Chandra's response was automatic. Her mind busily mapped out the floor plans for her apartment.

Excitement suffused Chandra as she stood in the center of the room. She knew it could work. As long as she had her computer, she could work from home. She liked the idea of a renter for the studio on the second floor and a restaurant on the main floor. Her thoughts returned to Kathy who was in mid-conversation.

". . . list of other properties . . ."

Chandra cut her off. "I don't think that will be necessary. I feel strangely centered with this one." She walked over to a mass of old doors neatly stacked in a corner. She was about to ask about them when they heard the sound of shuffling feet behind them. They spun around and saw an elderly woman who smiled at their startled reaction. Without Chandra asking for the purpose of the doors, the answer came.

"Those doors are from this building. This used to be an old speakeasy during prohibition." Chandra's mouth hung open.

The woman pointed to the oversized baseboard. "See how the baseboard goes up here," her finger pointed to the opposing walls as she continued, "and there? Those were the two stages, one for the band and one for the dancers." She pointed back to the stack of doors. "Those doors were placed anywhere the patrons entered or retrieved their bottle. See, they have bottle holes carved in them. They needed to be replaced often." She held her hand to her mouth as she whispered, "Because of overuse."

"How cool is that?" Chandra's voice escalated. Her mind filled with so many speakeasy questions that she did not stop to consider their uninvited guest.

The woman continued in a trance-like voice. "Salem actually had many speakeasies. Who knows the actual number? Some say five. I don't know. I've only talked to the people from this one."

A loud pounding noise interrupted Chandra's memories of that day. She sat in her bed and concentrated on the sound. After the third set of deliberate knocks, she realized it was not a dream. She opened her apartment door and ran down the long flight of stairs.

The same elderly woman from her memory now stood before her. Dressed in a simple housedress, sopping wet hat and a pair of saturated black shoes, Chandra gasped at her appearance.

Chandra tugged at her arm. "Please, come in." She watched the woman shiver. "You are absolutely soaked! Come upstairs with me. We will get you into something drier. Please be careful, though. The electric is out."

Together they climbed the stairs. Chandra's thoughts raced. She remembered seeing this woman several times in the past few months. Her first encounter was the day she looked at the building, and since that day she found her standing across the street, peering into the windows at dusk, or gazing up from the sidewalk. With each encounter Chandra tried to approach her, but the woman slipped away before Chandra could reach her. *What would bring her here on this dreadful night at this hour?*

Chandra moved the clutter from her kitchen table and placed a large candle in the center. She tried to make light conversation as she wrapped her guest in several blankets, but the woman sat still and silent. Chandra lit a few more candles. Soon a restful glow illuminated the room. Chandra slid into the chair opposite the woman and waited.

The woman's eyes remained fixed. After a long pause she whispered in defeat, "I am sorry it is so late. I had to come. They wouldn't let me rest."

2

"My name is Isabell Ramett. I am ninety-two years old. My sister, Anna, used to live in this apartment when a photographer rented the floor below her and a music store occupied the main floor. That was many years ago.

"When Anna had surgery and needed twenty-four-hour care, I volunteered to be her nursemaid. I spent many sleepless nights in this very room for this place is home to many restless spirits. Alone late at night they would come to me, only me. My sister was never bothered. When I tried to speak of it with her, she would scoff at my distress.

"Spirits?" she would question. "Dear Isabell, I have lived here for fourteen years. There are no spirits in this place."

"Yet, to me they would come. Some were angry, some sad, but most were happy to just share their experiences.

"At times they asked for my help. I delivered messages to their families. I spoke their confessions to their priests. Once, I went to a home to leave a box of letters, but the home no longer existed. A new building stood in its place. When I returned with the undelivered package, the spirit was furious. I tried to explain, but his eyes saw something very different from mine, so I returned and left the box by the front door. I guess that satisfied him because I never saw him again.

"One by one, my actions seemed to pacify them, until one evening I was bothered no more. The last three weeks I stayed with my sister were uneventful. I slept very sound without dreams, cries, laughter, or knocking. I finally felt peace . . . until three months ago.

"I knew of your coming one month to the day from when we met. Once again, my peaceful sleep had been disturbed. But these new spirits spoke only one name— Chandra."

Chandra held her breath at the mention of her name. She felt bewitched in this woman's presence, yet never threatened. Her pleasant countenance was oddly calming. Chandra hung onto Isabell's words as she continued.

"I encouraged them to let me help as I had the others, but they would not yield. They were anxious for your coming. The spirits spoke to me every night. At times they would stay until the early morning light layered its color on the horizon.

"The day of our meeting, I had no rest. They all came together. They knew you were close. My words would not comfort them. By six o'clock I was dressed and walking to this building. I sat on the bench across the street and waited for you to arrive. It was my only peace that day.

"I am old and I am weary. I can no longer hold them back. They are eager to tell their stories. When all is spoken, your role will become clear. My life is spent. It is your time now."

When Isabell finished speaking, her head rested in her hands. Chandra stared at the woman in disbelief. She then encouraged Isabell to come to the living room and sit in a more comfortable chair, but Isabell remained unmoved, silent, and waiting.

Suddenly Isabell's back stiffened. Her eyes suddenly opened wide and then her eyelids began to flutter. Her lips quivered and she mouthed words, yet she had no voice. She stood. Her chair toppled to the floor. She picked up a candle, carried it to the living room, and placed it on a lamp table.

7

"Come, come, my dear. Come sit with me a spell. There is someone here who wants to meet you."

The silhouette of the stepladder played across the unfinished walls as Chandra walked toward the wingbacks. A single white pillar placed on the table between them cast a dim light in the oversized room. Chandra pulled the other chair to face Isabell. On her lap was her mini, set to record.

The candle's wick withered until barely an ember remained. With a brush from something unseen, the light abruptly vanished. Only silence remained.

Chandra's heartbeat throbbed in her ears. The soft drumming sound slowly gave way to a faint hum of a male voice that grew louder and closer until Chandra felt his breath on her neck. Isabell's distant whispers reassured her as she covered her face in disbelief.

When Chandra opened her eyes, she stood in an empty bar. A lit candle sat on a table before her. Two large stages flanked the room. An old man pulled a trumpet from his weathered case and stepped onto a stage. He slid a stool to a microphone and began to play.

Music filled the room. His calloused, dark fingers pumped the valves with ease. He stopped mid-tune and tossed his request to a young man behind the bar.

"Hey, Mickey? How 'bout a tall one?"

"Ah, George. You know you can't have a tall one."

"It don't hurt to ask." He played a few more notes then said into the microphone, "Then a short one will have to do."

The young bartender swirled a jar of clear liquid and emptied it into a long-necked container. He tipped his head toward the liquor. "This stuff's for the payin' customers."

"What about the workin' man?"

The bartender laughed as he watched the last drop splash into a clear bottle. "The workin' man. Now that's a good song. Play it for me, George, and I'll give you a shot of courage."

George began to play his trumpet. He stopped to sing a few bluesy words now and again, and then played some more. He watched the bartender pour a shot glass of a darker liquid and carry it to him. The musician wrapped his thick fingers around the small glass, winked, and threw the fire to the back of his throat.

He coughed at the taste. "That suff'll kill you."

"Workin' man's liquor, George. Workin' man."

The room soon filled with people. Some came straight from the mills, their clothes sweaty, dirty and tattered. Others were dressed in the latest fashions—men in suits with matching hats, women in high heels, garter belts, and sequined satin dresses heightened with fringe. Even a few young children accompanied the adults.

The illegal liquor known as white lightning and blues and jazz music flowed throughout the room. Empty chairs sat at lonely tables while their guests gathered close around the bar. Many crowded the dance floor when the band played the Charleston.

Suddenly, the trumpet player leaned into the microphone and cleared his throat. "Ladies and gentlemen, for your viewing pleasure, help us welcome to our stage . . ." the drum roll gained strength, ". . . the Pussycats!"

Loud cheers and wolf whistles erupted as six women burst through the back door. They shrugged their cloaks to the floor revealing their costumes. Dressed in black and tan striped bustiers, black garters, and back-seamed stockings, the dancers wiggled their way through the crowd. Striped cat masks left only their eyes and ruby lips exposed. A long pussycat tail attached to the back of their ruffled panties begged for the drunken men to move closer, and follow them . . . all the way to the stage.

The ladies shimmied and bounced around the stage to the music. Their heels kept perfect rhythm through four music sets. Then with their bodies glistening with sweat, they picked up their cloaks. One dancer dragged her fur wrap on the floor behind her. They worked their way through the crowd and gathered their tips from the cheering intoxicated men while the women observed with interest. The children hid under the tables as The Pussycats disappeared through the back door. The room applauded for more, yet the dancers never returned.

"Last call," shouted the young bartender.

Waving patrons lifted their money or tokens high above their heads. Mickey worked feverishly to satisfy each request. When the final empty glass was slammed down on the bar, he began his evening count.

The room emptied as quickly as it had filled. The staff bustled, clearing the room of the evening's gaiety and drunkenness. With the ushering of the last man toward the entrance, the bartender picked up his own shot glass brimming with white lightning, tipped his head, and spoke to the woman leaning against the back wall.

"Speak easy, Lyla."

Without warning, a cold burst of air snuffed out the candle. Chandra and Isabell sat quietly in the darkness. Chandra's heartbeat thumped in her throat. She worked hard to suppress nervous laughter.

A faint light shimmered in the kitchen. She watched as Isabell rose from her chair and walked toward it. After waiting a moment, Chandra followed in silence. When she reached the kitchen door, she looked through the round bottle hole carved into the door. She saw Isabell seated at her kitchen table. A single candle burned in front of the woman. Chandra drew in a deep breath before entering.

3

Dressing tables filled the room. Six mirrored vanities lined the perimeter cluttered with lipstick, powder puffs, hairbrushes, combs, and various hairpins. Shoes, discarded, tattered stockings and feathered boas peppered the floor tossed amid a cluster of handbags, coats, and keys. Several empty shot glasses filled a tray.

Isolated in an unused corner sat a lone Windsor chair. A man's hat hung on its ear. A cane rested beside it. Folded neatly on the seat was a single white handkerchief. Chandra picked it up and ran her fingers over the red embroidered initials—*ALT.*

The door flew open. Excited chatter from two of the dancers bounced around the room.

"How much, Silvia?"

"Eleven dollars! Can you believe it? Four dollars again from my guy." Her whispers grew louder.

"Which guy?" Valetta eyed her reaction curiously.

"The one in the striped suit and black bowler. How about you? How much did you..."

"Shhh." Valetta held her finger over her lips in warning. "They're comin'."

Four more dancers entered the room—their hairdos disheveled, costumes askew, and red lipstick either smeared or missing. Valetta rolled her eyes.

The six women undressed quickly and slid into their street clothes. Within a few minutes the room was empty. Chandra listened as their chatter moved farther away. She took a few steps toward the door and froze when she heard someone running.

Silvia burst through the door. Her fearful eyes darted. She ran to her dressing table and rummaged through the paraphernalia. She picked up a pearl earring and clutched it in her hands. Her wet cheeks glistened.

She ransacked the other ladies tables though removed nothing. She ran to the door and pressed her ear against it. She stared at the lone chair, lost in thought, until she surrendered and moved closer to it. She wiped the tears from her face and grabbed the hat and cane. Her eyes fell on the white handkerchief. Her fingers barely touched it when she heard voices approaching. She replaced the hat and cane and hid behind the costume rack on the opposite wall.

"Why would it be in here?" Annoyance laced her strained voice. "This is the girl's dressing room. How could your hat be in here?"

His muffled reply made Silvia cringe. She held her breath when a hand rattled the doorknob.

"That's strange. It's never locked." Lyla responded.

Silvia felt faint. She held her breath and tried to keep the clothes rack from toppling over. She heard the key enter the brass lock. This time the door swung open. Lyla Timmons entered the room accompanied by a well-dressed man.

Lyla tapped her foot and crossed her arms, "Well?"

The man glanced around the room. He saw a hat setting on a chair. He picked it up and inspected the inside satin band. His fingers slid under it searching for his answer. He smiled in triumph.

"This is it," he snapped.

"I'll ask you again, Mr. Canter, how did it get in here?"

"I don't know. Maybe someone stole it."

Lyla's belly laugh rang through the room. "Stole it? Why would someone steal that ugly black bowler?"

He glared at Lyla without speaking. Once again, his fingers fumbled through the satin. He fanned several large bills inches from her face.

He sneered through gritted teeth, "For *this!*"

Lyla's mouth hung open. The large amount of money held barely an inch from her face was a foreign experience. She stammered to find words.

"Now show me out of here!" His tone was accusatory and menacing.

He gripped Lyla's arm tightly and repeated his command. Lyla stood firm. He pulled on her arm again. Shifting her weight, she lifted one leg and ground the pointed heel of her shoe into the top of his foot. He yelled in pain and bent to massage his foot releasing his grip on Lyla's arm. When he stood, his eyes met Lyla's .40 caliber Derringer.

Her hand and voice held steady. "It's mine and I'm not afraid to use it." Her eyes narrowed. "Now get out and don't ever come back. We don't want your kind around here!"

Skelly Canter stood and in a single move stomped his foot in her direction. Lyla never flinched. She fired a single shot.

"Consider that a warning. The next bullet has your name on it." She lifted her steady finger and pointed toward the door. "Now, get out!"

Skelly dusted off his hat, pulled on his shirt collar, and walked out the door. His deliberate footsteps pounded until they faded in the distance.

Lyla's eyes scanned the room. She noticed one of her white handkerchiefs lying on the floor. She picked it up and wiped the stock and barrel of her pistol. She lifted her long skirt and placed it back into her leg garter. She closed the door quietly behind her.

Silvia listened until it was quiet. She slipped from behind the clothes tree. She wiped away the sweat and tears; her face still held the burden of anxiety. She tiptoed toward the door and crept out unnoticed.

A second candle flickered and faded to an ember.

4

Chester Willis stepped out of the bank at precisely four in the afternoon. The copper clock on the corner chimed as he waited to cross the street. He opened the heavy oak door at the bottom of the staircase without any problem.

His footfalls became heavier, more deliberate with each ascending step. His leather work boots slid across each tread and thumped into the riser with a thud. When he reached the door, he paused, one hand resting on the door handle, breath labored. He tapped three times, and followed with a series of four loud knocks. A single eye peered through the peephole.

"What say you?" came in a whispered voice.

"Speak easy, Lyla."

With the correct password spoken, the hidden locks released. Chester walked into the small room. He walked to a narrow door and began a second and different sequence of knocks and taps.

Again, the same whispered voice spoke, "What say you?"

"Lyla, speak easy."

With the accepted reverse password, a hand appeared through a round opening. Chester placed three dollars into the hand and watched as the bottle passed through the same hole. The small round door closed with a snap.

Chester smiled as he entered the room. The two men sat at the bar. From the tone of their slurred speech, it appeared they had occupied their seats for quite some time. He settled into a stool three spaces to the left.

He watched the ballroom begin to fill with its colorful people. The speakeasy drew an unusual crowd. Its liquor was the best in town. Not a single patron had died from the white lightning it served and the owner was determined to keep it that way.

The proprietor was a robust woman in her forties. She stood only five foot two but her demeanor commanded respect from all who entered her presence. She had fiery red hair that matched her lipstick and nails and always stood in the back shadows. If a patron became unruly, just a glimpse of the red dress swishing in the offender's direction was usually enough to calm things. Only a few times did she need to draw her gun.

Her name was Anna Timmons, though all who entered whispered the name Lyla. She had never married or seemed to fancy the company of any man. Her laugh was as ruddy as her complexion and her voice was low and gruff. She intimidated other women, but the men revered her. It wasn't easy being the sole owner of a drinking establishment during prohibition, but if anyone could pull it off, it would be Lyla.

The idea for the password came to her in a dream. She preferred her middle name to her first but never used it because of its origin. Her first name came from her maternal grandmother, Anna, given for her sweet and honorable disposition. Her middle name came as her father's suggestion, and after his death, discovered the name 'Lyla' was his lifetime mistress. Her mother refused the speaking of the name and further jaded her daughter's view of men and their usefulness.

She had very few friends and many enemies. She did not flaunt her money to the outside world, except in her taste of clothing. She only wore red. Not the color choice for a woman sporting her hair color, but that was why she did it. She was a self-made woman who never followed the rules and most of the time it paid off, especially on the third floor of 378 East State Street in downtown Salem, Ohio.

When the government passed the laws against public drinking in 1920, she saw it as a huge opportunity. She quickly jumped on the purchase of a three-story building and by the summer of 1921 Lyla's speakesy opened its secretive doors. All of the carpenters were paid cash for their trade. Darkness covered the trash removal, and Chester Willis was named as the rumrunner.

Chester's most recent purchase, a black Ford Coupe with a flathead V8 engine, hailed one of the fastest cars in Salem. He purchased it a few weeks after the tragic loss of his beloved Nash 400. He worked at Mullins during the day but spent the evenings and early mornings traveling the back roads to a private dock on the Ohio River.

He arrived at the dock five times a week precisely at one in the morning. Two toothless men, whose real names he never knew, arrived by boat between one-thirty and two o'clock. Most of the time the craft held three five-gallon jugs of white lightning but occasionally only two appeared. On those days, Lyla scowled.

A case or two of brown bottles always accompanied the jugs. The dark liquid held the same hue as the bottle and served as the moonshine for the hired help. Its bitter taste signified a much weaker variety than the clear liquid served to the paying customers.

Once a week the two men gave Chester a single bottle filled with a pink liquid. A thick coating of red wax double sealed the spring-loaded cap. As it was Lyla's special prize, the bottle was refused if its hallmark displayed damage, be it broken or cracked.

Chester flashed his lights as the boat approached the dock. His engine idled in waiting. He jumped out of the car and handed the tall, gangly man a brown envelope. He stuffed it into a rusty box without counting the contents. He trusted Lyla. After all, he was her half-brother, child of her father's southern Ohio lady friend.

The stout man, whom he nicknamed Shorty, handed the special bottle to Chester. Both men stood silent as Chester carefully inspected the wax for any sign of tampering. Once satisfied, he nodded his head and gave the tall man he nicknamed Bean the sign. Within five minutes Chester's trunk was loaded with the 'shine. His idling car sped out of sight while the men paddled quietly down river.

Chester whistled as he rushed back to Salem. He parked his car around the corner and raced up the staircase to the speakeasy. After the knocking and passwords were accepted, he revealed Lyla's brew from beneath his coat.

His sigh punctuated his relief. He had made another successful trip. This was his one hundred and sixty-third trip of that year without any problems from the law. He hoped his one hundred and sixty-fourth would turn out the same. He smiled as he placed the bottle into Lyla's hands.

She lifted the clear container into the air and shook it gently. The pink liquid swirled in response. Her fingers traced each wax tendril closely inspecting the color until a thin smile passed over her red lips.

"Well this looks beautiful, Chester."

"Thank you, Ma'am."

"Any trouble?"

"Didn't see anyone. Real quiet evening."

"Good. That's what I like to hear."

Chester tossed his keys to Lyla's protector, Johnny Pasquel. His oversized hands snatched them from the air. He slipped out of the building and carried away the jugs and cases of bottles without detection.

Lyla's high heels clicked across the well-used floor. Chester followed her to her private office. As instructed, he waited in the doorway. Before Lyla finished counting his payment for delivery, he felt Johnny's breath on his neck. The ritual was always the same.

"Here you go, Chester." She placed thirty-five dollars into his hands.

"Thank you, Lyla."

She looked at her bodyguard, "Johnny, show Chester out." She turned from both men and closed the door. Her muffled voice echoed in the narrow hall, "See you tomorrow."

Chester did not reply. The door was already closed. With the completion of his transaction, he received a handsome payment. Johnny followed him to his car and watched Chester pull from sight.

Chester looked in his rear view mirror but never saw Johnny walk around the corner. He lit the evening's last cigarette and blew the smoke out of his window. The thin night air seemed restless.

His eyes darted in all directions as he slipped through the back door of his house. The floorboard groaned his arrival. He tiptoed into his bedroom. His wife, Sarah, was sound asleep. Listening for the tranquil rhythm of her deep breathing, he knelt at the bottom corner of the bed and fumbled for the tattered mattress covering. He shoved the wadded bills as far into the stuffing as he could reach.

Sarah stirred from the movement. "What time is it?"

"Shhh. It's late," he whispered. "Go back to sleep now." He slid between the sheets and held his wife in his arms.

"How was the double shift at the mill, dear?"

"Fine, Sarah." He patted her bare arm. "It was just fine."

The squeeze of wet fingers snuffed the candle flame to darkness.

5

Percy, the night janitor, watched Skelly as he brushed passed him. He sloshed the mop and grey water over the floor for the second time. "Until the water is clear," Lyla's words echoed in his thoughts. Normally, he was happy to have the work, but tonight he was tired. He wanted to go home. He wanted to feel the softness of his pillow . . . his blanket . . . and. . . . A tap on his shoulder interrupted his fantasy. He turned to face Skelly Canter.

"Yes, sir. Can I help you?"

A sinister smile covered Skelly's face. "Well, I certainly hope so." He extended his hand.

"The name's Percy, sir."

"Percy." Again, the smile returned. "Now that's a fine name. My name's Skelly."

The men shook hands. Skelly wrapped his arm around Percy's shoulder trying to persuade him to move away from any listening ears. Percy held fast.

"I gots to finish this, Mr. Skelly, sir, or Lyla won't pay me."

As if written for a film Skelly grinned at his luck. He quickly whispered a question. "And how much does Lyla pay you to...," he glanced into the murky water, "... mop the floor?"

"I gets six dollars a week."

"Six dollars?'

"Yes, sir. Six dollars." Percy straightened his stance at the proud vocalization of his weekly pay.

Skelly tightened his grip on Percy's shoulders and whispered, "How would you like to make an extra six dollars?"

Percy jumped. "Well, yes sir!"

Skelly held his fingers to his lips.

Percy leaned into him and whispered, "Doin' what?"

Skelly nodded his head and smiled.

A murmur of hushed whispers blew out their candles.

6

Mickey's responsibility as the lone bartender was immense. Not only did he watch the patrons for theft, inappropriate activity, or belligerent drunkenness, but he also held responsibility for the dancer's safety and effectiveness. He kept a keen eye on the band members and the unsupervised children, as well as the lady clientele. His most important duty was to be aware of the threat of a raid.

He had worked behind the bar for nearly a year without incident until one Thursday evening in July. The crowded room and lack of ventilation made the bar oppressively hot. But the heat of the milling bodies paled in comparison to his desire for Valetta.

She finished her third set and approached Mickey at the side of the bar.

"Mickey, I need something." She fanned her scantily covered body with her hands.

Mickey glanced toward Lyla and she nodded with approval. The look on Johnny's face told a different tale, but Mickey filled a shot glass with the dark liquid.

He watched Valetta scowl at the color, but she emptied the glass.

A man at the end of the bar stumbled off his stool. His words were slurred and slow. "Hey sweetie. Get out there and show us what you've got!"

Valetta smiled at the obviously drunk man and patted his hand. "In a minute, baby." She fanned herself again, "This girl's gotta cool down."

"Not you. You like it hot." He moved closer to her.

She ignored the looming threat and turned her attention toward Mickey. "One more?"

The drunken man lunged at her and tore what was left of her clothing. He wrapped his arms around her half-naked body and began to dance with her. The women in the room shrieked.

Mickey jumped from behind the bar while Johnny ran from the back of the room. Both men wrestled the drunkard to the floor, with Johnny adding a few punches to the drunkard's face and ribs. Mickey got up, wrapped his coat around Valetta and ushered her to her dressing room. His cheeks were speckled with blood.

The silent crowd parted for Johnny as he dragged the man's bloody body across the floor. No warning was necessary – all knew not to interfere. Johnny tossed the man onto the floor in the cloakroom and locked the door.

With Valetta's final set thwarted, the crowd grew impatient. Mickey's absence fed the patrons' annoyance, and the voices in the room escalated. They shouted for the missing bartender.

"Hey! How about another drink?"

"Where the hell is he?"

"Are we gonna see the little lady dance?"

"Hey Mickey! Where are you?"

Mickey walked behind the bar unaffected by their demands. He picked up a bar towel and started to wipe the spots off the shot glasses. All eyes were on him when he raised his hand in the air.

"One at a time, you wolves! One at a time or you'll get nothing."

His comment settled the crowd to low murmurs. He lined two rows of glasses rim to rim, emptied the contents of a bottle, and disbursed them to the thirsty crowd. The gaiety continued with a few evocative comments about Valetta's exposure. Mickey pretended not to hear them.

Johnny walked to the sentry post to check on Paul and immediately became irritated to find him missing. He groaned at the number of guests bidding for entrance and hurried with multiple knocks and passwords. With irritation lingering at the forefront of his thoughts, he did not notice the line began to dwindle.

"What say you?" he began in his usual mundane tone, wondering about Paul's whereabouts. He peered through the peephole and saw only the barrel of gun. The voice behind the weapon was gruff and low.

"Open up! Police!"

Johnny lunged at the copper rod that hung beside the door. Immediately the lights in the ballroom went out. With the second tug the chandeliers lit the room.

Lyla worked the crowd to settle the nerves of the newcomers. She whispered soft instructions to them.

Mickey opened a trap door built into the backside of the bar. He slid every shot glass full or empty into the void. With one push of a foot petal, all of the bottles of moonshine stored on the back shelf slid from view. Blaring music and the cries of the crowd muffled the clatter of the glass bottles with their illegal contents.

The sentry, Paul, a scrawny crippled man, appeared to relieve Johnny of his temporary duty. His faked nervous stutter held the law back just long enough.

"Wha . . . t . . c . . . c . . . c . . . can I d . . . d . . . d . . . do for you off . . . ff . . fficers?"

"Open this door and step aside."

"D . . d . . d . . . d . . o you ha . . . a . . . a . . . ave a res . . . s . . s . . . erva . . . a . . . a ...tion?"

"Open this door or we'll knock it down!"

Paul slowly turned each thumb lock. The officer's incessant pounding continued until the door swung open. The jolt forced Paul to the ground. No one bothered to help him stand.

They burst into the room to the joyous melody of the crowd leading the band. The only drink in sight was soda. One official grabbed a glass from a man's hand, smelled it, tasted it, and threw it against the wall where

Lyla was standing. Slivers of glass fell into her hair. All faces turned to the red-haired woman whose eyes hurled daggers at the offending officer.

Lyla swaggered toward the uniformed man. The swish of her red dress sounded her deliberate approach. He tossed orders to the crowd ordering them to line the walls, ignoring Lyla's clenched teeth. Drops of soda stained her bodice. She grabbed the police officer's flailing hand. Her red fingernails immediately drew blood. Surprised at her aggression, the man fell silent.

She sneered, "My patrons will do no such thing."

"Stand back, Anna, or you're under arrest."

Her laughter filled the room. "For what?' Before he had time to answer she added, "For having a dance party? For listening to the band? For having fun in this dreadful town?" Her body language left little doubt of her disdain for Officer Jack Little.

Jack leaned close to Lyla, mirroring her abhorrence and spit, "For serving alcohol."

She laughed aloud and turned toward the silent crowd. She swept her hand in the air and yelled, "This gentleman, as I so loosely refer, thinks I am serving alcohol!" Moans erupted from the people. "Have I served any of you alcohol?"

A massive "NO!" came from the patrons.

Lyla turned to Officer Little. "You will leave but not until you pay a dollar for my broken glass." She pulled a sliver from her hair and ground the shard into his hand. Unable or unwilling to suppress her smirk, she held out her hand for the money.

The officer huffed and screamed obscenities. He knew she served alcohol, but once again failed to prove it. As his mouth continued to spew his limited vocabulary of choice words, his mind reeled a plan to catch her and bring her to justice. Today Lyla had won, the next time she would not be so lucky.

Silence snuffed his candle.

7

Chandra felt her skin turn to ice. Every hair on her body tingled and stood at attention. Isabell's face was drawn and sallow. Her tired eyes revealed fear. "Gather all of your candles, dear. Every one you can find. It looks like we will need them all."

She ran through her dark apartment and gathered pillars, tapers, votives, jars, and a large triple-wick candle. With an armload of wax she dumped them on the table. Her hands shook as she struggled to set them upright. Isabell patted the back of her trembling hands.

"Soon, my child, you will have met them all. It will be difficult at times to follow for they will fight for your attention. Their candle will light when it is their turn to speak, but they may not be able or willing to share all they desire in a single lighting. It may take a number of occasions to expose their full story; be it because of their long hidden guilt, which will be difficult for some to openly reveal, or the restlessness of others anxious to speak, hastening them along. The intensity of the flame will give you a hint whether they are finished or still have more to say, but make no mistake only they can snuff their flame, and also be aware of their conversations when two candles are lit together. Do not give in to your frustrations if you become lost in some of their staccato revelations, for in the end, it will be clear. Why the spirits choose to speak this way is a mystery to me, but I have always found it to be so." She tapped on the red rim of the triple wick candle. "When this one is lit, all else will be snuffed. For this one is Lyla."

The pair sat in silence. Chandra jumped as a single white pillar burst into flame.

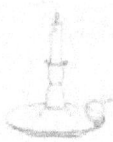

Valetta Hamilton carried a Chinese takeout container by the thin metal handle. Its fragrance filled the hallway as she knocked on the door.

"What say you?"

"Speak easy, Lyla." She waited impatiently for the opening of the locks. Her stomach growled as she sniffed the edges of the white cardboard box.

From the opposing side of the unopened door came a gruff voice, "Smells good enough to eat."

"Ah come on, Johnny. A girl's gotta have some time to eat before she dances for the wolves."

The door swung open. "I wasn't talking about the food." His grin spoke volumes.

She slapped his husky arm. "You're a real sweet talker, Johnny Pasquel. A regular ladies man." She made no attempt to mask her sarcasm.

Valetta carried her usual Chinese order of a 'Number One' to the girl's dressing room. She was always the first to arrive and sat alone to enjoy her meal before dressing for the night's show. As her chopsticks fished the bottom for the last morsel of ham mixed with scrambled eggs a quiet tap sounded on her door. It was Johnny.

She sat on the edge of her dressing room table and he in the chair in front of her. She wore only stockings and bustier. Their flirtatious notes lasted a few minutes. Johnny's comments were mostly off-color while Valetta tried to swing the topic away from sex. Johnny usually won. When their rendezvous ended, Johnny ritually hooked the back of her stockings and left with the empty carton of her 'Number One.'

Valetta was the first woman Lyla hired for the club. For nearly three years, she was the sole dancer. She performed a modest style of strip tease though never over-revealing. The men would hoot, "Take it all off!" or "Bare it all!" but Valetta left them wanting by never giving in to their requests. She slinked from table to table lingering long enough for the men to adorn her with their tips. The dragging of her fur punctuated her final exit. No matter how loud the requests for an encore, when she slithered her wrap between their chairs, they knew she was finished. Desire for nudity forced their return, and the liquor aided in their belligerence.

Lyla knew Valetta had her eyes set on one man, and Johnny would not allow his woman to be viewed as risqué. "Always leave them panting for more," he warned. "Believe me you will be paid handsomely for it." Moreover, he was right. Her bustier and stocking band burst with bills. Her tips paid for her rent and her wardrobe. The only gift she ever wore was a diamond ring from Johnny, but only after her act. She did not want her clients to know.

She danced six evenings a week and knew all of the staff. She was twenty-six, five-foot-four, and a green-eyed brunette. Her powdered cameo complexion accented her petite figure, though her legs were long and slender for her height. She wore her skirts tight and short and her neckline plunging. With her fringe strategically sewn to accentuate her shape, the men loved to watch her jiggle and swing. Although she pretended to be relieved when Lyla added the rest of the dancers to her act, she resented sharing the spotlight and the money with the "floozies."

On the celebration of her first anniversary, she arrived earlier than normal. She stopped at the bar before entering her dressing room. She tossed her words to Mickey.

"What's a girl gotta do 'round here to get a drink?"

Mickey wiped his wet hands on a white bar towel, "What'll it be?"

Valetta laughed, "It's my anniversary." She leaned into the bar, her bosom nearly spilling from her bodice.

"How about somethin' special?" She raised her eyebrow and slowly licked her lips.

Mickey choked on his thoughts. Her playful aura left him speechless.

"How about the payin' customer's fire, Mickey?" She batted her false eyelashes. "Would you do that for me?"

"Yes, Miss Valetta," he spoke in a near-trance voice. "I'd do anythin' for you."

Valetta wiggled on her bar stool as he poured a shot of the clear liquid. His eyes fixed on her cleavage. She threw the first shot to the back of her throat, swallowed, and licked her plump pink lips.

She slid the glass to Mickey and stroked his moist hand. She whispered, "How 'bout another?"

He poured two glasses to the brim, slid one to her, and wrapped his hand around the other. After a wink and nod they knocked back the liquid fervor together. He slid his fingers across the ruffle of her bodice allowing them to dip slightly below the surface. Valetta never flinched. Mickey grabbed the rest of the bottle and followed her to her dressing room. This marked the beginning of a Tuesday evening ritual. It was Lyla and Johnny's night off.

Mickey's hand cleared the bench in her dressing room. He watched as she popped each button open revealing more of her soft skin. She allowed him to touch and play until his obvious arousal. She turned from him and let her dress fall to the floor. She placed her hands on the wall and forced her body into him. He fondled her and pulled her hips to him. She moaned from the movement.

His gentle thrusts were pleasing to her. She clawed at the wall with pleasure. He moved her wet hair from her shoulders and kissed the back of her neck. He played until both were fully satisfied.

She lifted the bottle from her dressing table and took a long drink. She turned her naked body to her lover and offered him a drink. After briefly caressing what he desired, he took the bottle from her and finished its contents. They dressed in silence.

Heated desire filled most Tuesdays behind a locked door in her dressing room. Although she had accepted a promise ring from Johnny, her sexual passion fell to

Mickey and they acted on it as much as possible. The simple touch of Mickey's fingers skirting her bare skin along the edge of her plunging neckline was the only sign needed to ignite her desire for him. His footsteps and bottle were quick to follow but slow to be finished.

Laughter smothered Valetta's candle.

8

Chester woke in the middle of the night. Anxious sweat soaked his body. He crawled to the bottom of his mattress and forced his hand through a torn seam until his fingers found a thick wad of cash. He counted his bills. Satisfied with the correct amount, he relaxed his shoulders.

He had no reason not to trust Lyla. His pay of thirty-five dollars was always the same. He rarely counted it, but a whispered word from an unseen onlooker cast doubt.

As silent as possible Chester pulled as many rolls of money as his fingers touched. The dark room and Sarah's consistent tossing made the task difficult, yet Chester had to be certain. He managed to find seventeen payments for his rum rides. The rolls held the same amount—thirty-five dollars, except one. His hands trembled as he counted it for the third time—twenty-five dollars.

His hands shook at the thought of the missing ten dollars. He cursed himself for not counting it. The whispering faceless voice nagged him. He stared at the twenty-five dollars. Lyla had cheated him.

His candle went dark and then suddenly rekindled.

Chester cashed his thirty-dollar-and-seventeen-cent paycheck for one week's work at the mill. He had only five hours of overtime, but it made a difference. He pulled an additional five dollars from his rum money out of his pocket and added it to his week's pay. He handed the money to Sarah with a smile.

"Thirty-five dollars?" she shouted with a skip in her voice. "The extra money sure will come in handy." Sarah stroked his whiskery face. "You work too hard, dear."

Chester managed a smile. He hated lying to his wife, but try many times as he did, he could not tell her about the illegal runs.

Sarah was a woman of strong faith. She went to church every Sunday and Wednesday evening Bible study. She was great friends with the pastor and his wife and invited them to dinner once a month. She enjoyed their company but hosted them for Chester's benefit. He only accompanied Sarah to church on holidays.

He managed to keep his extra curricular activity a secret, but when he entered the large stone church for the first time, it was difficult not to choke on the communion wafer. He followed Sarah to her regular pew. To his surprise, the woman who passed the sacrament plate to his wife was Valetta Hamilton. She smiled at his presence and squeezed Johnny's arm. He leaned forward and nodded to Chester. That was last Easter. Chester made excuses for Christmas so Sarah went alone.

She never nagged her husband about church. Chester was a good man and she left it up to God to lure him into the fold. She spent many hours in prayer about her husband's faith. Sarah even hired a Christian housekeeper, Nora, who prayed daily for Chester's salvation.

Chester was a good provider so when he decided to buy a new car, Sarah never questioned his reasoning. She did not ask about the missing Nash 400, why the new Ford's engine had to be a V8, or why he needed to drive nearly eighty miles an hour.

Occasionally, on a sunny Sunday afternoon Chester took his wife on a joy ride. She did not care much for the speed in which he traveled, but after witnessing Chester's delight in the performance of his Ford, she sat quietly in the passenger seat and prayed for their safety.

Chester watched Sarah count his pay for the third time. She shuffled the dollar bills from one pile to the next until she was satisfied at her creative financing.

She smiled at her husband, "We will have seven dollars extra." She fanned the money in the air. "Did you hear me, Chester? Seven dollars extra." Her smile widened, "God is good."

"And so are you," he added with a smile.

"I am off to the market. Do you want to go?"

"No, I believe I will stay here. I have a few things to tend to."

"I'll return in two hours. I need to visit the butcher."

Chester smiled again. That would give him plenty of time to visit Lyla. "Two hours it is." He kissed her on the cheek and watched her walk out the door.

He drove downtown as quickly as he could, ran up the stairs, and knocked on the door to no reply. He knocked again and waited. After a few minutes he placed his ear against the door. He heard voices, but they seemed far away from the entrance. As often as Chester came to the speakeasy door, he was not permitted to have a key. Only three people had that right—Lyla, Mickey, and Johnny. Again, he knocked. He heard footsteps approaching and pulled his ear from the door. He began his series of knocks. An irritated voice interrupted the sequence.

"I heard you the first time!" The voice huffed, sighed, and whispered, "What say you?"

The gruff encounter made Chester pause. He knew that voice well, though he had never heard it come from inside the speakeasy before. Irritation in this voice was far from normal. A different voice interrupted Chester's thoughts.

"What say you?"

Chester jumped back from the door. Twice the question came, yet asked by different people. He moved into the stairwell. His reply was stuck in his throat. He wanted to see Lyla. He wanted to ask about the missing money, but something in the pit of his stomach told him to flee. His gut reaction won the argument, and he fled down the staircase never once stopping to look at the man watching from the top.

Out of breath, Chester burst through his kitchen door. Nora's hands tidied the kitchen, though her Bible lay opened on the table. Chester ignored her request to join her in the study and ran into the bedroom. With Sarah not expected to return for at least another thirty minutes, he knelt on the floor beside the mattress.

His fingers groped under the mattress and withdrew all the money he could feel. He moved to the opposite side of the mattress and began pulling clusters of rolled cash. Though he rarely counted it, he always wrapped a rubber band around each payment. He found each unspent money roll save one. With the wood floor littered with rolls, he began to count.

"One, two, three . . . thirty-five." He opened the next wad. "One, two, three, four . . . thirty-five." And another, ". . . ten, eleven, twelve . . . thirty-five."

Time after time the result was the same. He had seven more bundles to unwrap when he heard Nora and Sarah talking. Their voices came closer and Chester panicked. He tossed the last of the cash on the bed, stirred the covers and threw his body and blanket to cover the money. The blanket settled to its position just as Sarah opened the door.

"What is going on in here?" Sarah's hands were fixed on her hips.

Chester pretended to be startled from sleep. "What?" He rubbed his eyes sleepily.

Her voice immediately softened. She tossed Nora a disapproving glance. "Chester. Are you feeling all right?"

His plan had worked. He spoke in a groggy tone, "I . . . I don't feel very good." He added just before her next question, "I think it was something I ate."

Sarah walked to the edge of the bed as Nora stood in the doorway. She touched her cheek on his. "You don't feel feverish." She gently stroked his hair, "Would you like me to draw the curtains?"

"That would be great." Again, his nerves caused his face to flush.

Sarah pulled the curtains, kissed him on the forehead, and tiptoed out of the room. Chester heard the women discuss his actions.

He waited only a few minutes and pulled the money from underneath him. He counted the bills in the light from a tattered curtain. It was all there. Each stack held thirty-five dollars but one. He replaced the money into the mattress and walked to the window to fix the curtain as Sarah had. The last thing he saw was Nora standing on the front walk. There was no doubt that she saw him; her body language spoke volumes.

Chester's candle blew out with a sigh.

9

Skelly entered the speakeasy as one of the last customers of the evening. He made no eye contact with Percy as he walked through the password door. Importance and necessity scripted his part to avoid suspicion of involvement.

He took a seat at a table covered with empty glasses, two of them broken. He pulled his silk handkerchief from his suit pocket, dusted it over the glass shards on the chair, and watched as they bounced on the floor. This was the second night he visited Lyla's establishment in hopes of the opportunity to approach one of the dancers.

He set his sights on Silvia the first night. Her short brunette hair damp with sweat fell in sexy strings across her flawless face. She made no attempt to move them as their eyes met.

Skelly lifted four dollars in the air and wiggled his index finger signaling her to come closer. He watched as Silvia shimmied over to his table. She was beautiful to him. Tall, toned, but not horribly thin. Her hazel eyes twinkled when she danced especially when she had the stage to herself. Pretending to be a bit shy when she worked the room left most men vying for her attention. Skelly felt certain she was a master at the art and knew how to work the room as well as the customers and by the amount of money tucked in her bustier, he was right.

She held the tip of her fur tail in her hands and stroked its softness. When she extended it to Skelly, she exposed her moist skin. She leaned into him to accept his generous tip.

Skelly smiled and pulled it away from her lifting the bills into the air. She made a move to snatch it from his hands, but he pulled them further from her reach. He did it twice.

"Hey!" she yelled, half annoyed.

"Not so fast there, Sugar. This man wants something in return."

Silvia bent over nearly spilling from her costume. She stroked the bottom of his chin and continued to flirt.

"And what would that be?"

Skelly smiled and gently pulled her fingers from his face. He placed the bills in her palm and whispered, "I haven't decided."

Silvia tucked the bills into her bodice inches from his face exposing all she owned and smiled. "Well, Sugar, you let me know when you figure that out and I'll be there."

Skelly grinned to himself. They did not call him Slick for nothing.

His flame flickered and then stretched to a thin flaxen glow.

10

"Nothing speaks of innocence like pearls," Skelly repeated as he snapped the lid of a velvet box.

Seated in his casual room, he stared at the clock certain it had stopped. With each rhythmic tick, the minute hand hopped to the next position leaving that second lost in time forever. After an eternal movement of five minutes, Skelly left his apartment to take a walk, snatching his black bowler just before the door closed.

With each breath of the night air his confidence grew. He found his thoughts wandering to the smell of Silvia's skin more often than perfecting his plan but decided it was fine to allow that fantasy as long as he kept it to himself.

A howl of a cat in heat made him jump. A nervous frisson ran through his body. Where am I? He turned in a tight circle searching for anything that seemed familiar but found nothing. Convinced he could not have walked far; he turned to retrace his steps and ran into a brick-hard barrel chest.

"You lost, Slick?"

The sound of his nickname from an unrecognizable voice convinced him he had wandered into Irish territory.

"Nice hat," he spat with sarcasm.

His heart pounded as he slid his hand toward his revolver. His pocket was empty. A crooked grin covered Skelly's face. Forcing his body to live up to his nickname, he fanned his hands in the air allowing time for his eyes to search the perimeter. He saw no one.

"Nice night for a walk, don't you think?"

"A walk?" the big Irishman laughed.

"Sure. There is nothing like a walk to clear your head." Skelly raised his hands again and used the opportunity to reconfirm. He was right. The man was alone. "It's a clear night." He leaned into his opponent and added, "And we are alone."

"Yeah," he stumbled as he tried to lean into Skelly. "A long walk to nowhere."

Skelly's shoulders relaxed when he affirmed his suspicions—the man was drunk. Lucky for Skelly his reactions would be slow. After all, the big guy couldn't follow a simple conversation.

After a moment of hesitation, Skelly threw a heavy punch to the man's abdomen. He watched the man moan and fold in half. A swift kick on his back forced him into the bushes along the sidewalk. Skelly brushed a leaf from his arm and turned to walk away. When he reached the street corner, he molded his body into the shadows. The man's body lay still, yet Skelly felt no comfort. He changed his course and ran for blocks until finally resting in familiar territory.

Dismissing the shame he would feel if any of the family had seen his open show of fear, he fled up the fire escape to his apartment. Safely inside, he began to slow his breathing.

In his left bottom bureau drawer rested his Colt .38 Super. He admired the mother-of-pearl grip fitted for his hand. His silver cursive engraved nickname seemed to glisten no matter what the light.

His bowler placed gingerly on the floor beside him begged for its story to be brought to the spotlight again. Skelly picked up his hat, read the maker's name aloud, and slid his fingers around the silk interior band. Steady fingers opened the note penned in his handwriting stained with an odd shade of brown.

April 8, 1929,

I received this hat as a token

the day I bought my first car.

It was a frosty day in April despite the brightness of a cloudless sky. Often he peered out the sole window in the trivial office of mob boss Vincent Franciasco Sabino, also known as The Stag, and hoped the warmth of the sun would remove the incessant chill. Skelly, sitting at his desk, had just put his Colt in the top right-hand drawer when suddenly the door flew open with such a force that it bounced against the wall. Skelly got up from the desk and was met with the figure of a large Irish ruffian.

"Who are you?" Skelly retorted.

The man did not answer. His eyes moved over Skelly's body and attempted to peer behind him.

Suddenly Skelly recognized the thug. His weight had increased by nearly double since the previous year, but his body language left no doubt that this was the number three man in the Irish mob. Skelly silently cursed the fact that had the intruder barged in just a moment earlier, his Colt would be in his hand and not in his desk drawer. He forced himself to remain calm.

"Where's The Stag?"

Skelly held out his hands while taking two steps toward his desk. "Well, look around. Obviously he's not here."

"Says who?'

Skelly winced in disgust and shook his head. His feet took one more step. "Uh, that would be me."

The Irish moved into Skelly's personal space. His white teeth revealed his youthful age though his demeanor seemed old and unskilled.

"I've got a message for Vincent," the 's' sound hissed through his teeth.

Skelly rolled his hand in the air Vincent style. "I'm listening."

"Listen up, twerp. The message is for The Stag, not . . ."

Skelly pointed to his own chest. "Slick."

The man cackled and closed his eyes for a few seconds. That was Skelly's chance. He moved behind his desk and sat in his chair. The right-hand drawer was still open. The Colt was just a few, tantalizing inches away. He had to be careful.

"Ok, Slick, my message is for Vincent and Vincent alone."

"Well it's apparent he is not here so if you want to get a message to him give me a second and I'll write it down." Skelly pretended to shuffle the papers on his desk with his left hand, while slowly easing his right into the desk drawer. He picked up a fountain pen with his left hand and held it up. "Okay, I've got it." He found himself staring down the barrel of a Smith and Wesson revolver.

"I'm thinking instead of writin' it down I can get the message to him another way," said the Irish mobster.

Skelly pulled the trigger of his Colt. His bullet blew through the desk and lodged in the Irishman's leg. Recoiling in pain, the Irish mobster fired a wild shot that shattered the ceiling light bulb. Skelly fired one more shot. The thug lay dead on the floor.

Skelly watched the dark blood begin to form a puddle. Gore speckled his desk from the first hit. He tore a corner from a piece of paper and scribbled some words on it. Moments before ruin, Skelly rescued the man's hat from the growing pool. He folded the note and tucked it inside the interior satin band.

Vincent walked through the back door and smiled. "I see you've bought your first car."

Skelly nodded. He placed the black bowler on his head. It was his first hit, and it felt good.

That memory, mixed with the adrenaline of that day, saw Skelly to the bottom of Lyla's staircase without him recalling the drive. He opened the door just as two men walked through the threshold and fell onto the sidewalk laughing. Skelly stepped over the cackling drunks and climbed the staircase toward Silvia.

As usual, he was one of the last to enter. After the exchange of the knocks and passwords, he seated himself at the end of the bar.

Mickey hurried around the shouting mob. "Last call!" he bellowed, forcing the crowd into a frenzy. "One at a time, I said!" Annoyance surrounded their responses.

Mickey abutted shot glasses that stretched nearly four feet across the bar. Patrons placed a coin or token in front of their claimed glass. Mickey lifted the last call jug. It was an oversized container filled to the brim with white lightning. Its long neck gave great control for long-term pouring. He started at one end and finished at the other never lifting the bottle once. With the glasses full and payment placed the chant began:

"Drink, drink,
until the fire is gone.
Savor the flavor.
Join in our song.
For tomorrow will come
And we hope to be here
Drinking and singing
Without any beer!

Raising their glasses in unison they nodded their heads and tipped them toward Lyla. With one voice they shouted, "To Lyla!" All drank together.

The room shook from the multitude of glasses slammed together onto the bar. As usual, a few broke into splinters leaving tiny drops of blood to float atop the spent liquor. Mickey began to gather the unbroken glasses and clear the patrons away from the area.

Rarely did one linger after the last call song. It was an unspoken house rule that seldom needed enforcing. Skelly watched most of the patrons funnel toward the door while he waited for Silvia. He could hear her laughter before they made eye contact. Skelly motioned for her to come closer.

Something about him attracted Silvia. He was not particularly handsome, but his confidence made up for that. He stood a few inches shorter than she even without heels, but that did not bother her either. He had a beautiful smile and twinkling eyes that lit her heart when they met. He always wore a suit. His shoes were polished. Only his hat cast oddness. Yet to Silvia, she could live with the hat. Perhaps she would buy him a new one.

He held out his hand to her. "Hello, Sugar. Did you have a good night?"

"It's better now that you're here. I missed you." She crossed her arms, winked, and stomped her foot. "You're late!"

"Couldn't be avoided."

She waited for more of an explanation though none came. She smiled. That was what she liked the most—he was mysterious.

"Let's get outta here," she whispered.

"Where to?" He winked.

"My place."

"Your place?"

She batted her eyes and shook her shoulders. "Walk me home?"

Skelly grinned. "It would be my pleasure, Sugar."

They walked arm in arm to Silvia's door. Skelly watched her nervously fumble for her keys and took that as a sign to wait one more day. Cupping her hands inside his, he placed the velvet box in her palm.

She jumped in surprise. "What's this?"

"A token."

"A token of what?"

He nudged her hand. "Open it."

Silvia slowly opened the lid and gasped. "Oh, Skelly. They are beautiful!"

"I thought they would grace your ears perfectly." He fondled her ear lobe.

She placed the opened box into his hand and fumbled to replace her old earrings with the pearls. She shook her head until she could feel the dangle touch her skin.

"How do they look?" she toyed.

Skelly placed his hands to her cheeks to stop the swinging motion. "Perfect. They look perfect."

Silvia threw her arms around his neck. "Thank you, Skelly. I love them."

"I'm glad."

They stared at each other for only a moment before Silvia felt uncomfortable. Her smile turned to a frown. She hesitated to reply until she had enough courage.

"But why?"

He grinned forcing his eyes to dance. "What you mean is what do I want, right?"

Silvia stuttered at his presumptuous approach. "Well, I . . . uh . . ."

Skelly threw his head in the air and laughed. It echoed through the empty street. Once again, he placed the box into her hand and patted the back of it. He watched the look of concern melt from Silvia's face. That's what he wanted. Now she was ready.

He touched the long silver threads on her left ear and followed them down the large swinging pearls at the bottom. "This one is for keeping me company tonight."

Instinct made Silvia fondle her right earring. She added, "And this one?"

Skelly met her hand around the expensive gift, leaned into her, and gently kissed her cheek.

"This one? Hmmm. . . ." He stroked his chin. "I haven't decided, Sugar."

Now enjoying the game, Silvia echoed her response from last night. "Well, Sugar, you let me know when you figure that out and I'll be there." She gave Skelly a quick peck on his lips. "Good night. And thank you." Just before she closed the door she whispered, "See you tomorrow."

Skelly whistled all the way back to his parked car proud of his plan and its progression. Soon, all would be in place.

The resonating sound of "Shhh" snuffed the flame of both candles.

11

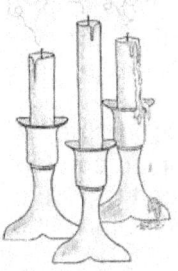

Chester followed the Ohio River to the dilapidated dock at Rockery Bay. He blinked his Ford's headlamps as he had done many times before. The responding light came on cue. He responded with the final flash and opened the coupe's door.

The sound of his footsteps on the wet planks echoed against the river's banks escalating the sense of unknown watchfulness. Twice he slid off the walkway to hide only to chastise his reaction as unnecessary. He continued onto the end of the slippery surface.

In a departure from the standard routine, he waited for Bean to secure the boat to the dock. Assorted river sounds—lapping waves, current gurgles, and occasional splashes of things falling into the water made Chester edgy. Low whispers carried over the water. He stared into the darkness until the lantern lit Shorty's face.

The man's stout body waddled up from the long bow. His hands were empty.

Chester hesitated when he saw that Lyla's bottle was missing.

"We ain't got none." Shorty's words fumbled from his lips. "None . . . nope, sir, none." His slurred talk continued while he lifted the first wooden box of moonshine.

Chester extended his hands for the first case of liquid fire. Bean walked past him and tossed it into Chester's trunk.

"Humph," he huffed. "This shit gets heavier every week."

Shorty managed a muffled chortle while he pulled the second case from the boat. His hand-rolled cigarette stifled his words. Only Bean understood his comment. The two erupted into hushed chatter.

The long-established routine quickly filled Chester's trunk with liquor. Staring at his empty hands he began to stammer.

"But, what of Lyla's bottle? What should I tell her?" His pathetic tone rippled across the oar's waves. Cruel laughter swirled around Chester.

"Tell her she can do without," a sneaky reply resonated. He jumped at the notion that it came from behind him. An eerie chill transfixed him.

Chester coughed at the thought of facing Lyla. "But . . ."

The men laughed. Their voices now sounded distant and hollow. "Tell her it wasn't ready. We'll bring it to her in person."

Shorty's sinister retort magnified Bean's comment. "Yeah. We'll git it to her in person." The men snickered.

Chester stood frozen in place as their laughter continued long after their shadows disappeared. He ran to his Ford. Even after he slammed the driver's door shut, he felt no comfort.

Once before he arrived without Lyla's special tipple. He shivered at the unpleasant memory and promised himself he would not permit the abuse again.

"I won't allow it!" He slammed his fist on the steering wheel. "They said they would bring it. I'll just tell her that." Convinced that he could calm her before her temper flared, his shoulders relaxed. "They said they would bring it," he whispered again.

Chester drove his coupe down Sugartree Alley with his headlamps off. His watch read ten minutes past three. He was early. He lit a cigarette and watched the paper's edges flare with the tip's glowing embers as he inhaled in deep draws. The smoke curled around his nose and wafted with the breeze out of his open window. Droplets speckled his windshield. He checked the time again.

He opened his car door, flicked his cigarette ashes, and stood. As he closed his door he heard footsteps approach from behind. Chester spun to face his opponent. The alley was empty. He listened for any movement. Convinced he had spooked himself, he smiled and flicked his butt into a growing street puddle where it fizzled and hissed until it became silent.

Lyla met him at the door. Her eyes searched his empty hands, but before she spoke, he offered, "They said it wasn't ready. They said they would bring it to you in person."

She offered no response, just a huff of disgust. She held out her hands for Chester's keys and tossed them to Johnny.

Chester followed Lyla into her office. His rehearsed speech about the missing ten dollars was difficult to start. After stammering for the words, he blurted his thought.

"Lyla, I was short ten bucks."

Clutching his pay in her hands, she sneered at his comment. "What did you say?"

Her red hair fell into her eyes.

Chester stuck out his chest. "I said I was short ten bucks."

"Are you accusing me of cheating you?"

Chester's face turned white. "I . . . I'm just saying I was short ten bucks."

"And who always gives you the money?"

"You do, Lyla."

"So if I always give you the money, then I cheated you?"

Chester felt Johnny's presence behind him though he dared not turn around. "This is not what I wanted to happen," he thought.

Lyla drummed her long, red fingernails on her desk. Each tap challenged him to advance. Her other hand slowly lifted her skirt searching for her pistol.

Johnny butted his chest against Chester's back. "Do you want me to . . . ?"

Lyla waved off his question with a nod of her head. Her hand found her gun and in a split-second drew it from her garter.

Chester held up his hand in defeat. "I don't want . . . trouble."

"Too late now, Chester." She gritted her teeth.

"Now, Lyla, calm down. I just thought you should know. I just noticed I was ten dollars short. I thought it was a mistake. I didn't think you cheated me." He lowered his arms. "I wasn't accusing you of anything." He attempted a laugh, though it sounded like nervous stutter. "I just wanted to tell you . . . thought it was a simple mistake. I'm sorry."

Lyla eyed Chester and returned her pistol to her garter. She crumpled his money in her hand and stepped toward him. She held his pay tightly to his chest. "Go on . . . count it."

She shook her head. "Mother always said not to trust a shifty man." She turned from him and tossed her final thought, "And I guess she was right." She could not resist adding, "You can't trust someone who can't trust."

Chester rolled the money and shoved it deep into his pocket. He wrapped his hand tightly around the wad of cash and followed Johnny in silence.

He replayed the scene. Why did he apologize? Lyla was the one who cheated him out of the money, and then aimed her gun at him?

Outside Chester's car, Johnny tossed him his keys and turned away in silence. He stood a distance away, arms crossed, waiting for Chester to leave.

Chester started the engine yet did not shift the transmission into gear. He stared at Johnny through the rain-coated windshield. Half of him wanted to rush back up the stairs and demand his ten dollars while the other half screamed at him to flee while he could. He struck a match, lit the end of his cigarette and counted his cash. Again, he was ten dollars short.

Enraged, he fought a silent battle within himself. He stared at Johnny, arms folded with his feet spread shoulder-length apart. Chester decided he would return on foot, undetected by Lyla's henchman. Anger forced him to confront Lyla and this time he would not be intimidated.

Johnny watched Chester light his cigarette and drive away. He took in a deep breath of the cool evening air and wiped the sweat from the back of his neck. He knew Valetta waited for him, and he smiled at what was promised.

With one step he kicked a stack of coins and watched them scatter across the sidewalk. The sound of metal on brick echoed in the empty alley. His eyes followed each coin until the last spun to a stop. He did not bother to look around. He was convinced he was alone.

He dropped to his knees. His thick fingers fumbled to pick up the loose change. As he reached for the last coin he heard a muffled pop. He shot to his feet but before he could confirm his fear, his body slumped to the sidewalk. The last thing he saw was the sight of a tire iron falling inches from his face.

Three candles blew out together in a flash.

12

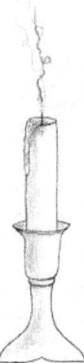

V aletta waited behind the building. Not only was she one of the first to arrive each night, but she was one of the last to leave. She impatiently waited for Johnny to escort her home.

She watched Johnny unload Chester's trunk and waited until the coupe pulled away from the building. Expecting to see Johnny walk around the corner at any moment, she tapped her foot on the sidewalk.

"Where is he?" she whispered to herself. She crossed her arms and turned toward home.

Valetta lived ten blocks from downtown. She walked east on Sugartree Alley until reaching the rear of the theatre. She slipped through the narrow alley and headed north.

The damp air built to a dense fog and by the time she reached the open area of Third Street, it was difficult to see three feet in front of her. She tripped over the uneven bricks and tumbled to the ground.

"Ouch!" she yelled into the emptiness.

The falling mist soaked her new dress and some type of grease soiled it. The same covered her right palm. She rubbed her scraped knee and stared at her shoe's broken heel in disgust. She kicked off her other shoe and continued in her stocking feet.

Without the echo of her heels the night seemed eerily silent. Fear gripped her. She slipped over a garden fence and waited.

Two men appeared within moments. Their hurried footsteps moved in muffled silence. Both were close to the same height, though one was visibly heavier. She may have dismissed their appearance as a coincidence until she saw their hands. Each held one of her shoes.

She placed her hand over her mouth to silence any sound or breath. She counted to ten after they slipped from sight. When she was convinced the men were gone, she jumped over the fence. The rose thorns tore at her new stockings, pulling one from her leg. Her half-empty garter swung free. Its clips pinched her skin. Each sound seemed magnified as she worked her dress free of the rose thorns. She glanced in all directions before attempting to stand. She decided to return to Johnny's safety and began to make her way back to the club.

She stumbled through the city streets making certain to take a different and well-lit path though she did not meet anyone else. She hid behind several garbage cans when she felt followed. The back alleys held not a single car. She felt open and exposed.

She was breathless when she approached the building. She tripped over a soft lump on the sidewalk and fell to the ground.

A sudden burst of air blew out her candle.

13

Mickey wiped the bar with his damp towel. He finished buffing the water spots off the evening's glasses and placed them in their suspended rack. He smiled at his contorted reflection in their gloss.

The speakeasy had a strange atmosphere when empty. Whispers seemed to linger and skirt around the room. Shady deals gone awry threatened the darkness.

Hanging in the center of the room was a blown glass chandelier. Its surround, made by The Mullins Company, featured winged cherubs and leaf gatherings that sprinkled throughout its oval shape. It was four feet wide, six feet long, and the perfect balance to the nine-foot chandelier. Six single milk glass globes hung around the perimeter of the room. Each of the drops boasted of their own Mullins' escutcheon that complemented the centerpiece.

Mickey watched the lights flicker to dark with the push of a button. The click of his heels echoed down the hallway to Lyla's room. Her door was ajar.

He knocked as he entered, "Miss Lyla?"

The door swung open wide. Her dressing room lay a bit disheveled, but not much out of the ordinary. He checked her office next. The only thing missing was Lyla.

"Lyla?" he questioned louder. "Hmmm." He shrugged his shoulders and walked out of her room.

After a few steps down the hall, he began to yell her name. His voice echoed throughout the empty building. He checked each room leaving the obvious for last.

He unlocked the cloakroom door. Darkness greeted him. In his first step his shoe crunched broken glass. Remnants of a light bulb swung from the ceiling.

"Lyla?" he whispered. "Are you in here?"

He heard a slight moan. An unseen force threw his body to the floor, driving his head into the doorjamb.

Stillness snuffed his candle.

14

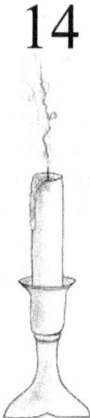

Skelly waited for Sylvia to round her usual corner. He was happy to wait.

He counted the minutes by rehearsing his speech. He practiced sneering and clenching his teeth, confident and ready, but she never came. He checked his watch for the fourth time. Twenty minutes past their meeting time, he walked toward his '27 Buick. His heart pounded. His throat constricted. He knew his boss would be furious, yet he continued with his plan.

He turned the key and the engine coughed into action. He maneuvered down the quiet streets looking for Sylvia. He drove past her apartment and jumped in surprise when he saw her upstairs window was lit.

He stopped and extinguished his car's headlamps. He watched Silvia walk to the window and pull down the blind. The fabric panel created a soft silhouette. She walked away from the window. He watched her body shimmy as she dressed for bed. He tapped his steering wheel and counted.

"Four, three, two, one."

On cue her room went dark. His face held a crooked smile. He lit a cigarette and took a long drag. Slowly its smoke curled from his nostrils. He took a second hit before finishing his exhale. Satisfied that tomorrow night would be perfect, he moved his idling car farther down the street. He tossed the last of his cigarette onto the vacant sidewalk. It sizzled on the damp surface until its embers faded to a soft glow. His car disappeared around the corner.

Skelly's face was inscrutable when he opened the back alley door of Maria's Place. A sharp tone of disgust greeted him.

"Well?" scoffed a man with an aging, well-shaven face who was settled deep in the shadows of the dim room. The drumming of his manicured nails on the heavily carved armrest added to the room's silent tension.

"Missed her." Skelly shrugged his shoulders and held his empty palms skyward.

The drumming stopped. A long pause followed by the sound of Vincent Franciasco Sabino sucking his teeth caused a lump to form in Skelly Canter's throat, but he refused to let the Don see him sweat, so he waited.

Slowly Vincent moved his face into the light. He rolled his hand in the air and spoke only one word—the word all knew and feared. "And?"

Skelly swallowed hard at the question. In the seven years he worked for Vincent he heard that word only three times, and three men lay dead at his feet shot with a single bullet in the forehead. He also understood that consistent stammering at Vincent's famous question infuriated him. If he could get through the next minute, he had a good chance of walking out of there.

"Tomorrow is the night." Skelly added and held his breath.

Vincent slid back into the shadows. His rolling hand hesitated and then moved to dust the sleeve of his white silk jacket.

Skelly also recognized this hand gesture. He met Vincent's approval. He would live to see the task completed with the Don's blessing. He walked outside, and vomited.

A sinister snicker came from behind the half-closed door. A sharp slap on Skelly's back accentuated the sound.

"Not feeling well, eh Slick?" he cackled.

Skelly's back stiffened at the sound of the voice. He wiped the putrid saliva from his mouth.

"I'm feeling just fine."

Raffaldi Sabino laughed again. "Sure. Looks like it." He crossed his arms and waited for a rebuttal. None came. "Is she set?"

Skelly lowered his arm from his face. "Who?" Part of him loved to agitate Raffaldi; the other part feared the response so he treaded lightly.

"Don't screw with me, Slick. Do you think I'm in the dark?"

"You mean like a mushroom?"

Raffaldi grabbed his collar and pulled Skelly toward him, his mouth twisted in knots. He knew this was the nickname spoken behind his back, yet no one dared speak it to his face. Skelly was the only one bold enough to dance around and get away with it. He stood a generous seven inches taller and forty muscular pounds heavier than Skelly so pulling him to his toes was an easy, true pleasure.

"Is Silvia set?" oozed from his clenched teeth.

"Tomorrow night." Skelly answered from his tiptoes never wavering from his collected demeanor.

"It better be, and you better be convincing. That redheaded twit is crowding our territory. She is a small town operation with big ideas. Thinks we'll play nice."

Each word grew in volume and sarcasm. His eyes narrowed to hollow black holes, yet his face never flushed.

Raffaldi had learned a thing or two from his father, and because he also had a violent temper, Skelly knew when to stop pushing his buttons. He also knew Raffaldi resented his position and secretly resented Vincent for bringing Skelly into the family business.

Skelly's so-called recruitment came from an opposing Irish bootlegger named Aidan. Skelly was the only survivor after a brutal holdout of the Irish versus Italians over 100 barrels of whiskey smuggled from Ireland. Ironically, each cask held the Irish family crest—a white stag rearing in front of a wall of fire. It was after the liquid triumph that Vincent fully embraced his nickname, The

Stag, and since the dawn of the following day, Vincent only wore white.

The next morning in a west side warehouse, Vincent found Skelly barely breathing. He remembered staring into Vincent's gun barrel, his hair soaked in all twelve of his associates' blood. He closed his eyes expecting the end, yet it didn't happen.

Some surmised Skelly's salvation as a reflection of Irish ties, other guessed his use as a mole, though only Vincent understood the true reason—the meaning of his name—storyteller. He knew Skelly's reputation of convincing calmness with an uncanny way with women, and he knew exactly how to use him.

Vincent assumed full responsibility for Skelly's recovery. He paid for a private doctor, assigned him a full-time nurse, and when Skelly's strength returned, Vincent awarded him a position just below his own son, Raffaldi.

Grumbling within the organization of Skelly's lofty promotion began, spurred mostly by Raffaldi's jealousy. Vincent called a family meeting to solidify his decision. Nine men were present. Only one was missing and would remain so for his vocal opposition.

Vincent began the meeting with ten minutes of silent stares. No one dared fidget. Vincent viewed that as an outward sign of weakness, one few survived. Finally, one word from the Don echoed through the room.

"Come." His hands flaunted his rolled signature.

Skelly opened a heavy paneled closet door and the dead man's body fell to the floor. All jumped but Skelly and Vincent. The man had endured sadistic torture—rope burns around his wrists, two broken legs, crushed feet, missing fingernails, and an empty eye socket—yet the obvious cause of death came from the position of his head. It was sewn on backwards.

Then it came with a voice calm and guiltless, "And?"

Eighteen eyes slid to the floor, including those of Skelly and Raffaldi. Not a word was spoken. It wasn't necessary. Acceptance met Skelly's position.

His candle fizzled in hushed whispers.

15

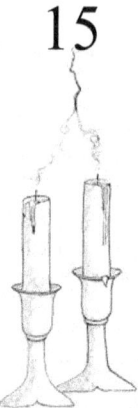

Valetta rubbed her twisted ankle. She struggled to stand and finally decided to pull herself up using the object that tripped her. It was warm and soft to touch. She screamed at the thought of a large dead animal.

Johnny moaned.

"Johnny!" Her voice was elevated and strained. "Are you okay?"

He answered her with a series of snorts and grunts but no words. Slowly he pulled his aching body into a sitting position.

Valetta was more impatient than concerned. She repeated her question. Realizing the answer was not coming soon, she redirected her thoughts. "What happened?" she asked softly, trying to mask her irritation.

Johnny rubbed the back of his head. He shook his head and shrugged his shoulders. His tight fist squeezed the coins.

"I found some money on the sidewalk." His words were slow and deliberate. "I . . . I guess I kicked them or something." He opened his hand to be sure he was remembering correctly. "I bent down to pick them up and someone hit me over the head." His glance accused Valetta.

Immediately, she was enraged. She knew that look. It came too often.

She shrieked, "Don't look at me! I had my own problems tonight." She eyed him suspiciously. "But I guess you don't care about that!"

Realizing that she was supposed to wait for him in her dressing room, he became irritated. He narrowed his eyes.

"Why are you out here?" He hesitated for only a moment and added, "Weren't you to wait for me inside?"

Valetta knew Johnny all too well. Calmness occupied the majority of his personality. Only if provoked or confronted with her independence did he display anything different. Darkness covered her smirk. She knew how to handle him.

"Baby," she stroked his shoulder. "You know how impatient I get." She moved her fingers to twirl his thick black hair. "After the night I had, I just needed some air. I waited for you, but you never came." She lowered her eyes. "I had no idea you had been assaulted or I wouldn't have left."

"Left?"

"That's what I have been trying to tell you. I started to walk home alone, but . . ." she looked in all directions and moved close to his ear, ". . . someone followed me."

Johnny jumped to his feet. "Where is he?"

"There were two of them. They had my shoes."

"What? Your shoes?" He slid back to the sidewalk and rubbed his head.

Valetta spilled each detail of her walk home. She loved the drama and built it to a climax. ". . . and that's when I found you." Proud of her tale with a few embellished details she waited for his response. When none came, she was disappointed. "Johnny? Are you okay?"

His head, slumped over, nearly touched the sidewalk. He tried to recall the events. Suddenly he remembered the sound of the muffled pop that came from inside the speakeasy. He jumped to his feet and ran toward the staircase.

"Lyla!"

Only thin, smoke trails remained of their flames.

16

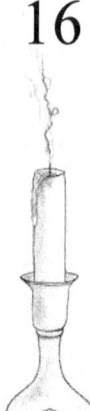

Mickey woke with a pounding headache. He pulled slivers of glass from his cheek and cautiously rubbed the growing bump on his head. He sat upright in the dark cloakroom. It was empty. He shook his head disbelieving his attack.

In the shadows of the darkened room the hidden door in the back paneled wall looked ajar. Mickey staggered back to the bar to retrieve a flashlight. Groping over the shelves, he felt its cool metal handle and flicked on the light. Fighting back the vertigo that dogged him, he crept back to the cloakroom.

Illumination from his flashlight lit the back wall. The concealed door remained closed. He checked the hidden lock, wiggling its lever. It was locked. His sigh reflected his draining tension as he walked toward the hallway. He traced the room's four corners with his flashlight before he closed the door.

Mickey had only taken three steps when a loud crash came from inside the cloakroom. His hands shook as he fumbled with the keys. Near the floor's center lay a broken trap door. He moved the light to the ceiling and gasped at the opening.

Instinctively he walked under the two-foot hole shining the light into its darkness. Attached to the wall was a ladder that could be lowered on rails but its only access was from above. He scanned the walls more closely for a trigger—a rope, a loose panel, or a lever—anything that would lower the ladder out of the way for an accidental advance. He found nothing.

Perplexed he retraced each earlier move to be certain he was not the cause. He moved into the entrance of the cloakroom and tried to remember. He approached the hidden panel door and fumbled for its lever. The door sprung open.

Mickey jumped back. He had tried this door a few minutes earlier, and it was secure. Now it swung open bidding him to enter. He held his breath and walked in.

He heard shuffling footsteps behind him. The cloakroom door slammed shut. A surprised face stared into his light.

"Who goes there?" the voice urgently whispered.

His stammered reply came in a rapid burst. "It's me, Mickey, you idiot. What are you doing in here? I thought you were long gone."

George, the trumpet player, stared at the bartender. "I was," his words were hurried. "But I forgot my horn."

"Your horn?" Mickey questioned. "You never let that baby out of your sight."

"I know." George looked at the glass on the floor. "I gots a bad feelin', Mickey. A bad feelin'."

"Why?"

"Well . . . ," he hesitated. "Jus' seen lots of funny stuff."

Mickey was annoyed with this game. "Like what, George?"

"Well," he slid closer to Mickey and whispered, "I seen a guy waitin' in the shadows, couple of days now. I ask him if he needs somethin' and he jus' mumbles and turns his back."

Mickey laughed, "He's probably drunk and can't find his way home."

George shook his head, "I don't think so. He seems shifty. Like he's up to somethin'."

"And what else, George?"

"Well, Miss Lyla, she's been lookin' a bit peekid. She's jus' been downright mean if yo' ask me."

Mickey laughed and placed his arm around his old friend. "Everything is fine, George. I promise. You'll see. Everything is just fine." He rubbed the growing knot on his head and tried to find some peace in his words.

"I'm hopin' you right, but I dunno. I thinks somethin' fishy's goin' on."

Mickey started to escort George out of the room but remembered that he needed to be certain the hired man's liquor supply was secure, and he wanted to check on his personal 'shine stash.

"You go on ahead now, George. Grab your horn and go home. I'll see you tomorrow."

"I will. But you jus' be careful. Watch yo' back now, hear?"

Mickey listened to George shuffle his feet as he walked down the hall and into the ballroom. He waited until his footsteps moved toward the stairs. Silence pounded in Mickey's ears. His head ached. Something in what George said made him feel uneasy.

Each creak in the floor, or scurry of a squirrel or mouse overhead caused him to jump. He listened for any odd sound, anything out of the ordinary. When all was silent, he convinced himself that he better calm his imagination.

Then he heard it. Voices overhead muffled by the sound of dragging. He redirected the beam into the dark hole. He jumped when it lit the bottom of a shoe. He dropped the flashlight. The lens cracked, flashed, and went dark.

Darkness filled the room.

17

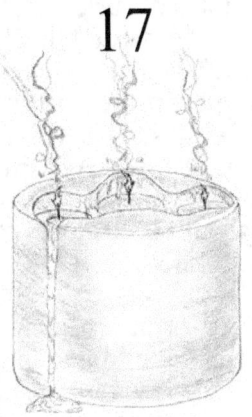

Chandra and Isabell sat wide-eyed in the darkness. Chandra jumped at any sound. With the storm outside settling into a soft rain and the lightning moving east, the mood should have softened but did not. With each lit wick the story grew more intense.

Remembering Isabell's earlier warning of the candle's significance and purpose, Chandra inhaled deeply. Isabell's assurance that 'In the end all will be revealed' brought her little comfort. She glanced at her watch. It was 3:37 a.m.

Isabell stared at the dark candles. Her trance-like state cast an eerie ambiance over the table. The triple-wick bowl burst into flame. She curled the corners of her thin lips and mouthed the word 'Lyla.'

Lyla sat on the edge of her dressing room table and stared at her dress choices for the evening. Her eyes traced the seams of each red dress. Her initial choice was a heavily beaded bodice that repeated its ten-inch pattern to the hem and finished with large teardrop crystals that swung from thin, nearly invisible threads. The second option was two separate pieces, though when worn looked as one. Its multiple folds of curled chiffon hid all of Lyla's weight issues, or so she dreamed. The last of three she had purchased that afternoon. Its exaggerated length was a refreshing change from the current fashion of barely above the knee. Its lines were simple, yet elegant and seemed to add a bit of mystery with its modified train if she chose to allow it to drift across the floor behind her. The audaciously diminished neckline exposed Lyla's finest characteristic. Looking at the new dress made her decision easy.

She pulled her red-printed cotton dress over her head and hung it on a cushioned hanger. She caressed each wrinkle until it yielded. Lyla whistled with satisfaction. Just as she was about to step into her new creation, a loud knock came at her door.

Disgusted with the interruption she shouted, "What now?"

Mickey's confident tone answered, "It's me, Mickey."

She tapped her red nails on her powder jar and waited for a reply. When none came, she emitted the obvious question. "What do you want," and added, "Mickey?" with exaggerated sarcasm.

"You have a visitor."

"Who is it?"

"Ummm," he stammered. "He says he's your brother."

Lyla waved her hand in the air. "Tell him I'll be with him in a minute. This girl must get dressed."

She heard the heels of his shoes click as they moved farther away from her door. Irritated by the interruption, she slid back into her red cotton dress knowing she would have to re-smooth its wrinkles. She slammed her dressing room door and pounded her heels as she raced down the hall.

When Lyla crossed the threshold, her half-brother and Mickey were involved in a hushed conversation. If her entrance had been a bit quieter, she may have been able to eavesdrop, but both men heard her. Mickey straightened his stance while Hank remained slumped on a stool with his back toward the door.

Lyla sauntered toward the bar. "Hank?"

He lifted his shot glass of pink liquid, saluted his sister, and threw the liquid to the back of his throat. He did not appear to swallow when he wiped his mouth with the back of his hand, but his mouth was empty. "Ahhh," he toyed. "Now that's the good stuff."

Mickey's eyes made a silent plea to Lyla for forgiveness. She glared at the bottle and then looked back at him with disapproval.

Hank spoke first. "Now, Lyla," he sneered revealing his missing teeth. "Don't be mad at your boy here." He waved his gangly arm toward Mickey. "He only did as he was told." His laughter filled the room. He placed his sweaty arm around his sister's waist. "I just wanted to taste it here in your special place."

His blood-shot eyes traced the amenities in the room. Again, he filled his shot glass from Lyla's special bottle, drank, and wiped his mouth. "Nice place you got here, sis."

With her hands on her hips she snapped, "What do you want, Hank?"

"Well," he slurred. "I just wanted to check out your place." He lifted her bottle into the air spilling some of its contents. "And to bring you this . . . as a present." He smiled.

"So you came to drink my present?"

"No, to toast your success!" Again he grinned, proud of his response.

"Hank, I don't have time for this nonsense."

"So you don't want to drink with your brother?"

Mickey stared at the growing rivalry pained by the guilt of losing sight of Hank earlier and finding him alone in Lyla's office. He feared Lyla's reaction. Mickey wiped the same shot glass for five minutes.

Unnerved by his persistence, Lyla walked to his side and pressed her elbow deep into Hank's ribs. She bent close to his ear.

"Only one drink."

"Get the lady a glass," he announced to the empty room.

Mickey placed his well-polished shot glass in front of Lyla. He tipped the bottle and immediately Lyla waved him off. Her glass was barely half-full.

"Tell me the reason you came is to show me that you have perfected this recipe, Hank, or I'll find another, more experienced 'shiner. It tastes flawed as of late."

Lyla avoided his sneer and held her shot glass in the air while she watched Hank clumsily crash his sixth drink into hers. She nodded and drank its contents. The raw liquid seared her throat.

"Ahhhh . . ." Hank crashed to the floor.

Lyla clutched her burning throat with one hand. "Mickey! Water!"

He dipped a tumbler into a tub of melting ice, handed it to her, and watched Lyla down it and plead for another. He paid no attention to Hank.

"Miss Lyla, are you okay?"

Pointing to her present in disbelief, Lyla shook her head. "That was horrid."

Mickey picked up the pink bottle and smelled its contents. He shrugged his shoulders. "What's it supposed to taste like?"

Lyla grabbed the bottle from him and sniffed its contents. "A lot better than that."

The tips of her long red nails followed each red tendril. She stopped cold when the last had a single bead of white wax at the end. She kicked Hank's leg. "What did you do to my present?" She narrowed her eyes and spit on him. "Get him out of here. But first find out what he did to my raspberry blaze."

Mickey looked at the half-empty pink bottle. "Raspberry blaze, huh?" He sniffed the bottle again. "So that's what she calls it."

Lyla's wicks blew out one at a time. The rising smoke smelled like alcohol.

18

Hank woke in the cloakroom. A bare light bulb swung over his head and added to his feeling of nausea. He tried to focus but was unable. Finally, Mickey's outline came into his hazed view.

Mickey's red face moved within inches of Hank's. His teeth were clenched.

"I'm only going to ask you one more time, Hank." He shook the man's shoulders and pleaded, "Stay with me, Hank. What did you do to Lyla's blaze?"

Hank stammered and tried to speak. His words were gibberish and staccato interrupted by waves of nausea. "Its almos . . ." his eyes rolled to show their whites. ". . . all red . . . jus a lil' . . . white." His head hit the floor with a heavy thud.

Mickey opened the door and shook his head. Johnny stood at attention.

"I've tried to get him to talk. As many years as I have spent behind the bar, I have never seen a man drink so little and be so drunk."

"Maybe he started before he got here." Johnny added with a shrug.

"I don't know. He seemed to be sober when he knocked on the door." Mickey tried to recall his encounter. "He spoke the password without hesitation, not a bit slurry. He didn't stagger when he walked in." He shook his head again. "I don't know, Johnny I think he was sober."

"Well, something's off." Johnny looked at the pathetic man lying in a crumpled heap on the cloakroom floor. "Maybe he can't hold his liquor."

Mickey chuckled at Johnny's remark. "The man's a 'shiner. It's his living. Don't you think he has had more to drink this week than ten men put together?" He huffed in disgust. "After all, I'm sure he samples every batch before he sells it."

"Well," Johnny added without feeling, "I guess I'll see what I can get out of him. We have to have some answers to keep Lyla happy." He flexed his muscles. "And Mickey?"

"Yeah?"

"Lyla says he is not allowed in here any more. She says he makes her nervous. He's a little," Johnny brought his finger to his temple and twirled it in a tight circle, "titched."

"You can say that again."

Hank's candle sputtered but refused to surrender. The flame spewed a cinder that seethed across the table. Chandra placed her hand over the ember before it burned her antique tavern table.

"Ouch!" She recoiled and shook her hand from the shock of the burn. "That hurt!"

His candle's flame burst into action. He had more to share. His menacing laughter filled the room.

"Joey! Get over here!" Hank screamed at his partner. "This thing's gonna run!"

The men hurried around the still. The fire had jumped the barrier and quickly moved through the dry leaves. Within minutes the blaze burned out of control. It licked the base of the surrounding trees turning their bases black while their sap beaded and dripped.

Joey ran to the still and tried to salvage anything that was cool enough to pull off the still. When he reappeared, his shirt was on fire.

Hank jumped on his back and jerked the flaming shirt from his body. In the tussle Joey threw the only thing he managed to save—the copper worm. It rolled until the coil settled into the middle of the blaze. The men ran in the opposite direction.

The fire caused a lot of attention. Before the firefighters gained control it consumed thirty acres of a virgin state forest. The local town crawled with sheriffs who worked closely with investigators. They interrogated Hank and Joey first.

Suspicion of them making 'shine had surrounded the pair for many years. Although they seemed simple men with a comedic display of backward social skills, they were masters at the art of evasion. Each time the investigators questioned them, they acted as though they did not understand their questions, which made the conversation extremely frustrating for the law. When interrogated, the straightforward question 'Are you running moonshine?' came as rehearsed. Hank's answer was nothing short of brilliant.

"Yes, sir," he said. "We've run from the moonshine a lot." He grinned and closed his eyes as if recalling a factual memory. "We haven't done it much since Joey here," he swung his thumb in his friends face, "lost his brother in the river. We was swimming in the moonshine, and a storm came up. We wasn't paying no attention and 'for we knew it Jack was swept downstream." He hung his head and pretended to wipe a tear. "We saw his arms a swinging and screaming for help, but without the shine of the moon we lost him." He watched the faces of the police gasp in horror and annoyance as he continued his tale, "We done lost him down the river. They found his body four days later all blowed up from drowning." He placed his hand on Joey's shoulder and gently squeezed it. "Joey ain't said a single word since then. It made him a mute." Proud of his embellishment to a story he recanted many times, he grimaced. "Yep, it done made him a mute." He elbowed Joey who responded with a nod.

The hour-long questioning yielded nothing but more ridiculous stories, until the police threw their hands up in defeat. Hank had won once again. Aware that the police would be on their heels, the men hopped in their rowboat and paddled downstream to search for another spot to start their operation.

Many 'shiners used their own property to make permanent stills, but unless they owned several hundred acres and could operate far from property lines it was safer to build temporary distilleries on state property. Hank never used the same location twice. With thousands of acres of accessible state game land available, the need for a permanent location was not necessary. As long as they had a boat, oars, copper, corn, raspberry syrup, and sugar all within a limitless supply of cold mountain water used to cool the copper worm condensor, they were in business.

Joey's sense of looming danger was a necessary addition to Hank's persuasiveness. He seemed to know when they were under surveillance. He warned Hank as they approached the still. The men jumped back in their boat, picked up their fishing pole and pretended to be having a disappointing day on the water. Joey had thwarted their certain arrest three times in the past year, all under Hank's growing suspicion.

The week after the unfortunate fire, the frenzied men worked for days to build another still. They had two five-gallon jugs of white lightning to deliver to Lyla but lost every bit of her raspberry blaze in the fire.

Hank knew his half-sister would not be amused with any excuses so he decided to keep their unfortunate set of circumstances to himself. However, he needed to complete the order because Lyla must have her pink fire. She could not go without or there would be hell to pay.

By Friday Hank had the still in operation. He started the fire just as Joey brought the last fifty-pound bag of sugar over the river's embankment.

Hank's hand suspended a full Mason jar. The reward of Joey's sweaty exertion came in the form of the new moonshine. It was strong, clear, and exceptionally potent. The clear liquid ran smooth in their mouths and through their veins until both passed out onto a mossy knoll.

Lucky for the pair, the law was not in the woods that evening. Hank woke near midnight to the smell of over-burned raspberry blaze. Panicked, he ran to the spout and spilled the disappointing contents into a jar. The liquid was brown.

Joey staggered to join him. "Now what are we gonna do?"

Angry with the responsibility Hank hollered at his partner. "Why is it my problem?"

"Cuz she's your sister?"

"My sister, our money." He held his hands out, palms up. "Now whose problem is it?"

Joey hung his head in defeat.

Hank's tone continued, "Now whose problem is it?"

Joey priding himself as a fixer said, "Let's jus' color up some lightnin' by add'n a bit of dye." His wide smile taunted his partner with his full reveal of missing teeth.

"And where are we gonna get some dye out here?" Hank swirled his hands through the air.

"We gotta go back and get the wax on it, don't we?" Joey didn't wait for Hank to answer. "I got some red cotton dye at my house. Wilma was want'n to dye her old dress so we bought...."

Hank stared into the night sky and cut him off. "Well, why are we still standing here? We have to get it fixed up. It's gotta be getting close to one o'clock."

The men rushed the jugs of liquor to their boat. Fortunately, their river path took them passed Joey's shack. They hurried up the riverbank with one of Lyla's lidded bottles filled with the evening's batch of white lightning. Hank melted the wax for the seal while Joey ran into his house after the dye.

Joey's face flushed as he met Hank in the outbuilding. He handed Hank a dark brown bottle with the label partly missing. "Here's the dye!" he announced, smirking.

Hank took the bottle, unscrewed the lid, and sniffed the contents, "Whew! This shit stinks."

Just as he tipped the bottle Joey screamed, "Wait!" He snatched the container from Hank's hand and brushed the debris from the half label. "It's a good thing I seen this." He lifted the bottle within inches of Hank's face. "You coulda poisoned your sister!"

Hank read the label, "Cyani." He squinted as he tried to finish the word. His eyes popped open, "Cyanide!" He turned to Joey with a crooked smile and whispered, "We could have killed her."

The men stared at the open bottle of poison. The smell of bitter almonds filled the air as Joey brandished the bottle. He picked up the lid, capped the bottle, sealing in the deadly odor, handed the bottle to Hank, and quickly ran back to his shack for the clothing dye.

Hank shook the poison and watched the liquid swirl inside the brown bottle. He smiled as he shoved it into his pocket.

Breathy laughter snuffed his candle.

19

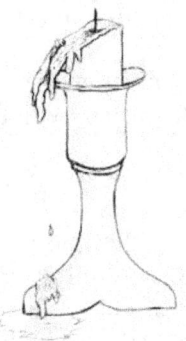

Silvia's eyes darted around the room searching for
Skelly. She found it difficult to keep her mind on
the music and on her dance steps. Three nights had
passed since he gave her the pearl earrings, and she waited
for him each night since, but he did not come. She finished
her fourth set with a half-hearted effort and walked off
the stage in mid-song.

The crowd groaned at her inattention. With one dancer
missing, the set quickly fell apart. Miscues and missteps
plagued the other girls. Without warning Valetta's high
kick landed on the shoulder of the woman in front of her.
Both tumbled to the floor. Sighs of surprise and cheers
for a fight filled the room. Men jumped to their feet to
witness the possible squabble.

Valetta's face landed only inches from the first table.
Loose bills spilled from her corset settling at and under
the tablecloth's hem. A youthful hand emerged from under
the skirt and snatched the money seconds before Valetta
had the opportunity to do the same. Her face flushed as
she lifted the tablecloth to six startled eyes. Laughter
spilled from her lips at their exposed faces. She withdrew
her demanding hand and whispered to the three children.

"You can keep it." She placed her finger over her lips. "It'll be our secret."

Suddenly aware of the agitation in the room, she stood and waved her hands in the air. "I'm okay." She extended her hand to her toppled partner and pulled her from her knees. "And so is she." She looked at the horn player. "George, play this group something soft, while we go powder our noses."

Groans erupted. The men knew that when the dancers left, they would not return. Valetta tried to ease their growing agitation.

"Unlike normal," she smiled, "because of our . . . ummm . . . interruption, we will return for one more set."

An outburst of loud applause joined their pulsing beat. Even Johnny joined in the celebration.

When the dancers gathered in the dressing room, Valetta scolded her partners. Then she turned to Silvia who sat with her back to the rest, running an emery board over her fingernails.

"What is wrong with you?" she spit in frustration.

Silvia admired her perfect left hand unaware that Valetta had moved within inches of her face. Startled by her anger and close proximity she flinched. "What?"

"I asked you a question."

"What?"

Valetta screeched, "What's wrong with you?"

"Nothing, why?"

"You walked off the stage in mid-set! You irritated the crowd and caused so much distraction that Glory and I fell on our faces, I lost my tips to the grubby little hands that always hide under the first table, and my cheek is going to have a nice bruise by morning if my eye isn't swollen shut first!" After a brief sigh of disgust, she added, "And I had to promise the crowd another set to quiet down the growing riot." Infuriated with Silvia's inattention Valetta's face burst with color as her voice grew stronger. "And you just sit there and act innocent?"

Silvia eyed her curiously. As long as she had known Valetta, she had never witnessed her lose control. Sure, she should not have walked off the stage, but if she felt like being honest, she would explain to Valetta that she was looking for Skelly. That's all. Instead, "Yeah," was all that spilled from her lips.

Valetta stammered around the room. Her voice ascended into the ballroom. A loud thump on the door startled her to silence.

"Everything all right in there?" Johnny's voice hushed the room.

Valetta's response was anything other than automatic, "We're coming out."

She motioned for the girls to walk toward the door. All obeyed but Silvia, her eyes were fixed on her right hand. Valetta pulled on her arm.

"You too, Silvia."

"Not me. I'm going home. I'm tired."

"Oh, no, you are not. You started this mess, and you will finish it with the rest of us."

"Who made you boss?"

Valetta grew more agitated. If Glory had not opened the door for Johnny, no telling what she may have done.

His deep, matter-of-fact tone sent chills through Valetta though not nearly as much as his single word reply to Silvia's question, "Lyla."

Though the sound of that name had an ill effect on Valetta, it seemed to fuel Silvia's courage. Sarcasm laced her response.

"Lyla? Yeah, where is she anyhow?"

"Visiting a sick friend," Johnny snapped.

Silvia dismissed the pair with a whisk of her hand. "Geez, what's gotten into you two?" She wrapped both of her hands around her neck. "I'm about to choke from the tension." She clicked her heels and followed the dancers out the door. "Are you coming Lettie?" she mocked.

They walked to the stage in slow motion through the pawing crowd. Valetta danced the first song without having memory of it. Twice she imagined the flash of Lyla's red dress as it disappeared through the doorway.

Before the start of the second song, Silvia spotted the top of Skelly's black bowler moving through the standing crowd. He sat at the end barstool. Mickey placed a shot of white lightning before him without asking. Skelly tossed the fire to the back of his throat and then lifted his empty glass toward Silvia with a wink.

When Silvia's number was over, she floated straight toward the bar, not for a drink but to be close to Skelly. She watched his eyes brighten with each advancing step.

Her fingers ruffled along his brim. "Where've you been, Sugar? Thought you disappeared on me."

"Never." He patted her arm. "You've got me spellbound."

His candle fizzled with a hushed snicker.

20

Chester drove a few blocks and parked his Ford in an unused alley. He crushed his half-smoked cigarette into the brick sidewalk, exhaled, and ran back quietly to the speakeasy. Anxious to avoid another confrontation, he scurried one block past Johnny to Broadway Avenue. He hurried around the corner to the wooden door that led upstairs.

He stopped at the landing half way up the narrow staircase and listened. He heard voices. They were shouting. Several minutes passed as he carried on his silent battle—stay or go? He closed his fist around his reduced pay packet. Leaving was not an option. He drew in a deep breath and walked the second half of the staircase.

He recognized Lyla's voice as well as Mickey's. Although it was difficult to tell it seemed there were at least two additional people, perhaps three, though their voices were faint.

When he reached the top of the staircase, the speakeasy door was ajar. Surprised at the lack of security and ignoring all of the alarms that rang in his head, he slowly swung the door open and slipped into the adjacent cloakroom.

Chester's throat tightened and beads of sweat gathered and slid down his forehead. The salt burned his eyes. His heart seemed to catch in his throat. He held his breath as the speakers drew nearer.

Panicked over the fear of certain exposure and raising suspicions with his unannounced return, he slid farther into the room and pressed his body against the back wall. Nervously his hands felt the panels for any place to hide. His belt loop caught on the hidden switch and released it. A veiled door sprung ajar. He fully opened it and slid into safety and darkness.

Lyla pulled the string to turn on the light. She huffed in disgust.

"Get me a flashlight!" Her order bounced around the room until Mickey heard her. "Didn't you just change this?" she nagged.

Lyla fumbled through the dark room muttering obscenities about incompetence. She complained about Mickey, Johnny, and had an especially lengthy fit about Chester. She shuffled her feet across the floor toward the back wall while she finished her tense solo conversation. She heard Mickey's clumsy approach before she saw the irresolute beam.

Mickey was breathless when he entered the room. "I forgot where I put the other one. I had one but I dropped it when . . ."

"Just give me the damned thing! I don't want excuses. I need to see!"

Mickey spun the handle toward Lyla and illuminated her annoyed face. He watched her recoil from the beam.

"What are you doing?" she screamed at him. She covered her eyes, took one step backwards, and stumbled. The flashlight hit the floor and blew out.

Mickey did not need to see her face to know she was furious. He also knew it would be his fault.

Through the darkness her screech chilled the air. "Now, look what you've done! I can't see a thing. Get another light, Mickey!"

"But Miss Lyla, I only had two and they're both . . . busted."

"What?" her tone reached an octave higher. "Then, go get another one!"

Mickey rolled over in his mind where he could find a third flashlight. Lyla's incessant ranting closed his mind to any other option. The thought of simply replacing the light bulb never presented itself. He felt his neck and face burn. He hated it when Lyla chided him like a misbehaving schoolboy. Losing his temper. he clenched his fist and lashed out in the dark. The blow knocked her to the floor.

"Miss Lyla!" Mickey gasped, "Oh my God!"

Garbled mumbles spilled from her lips. Their aggravated pitch rose and fell while Lyla's dress swished across the floor. Without warning a shrill bawl pierced the air. She clasped both hands around her left leg. She felt her dress become moist. Waves of sickness raced through her body. Her fingers brushed over a protruding bone. Groans settled into soft whimpers.

Mickey covered his ears until the echo ceased. With vacillation he whispered, "Miss Lyla? Are you all right?" He held his breath awaiting a reply.

"Oh my God, Mickey!" her voice was strained and near panic. "I broke my leg!"

Mickey gasped.

"I can't move. Turn on the light!"

"But . . . I can't. The flashlig—"

"Don't talk. Just listen!" If he were closer, she would have punched him. She gritted her teeth and hissed, "Go to my office. Under my desk . . . on the floor is another flashlight. Grab it and bring it back." Her tone softened slightly, "Hurry, Mickey. I'm bleeding."

Mickey ran from the room but she called him back. She tossed her keys in the direction of his voice. They hit the floor and skirted into the hall. Mickey dropped to his knees and groped in the darkness. He closed his fist around the cluster of keys and ran to her office.

Chester could only imagine what was happening a few feet from his hiding place. He placed his ear against the door, held his breath, and listened. After much commotion, it was now quiet. He lifted his hand to wipe the sweat from his brow when he heard a loud crack. Jammed in the tight quarters, his elbow rattled some glass bottles beside him and knocked one bottle to the floor. Sharp slivers littered his wet shoes. He jumped and covered his mouth with both hands to ensure no sound escaped.

Overcome with the need to flee, he popped the door open and gasped at the outline of Lyla's body. It, combined with the foul smell of the hired man's moonshine, caused him to gag. He covered his mouth to suppress the nausea.

Only a few feet separated them yet Chester's feet refused his will to move toward her. With his eyesight well adjusted to the darkness, he saw the flashlight lying on the floor a few inches from her hand. He picked it up and shook it. It remained dark. He tapped it against his hand and jumped at the brightness of the beam. It lit the ceiling.

Chester knelt beside Lyla and placed his hand on her chest. Its rise and fall was shallow, but present.

"Lyla," he whispered. "Can you hear me?" She remained unresponsive.

Chester looked around the room, only he and Lyla were present. He replayed all he had heard and tried to make sense of it. Their argument was short and no more heated than any other time that Lyla chose to chastise an employee. He didn't know Mickey well, but his impression of their relationship was one of trust. He shook his head at his questions.

Again, he leaned into Lyla. "Why did Mickey do this to you?" He tapped the side of her cheek, yet she refused to respond. "Lyla, can you hear me?" he pleaded.

Chester was not a religious man, but he felt the need and muttered a prayer for Lyla. He pushed the missing ten dollars from his thoughts. He only felt concern for his employer. After all, without her money Chester would not enjoy his current financial position.

He glanced around the growing pool of blood and recoiled before it touched his shoes. "Lyla . . ." He patted her face. "Please wake up."

Chester placed his hand behind her head and brushed her red hair from her eyes. He watched as her eyes fluttered. Filled with hope, he spoke in his normal voice, "Lyla, can you hear me?"

Her neck and arms began to twitch. Her eyes snapped open and closed. Her red lips parted and trembled, but no words came.

Chester spoke softly to her. "Be still, Lyla. Don't try to speak. Save your strength. Help is coming." His voice quivered.

Again, he lifted his eyes in prayer. It was then he noticed the gaping hole in the ceiling. The flashlight's beam lit a partially lowered ladder. He strained his eyes to see and moved his hand from Lyla's head. He stared at his blood-soaked palm in disbelief. When his eyes found Lyla's, they remained fixed on him. A wide stream of blood trickled from the corner of her mouth. He stood in a panic.

Hurried footsteps sounded down the hall toward the door. He heard Johnny shout Lyla's name. In a panic he jumped for the ladder and pulled his weight toward the top. His feet disappeared out of sight just as Valetta entered the cloakroom.

Chester held his breath as he fumbled for each rung. Slowly and quietly, he moved his body away from the light of the flashlight. He forced his trembling hands to pull his body's weight. Heavy air settled on his shoulders as his nerves ran with the fire of guilt.

His thoughts raced. Why did he leave? He didn't do anything. He just wanted to talk to Lyla. He wanted to ask why she shorted him ten dollars. Why would she do that?

He remembered her rant. His body raged with anger. He had done nothing wrong. It was Hank's fault that he didn't have her special bottle, not his. Was that why she shorted him?

The top of his head slammed into something hard. He raised one hand and felt a trap door above him. Running his hand over it, he found a seam and traced it with a finger. It felt small, but large enough to push through.

He heard another loud pop and a woman's scream. A second voice joined Johnny's muffled tirade. Their tone rose and cadence quickened. The sound of multiple feet shuffling far below reached him. His thoughts bent only on escape and grateful for the distraction, he pushed against the trap door, opening it.

The cool night air was a welcome change from that of the stifling shaft. He crept out of the opening and stood on the roof. In the distance, he saw a tall man limping away in the opposite direction. He strained his eyes to focus but lost sight of him in the growing darkness. The hatch swung shut, muffling the shouts below.

From the edge of the roof, he saw a second ladder, somewhat wider. It was the fire escape from the second story window, though there was no way to reach it. He paced the roofline and stroked his beard stubble. His palms were sticky with sweat and blood.

"Blood!" He whispered instinctively wiping his hands on his shirt. "Lyla's blood." He pulled his shirt over his head and wiped her blood from his face. Glancing in all directions, he noticed a pipe protruding three feet above the roofline. Its position seemed curious. But desperation overriding puzzlement, Chester crawled over the edge of the roof and shimmied his way to the fire escape below.

Fearful of making a sound, he moved quickly through the ladder's series of stairs. The bottom rung hung ten feet above the street. He swung his body over the edge and jumped. The iron rattled from the movement and Chester's feet fluttered before they hit the ground. When he reached his car and sat behind the wheel, he took a deep breath, having felt that it was his first in ages. He drove to his home with his headlamps off, fearful to light a cigarette.

Chester's candle fell onto the floor and went out.

21

Two candles burst into a wide flame and then settled to a soft glow. Hushed whispers filled the room, barely audible over the rushing wind.

"I said I will give you the money to rebuild your still."

"Why would you go and do that?"

"We need a local man to subsidize what we . . ." Skelly cleared his throat and lowered his voice, ". . . smuggle from Ireland."

"Ireland? For moonshine?"

Impatience lit his face. He flung out words like balls of fire. "Whiskey, not moonshine!" He wondered why his boss made him deal with these kinds of idiots. "Irish whiskey!" He shook self-pity from his thoughts. "Look. We need a local source. You've lost your still. We can make this work—together."

"What's in it for us?"

"What?" Skelly's patience was near its end. "If I don't pay for your new still how are you going to continue your business?"

"I got a little money."

"Enough to rebuild?"

"Well . . . uhhh . . ."

"Enough to continue to supply Lyla?" Skelly suppressed a cough. The sound of her name spilling from his lips made him want to choke. "Well?"

"Maybe with Hank's money too?"

"Hank? Why do you need Hank?"

"Cuz we's partners and he's the brains." He curled his arms to reveal his biceps. "And I'm the muscle."

Skelly's annoyance melted to amusement. "Is this guy for real?" he wondered. He formed a crooked smile. "So you're the brawn, huh?"

"Yep," he answered while continuing to flex.

"Ok. I got it. You are the muscle." Skelly laughed. "But why can't you be the muscle and the brains?"

"I'll needs to talk it over with Hank."

"Why? Can't you make any decisions on your own?"

Joey's face twisted into a grimace. Skelly had struck a nerve. Redness crept up his neck, over his chin, onto his cheeks, and finally settled deep into his eyes. The outburst expelled from his lips manifested itself in large spouts of saliva, most of which landed on Skelly.

Suddenly sober, Joey's voice echoed through the empty woods bouncing from tree to tree until settling around the pair like a blanket. "Of course I can makes decisions!"

Skelly grinned. "Well then. Let's make a decision."

"What's in it for me?"

Skelly put his arm around his pseudo friend. "Me?" Skelly laughed, "Now, that's more like it."

In a hushed whisper Skelly proceeded to reveal his plot. He would fund Joey for the building of the new still in exchange for two things. First, he wanted a limited source for local moonshine. The whiskey stolen from the Irish was depleting rapidly and Vincent demanded a larger supply. Of course, Joey could continue to supply Lyla, which brought him to the second, unfeigned reason. Vincent wanted Lyla out of business and the best way to get to her was through her raspberry blaze.

After an hour of intense persuasion, Joey nodded his head. His hair on his neck suddenly stood at attention. He felt watched.

He tried to shake the feeling by exuding brilliance. "I gots just the thing, Mr. Skelly."

"You do?" he retorted enjoying the build-up of Joey's loyalty. "And that would be?"

"Cyanide."

Skelly stroked his day-old whiskers thankful that Vincent could not witness his poor hygiene. "Cyanide, huh?" Again, he nodded his head. "I like it, but how are you going to get your hands on some?"

"Already gots it." Joey's smile was wide. He puffed his chest out nearly matching the protrusion of his belly. "I figures I only needs to taint a couple of bottles, switch 'em out 'fore she knows it. It won't take but a couple of sips or two to do her in."

The more Joey talked the stronger Skelly's confidence grew. It was crystal clear this stout man enjoyed the façade of being in charge. Skelly guessed the man never made a single decision his entire life and after listening he could understand why—the man obviously never had finished school. Skelly joined in the conversation just as Joey showed defeat.

"But I jus' don't see how I can do it. I ain't never been in her speakeasy. Hell, I don't even know where it is."

Skelly placed his arm around Joey's shoulders once again and squeezed. "I do."

"You do?"

"I sure do. And I know a secret way to get in." He winked at Joey and squeezed his shoulder again. "No one will even know you were there."

The men laughed together, happy with their well-laid plan.

Skelly's flame burst into a shower of sparks giving the appearance of a low-end sparkler. When its excitement settled, the flame flickered in a romantic dance.

Skelly placed his arm around Silvia's waist and squeezed gently. Her playful giggle signified his success. She was ready.

They talked of plans in the not-so-distant future. Silvia played with her earrings as Skelly spun his tale. She listened intently to his ideas. Her mind drifted to a life with him, their house, and children—a life without dancing, without the speakeasy.

Skelly's crafty web drew Silvia deep into his poisonous embrace. His whispered sugared words flowed past the pearls that graced her ears.

"You have too much to offer, Sugar. We will be a great team."

"But what will I do?"

Skelly grinned but covered it with a look of surprise. "Have you not been listening to a word I said?" He hesitated and waited for her nod. "You will be my wife."

"Why I . . ."

Skelly placed his finger on her lips, "Shhh. It's not a proper question yet." He kissed her. "That will be soon."

Silvia's heart leapt as the telling nerves flushed her face. She placed both hands on her cheeks to cool them.

"You take my breath away," she whispered.

Skelly smiled. It had been easy to court Silvia. He worked hard to create this assignment and truly enjoyed the entertainment. His sweet words were easy to speak because if he told the truth for once in his life, he was in love with Silvia. The only difficulty seemed to be holding to Vincent's time frame. Grateful for the quick turn in the conversation he decided to set the bait. His delay left him short on time.

"Look, Silvia, I don't know how to say this gently." He sighed. "We have to do something about Lyla."

Silvia jumped at the change in conversation. Her head swooned with wedding bells, a lace dress, flowers, and the band playing, and then tumbled to a broken pile on the night's sidewalk at his comment.

"What do you mean . . . do something?"

Skelly held her hands within his and with a hushed whisper fired his words rapidly. "She is never gonna let you go. You are her best dancer." He watched her eyes begin to light with admiration. "If you try to leave, she'll find a way to keep you. She never loses the best."

"But, I think Valet . . ."

"Valetta, smelletta. You're ten times the dancer than she. You know it. Look at the crowd. Do you ever pay attention to how they stare at you? They wave their money in the air and force you to come to their table. I watch their faces as you close in on their waving bills. They undress you with their eyes. Their fingers caress your skin." Skelly's words became desperate. His words were raw truth and it felt good to utter them. He kissed her hand and lifted her chin. "They touch you, Silvia. They touch you and it hurts me."

Small tears gathered in the corner of his eyes. Silvia threw her arms around him.

"What can I do? I have to work." Surrendering to his thoughts, she added, "She won't let me go."

"No she won't cause you're that good."

"What can we do?"

"I don't know. We'll have to think of something."

They continued to walk toward Silvia's apartment in silence. Skelly waited until her front door came into view.

He whispered, "I think I've got it!" Silvia's eyes pleaded for him to continue. "It may not be easy though."

"To be together and free of her control . . . I didn't expect it to be easy."

Skelly could not have scripted a better response. The confirmation of his nickname flashed through his mind.

"What can I do?" Silvia whispered.

Skelly looked around suddenly paranoid of listening ears. "Shhh, keep your voice low." He glanced around again. "They may be listening."

"They?"

"Yeah," was all he offered. Trying his best to lead in to an inside invitation, he hesitated a bit longer. "Can't be too careful. If this is going to work we can't talk about it out here."

Silvia fumbled for her keys and handed them to Skelly. "Then we must go inside."

Skelly grinned at his success. He watched Silvia glance around nervously and let out a sigh when he swung the door open. He ushered her quickly inside. Just before closing the door, he held up three fingers signifying the third stage of his plan had been set.

A tall figure emerged from the neighbor's bushes. He brushed off his hat and placed it on his head. A second man watching from an upstairs window directly across the street moved away from the curtain, the quick movement spotlighted his large frame in the backlit room—both signs that all plans were set. Raffaldi waited in his parked car anxious to return with news to his father. He tossed his lit cigarette out of his 1928 Cadillac Town Sedan's window and murmured, "Good for you, Slick. You did it."

Once inside, the couple drew the curtains closed, turned out each lamp, lit a single candle, and settled on the sofa. Their hurried and hushed conversation lasted for only a few minutes. As the first accepted indoor invitation, Skelly had other things on his mind.

"Okay. This is what I am thinking," he began. "The only way Lyla will let you go is if she herself is gone."

Silvia gasped, "Killed?"

"No, Sugar," he lied. "Run out of town. I gotta friend in Youngstown that would pay dearly to have her speakeasy put out of business. I'm thinkin' I'll get enough money for us to go away . . . far away."

Silvia smiled, "And get married?"

"Of course."

"And buy a house?"

"Sure."

"And have a family?"

"Whatever you want, Sugar."

"But how do we run her out of town?"

"Why don't you leave the details up to me?"

"O . . . kay, but . . ."

"But I will need your help."

"Anything for you."

This conversation worked even better than his plan. He pulled her closer and whispered her part.

"When all the details are worked out and the plan is ready, I'll need you to do three things. First, I need to leave the cloakroom unlocked."

"But Mickey guards that key with his life! I'll never be able to get . . ."

"Do you trust me?"

"Of course I do."

"Then you must believe me. I have a plan for you to get his key."

"But how?"

Skelly laughed. "It's gonna take me all night if you won't let me finish."

"I'm sorry. I'm just anxious, I guess."

"Me too, but we must wait for the right moment. Okay?"

"Okay. Go on."

"The second thing is a bit easier." He watched the tension slip from her face. She even managed a sliver of a smile. He patted her shoulder. "Now that's my girl!"

He also permitted his body to relax. He no longer spoke in hushed tones but spoke openly, with more confidence.

"The second thing is I need you to steal one of Lyla's handkerchiefs."

"But I . . . I thought you said it was easy!"

"Relax, Sugar." He held her hand and gently stroked it. "I said it would be easier, not easy."

"What do I do with a stolen handkerchief and why?"

"I want you to put it in your dressing room with this." He held up his hat and cane.

Silvia looked at him puzzled. She was tired, and something about this whole situation seemed off to her. She stared at Skelly's face. He seemed sincere. He certainly had charm. She wanted to believe him, trust him, but most of all she wanted to fall asleep in his arms.

Finally, she conceded. "Okay. What's the third thing?"

"That's it. I already told you. Place my hat and cane in your dressing room."

"I guess I'm tired. I just don't see why . . ."

"Sugar, I said to leave the details up to me. When the time is right, I just need you to leave the cloakroom unlocked, get one of Lyla's handkerchiefs, and put my hat and cane with the handkerchief in your dressing room.

"Just that, huh?" She toyed.

"Yep, just that. Except for one more thing."

Silvia sighed in disgust but spoke not a word. She waited patiently for her next request, her face downturned.

Skelly pulled her chin upward to face his. "Silvia, if anything I have asked you to do settles on you as anxiety, I want you to let me know. Even up to the last minute, if you have second thoughts I want you to grab my hat and cane and bring it to me personally. Leave the handkerchief as a sign. When I enter the dressing room and find it not there I will know you had a change of heart that you decided against the idea, against us." He sighed, "I won't pressure you. I won't question you. I won't ask for an explanation. I will simply slip away into a memory."

They sat quietly for a few minutes, each lost in their thoughts. Silvia spoke first.

"I'm thinking three."

"Three?"

"Yes, three. Three children."

"Whatever you want, Sugar."

As Skelly's candle began to smolder another burst into a vivid orange flame.

"So all is in order?" Vincent's question came as an exaggerated murmur.

Skelly shifted his weight from one foot to the other. He remained silent.

"Why are you nervous?"

"I . . . I'm not."

"Oh, so you're always shifty?" Vincent heard no reply. "I'll ask again . . ."

"No need." Skelly found his confidence and his nerve. "Everything is ready. If the dame shows up with my hat and cane," he patted his piece in his pocket, "I'll be ready. She'll never see it coming." The knot in his stomach made him want to vomit, but he remained true to his nickname.

Vincent smiled from the shadows. Although his face remained hidden, his tone exemplified approval. "I knew you could do it, Slick." He laughed aloud. "I knew it."

The room became eerily dark as both flames diminished to smoke.

22

Mickey sprinted down the hall into the ballroom. He jumped over the bar, his black heels dragging across its polished surface. He plunged a bar towel into the glacial water and filled it with as many ice chunks as he could find and then snatched a second dry towel.

He raced around the end of the bar and tripped. His wet rag slapped his cheeks as the frozen chunks skirted across the floor. When he pulled the towel from his face, he found his nose pressed against a wet shoe. The cackle of mockery startled him.

"Have a nice trip?" the voice taunted through the glowing embers of his cigarette.

Mickey chased the skating ice on his knees. The laughter continued. He closed his fist around the largest piece and hurled it at his target.

The man dodged the projectile. "Got any more?"

Mickey stood with his hand positioned for a second catapult. He recognized the man by his outdated bowler. "What are you doing in here?"

"I came for a drink."

"You were told never to come here again." Mickey forced the strain from his voice and lowered his pitch. "And besides," his eyes narrowed, "we're closed."

"Nope, the door's wide open." He lit a second cigarette with the butt of his first. "Didn't even have to say the password."

Mickey got up, grabbed the man's collar and pulled him from the stool. The man laughed at his futile attempt.

"So you're gonna throw me out . . . without the big guy?"

His cackle taunted Mickey. On impulse, Mickey threw a punch. A distinct loud crack left no mistake. Mickey watched the blood gush from the man's broken nose.

Skelly snatched the wet towel from Mickey's hands and wiped his face as smoke curled up from the floor where his just-lit cigarette had landed. Skelly crushed it with his heel.

"Christ's sake. I just wanted a drink!" came the muffled response from behind the damp bar towel.

"It's long past hours. You know that. What the hell are you doing here?" His hurried, jumbled words caused delay. He felt nervous and needed to return to Lyla with her flashlight, and this idiot kept him here.

With rising aggravation Mickey shoved Skelly and shouted, "Get out of here!"

Skelly staggered with his first step but quickly gained control. He pulled the cloth from his face and threw it at Mickey. Deep red blotches covered his white shirt and speckled his cheek.

Mickey pointed toward the door, "I said get out!'

"I'm going . . . I'm going," Skelly stammered as he disappeared from the ballroom.

Mickey hurried to reclaim the melting ice. He kicked the bloody bar towel across the floor and pulled a third one from a shelf. He heard a loud bang and spun toward the door expecting to see his uninvited guest reappearing. No one was there. Dismissing it as an echo, he finished gathering his makeshift compress and ran down the hall to Lyla's dressing room.

He fumbled with the keys at her door. "C'mon . . . c'mon. One of these has to open it." He tried several until one worked.

A sense of reverence filled him when he entered her room. Although invited to enter several times, this was the first without a guard. This room whispered of secret deals and broken laws. Many hushed meetings were held behind this locked door.

His mind wandered to the keys. It was a curious bunch—two silver ones, three gold, one rusty brown, and one of tiny silver. He held the small key close to his eyes. A crooked smile covered his face.

"What are you doing, Mickey?" he chastised himself. "Get her flashlight."

Lyla's oversized chair was nestled into the center of her desk. He forced it to the side while he dropped to his knees. "It's supposed to be under her desk," he mumbled to himself. With his face pressed against the wool rug he shoved his arm under the right-side drawers. He swept the underside, skimming the carpet but felt nothing.

"Must be over here," he whispered as he shimmied to the left-side drawers. Again, he fumbled for the flashlight. He felt its metal base and slid it to him. Thinking about the other two broken ones, he flipped the switch to be certain it worked. The lens remained dark.

"Ah, come on!" he yelled in frustration. He slammed the side of the flashlight against the center drawer of Lyla's desk to no avail. "Come on!"

Guilt from his lengthy delay caused him to sweat heavily. He fumbled with the switch multiple times. He shook the flashlight one last time, screaming obscenities at it. Finally the batteries and circuit connected. The bulb, dim at first, slowly brightened.

Thrilled that it worked, he abruptly sat up and slammed his head against the underside of Lyla's desk drawer. Wincing in pain, he saw that the flashlight illuminated a keyhole in the backside of the center drawer. With his head pounding and shirt soaked with sweat, he just sat there staring at the tiny hole.

Suddenly the image of that odd little silver key popped into his mind. It would open the lock! His fingers fumbled in his pocket until he fingered the cool filigreed metal. He inserted the key into the escutcheon. The lock snapped open. A single sheet of paper rolled up document style and wrapped in a red thread dropped to the floor. Beside it also fell a black box.

Overwhelming curiosity seized Mickey's attention. He forgot about Lyla. He forgot she was bleeding. He wanted to read the note.

He slid the thread from the paper and began to unroll it. A shot rang out in the distance. "Oh, my God! Lyla! What the hell am I doing?" He struggled to replace the string around the paper. His wet hand trembled. He shoved the two items back into their furtive space and locked it.

He slid out from under Lyla's desk clutching her flashlight. He did not bother to close her door. He had been gone too long. Lyla needed him and he had forgotten about her. He ran toward the cloakroom with the fading flashlight in his hand unaware that the red thread wound through his fingers.

Mickey's candle flickered but remained lit.

23

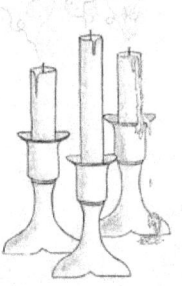

Johnny took the speakeasy stairs three at a time. His sweaty palms slid across the walls of the second set of stairs. When he reached the top, he burst through the half-opened door. He yelled Lyla's name, though no response came.

Valetta yelled from the bottom, "Wait for me!" She knew he replied but could not hear what he said—something about looking this way. Disgusted, exhausted, and flat out irritated, she shuffled her feet as she climbed each step. She sighed at the sight of her dress, her missing and torn stockings, sore ankle, and bare feet. Again, she sighed. She loved those shoes.

It was an eerie feeling to be inside the speakeasy this late at night. She was usually snuggled in her bed by now after spending the walk home warding off Johnny's advances.

Her pink-lacquered finger tips caressed the password door and pushed it open. She walked quietly down the hall toward the cloakroom. A rising anxiety kept her from calling Johnny's name. When she came to the cloakroom, she found the door ajar. A dim flashlight beam cast a small circle on the paneled back wall.

When Valetta stepped inside, her nostrils flared from an odd smell that permeated the cloakroom. It smelled damp, slightly musky or burnt, and mingled with the unmistakable fragrance of the hired man's liquor. It made Valetta queasy. She fumbled for the light cord.

Her bare foot stepped in a pool of goo. She suppressed a scream. She detested wet, slimy things. She took one step forward but refused to place her weight on the soft object beneath her foot. She whimpered as she shivered remembering a similar feeling on the sidewalk earlier that evening. She whispered Johnny's name.

Johnny ran into the ballroom. Puddles of water mixed with chunks of ice littered the floor. He slipped twice and fell. His arm rested on a bloody towel. He stood in a panic and no longer shouted Lyla's name.

He held his breath and pressed his body against the wall. With his arms outstretched he slithered around the doorframe and into the hall. A light from Lyla's open door lit the corridor. Each step moved him closer. Her room was quiet.

Suddenly, Johnny jumped when he heard the sound of a hard thud. He silently wished for a gun. Fear of the unknown stopped him in mid-motion. Lyla had a gun; in fact, she had two—one in her desk and one in her garter. How could he get his hands on either of them? Lyla was missing and someone was in her office.

He placed his hand on the oak door and drew in a deep breath. Poised for a fight he stepped into the room and listened. It was silent. He relaxed his shoulders and took another step.

His body jumped at the sound of a gunshot. He spun and ran toward it. With each stride Johnny felt as if he moved backwards. The shot's report reverberated inside his head. His rapid pace struggled to match his heart rate. He pleaded for Valetta's safety, for Lyla's safety, and for this nightmare to end.

The sight of the dimly lit cloakroom gave him little comfort. He heard Valetta's murmurs long before he reached the door. His feet slid passed the opening as he tried to stop, desperately grabbing at the oak frame to slow his motion.

The sound of hurried footsteps made Johnny turn. A dim light bounced off the polished floor as it moved closer to him. Mickey appeared breathless, bloody, wet, and carrying a useless flashlight.

Valetta stood with her back to the door. Her rounded shoulders forced her head to bow. Her hands held a gun.

Three candles dissipated in unison.

24

Joey ransacked his tarpaper shack for the bottle of cyanide. He recalled having a conversation about it with Hank and felt certain he noticed it on the shelf since that evening. He mumbled to himself while his hands covered every inch.

Hank watched him curiously from the entrance. Inside his pocket was a bead of white wax. He fumbled the pea-sized ball until it was soft and pliable. He slipped around the corner confident in two things—Joey didn't know that he had been watching and the cyanide was gone. He walked back to their new still.

Joey continued to search for another thirty minutes. Once certain he had touched every bottle on the shelves at least four times, he threw his hands in the air.

"I ain't got it. Where'd it go?" He covered his face. "Mr. Skelly's gonna kill me if I don't do somethin'."

He crumpled to the dirt floor. He wrapped his arms around his legs and rocked. Disgusted, he placed his head on his knees. A faint shine of a brown bottle, slender and tall, taunted him from under the bottom shelf built barely six inches above the dirt floor. The container rested against the back wall. He placed his face on the dirt floor and stretched his arm as far as it would reach. His fingers barely touched the glass and rolled the bottle in place repeatedly. In frustration he strained his hand to its limit forcing the lowest shelf deep into his face. He grunted and spit. "Aww c'mon!' he screamed, "Just a lil' bit more. Jus' a bi—you can git it." With the last thrust his fingers managed to roll the bottle within reach. He squealed, "Got it!"

Scrunched like a cripple, Joey's body remained twisted to his knees. He spat on the bottle and wiped the mud from the label. He read aloud, "Arsenic." He stared in disbelief. He had been certain it was the missing bottle of cyanide.

He shook his head. "I didn't even know I had arsenic." He shrugged, "Oh well. It'll has to do."

He slid the slender bottle into his pants pocket, crawled over the riverbank, and plopped his exhausted body into his canoe. He walked toward Hank as he tended the still's fire.

Hank's disgust filled the air. "Where in the world have you been?"

Joey stammered, losing confidence with each breath. "I got lost."

Hank mocked, "You got lost?" He shook his head and eyed Joey from under his wide-brimmed hat. "Sounds 'bout right." He tossed Joey an empty jug. "Come on. Get busy. We've got a lot of 'shine to bottle. Made a double batch."

Joey perked up at the task. "Hey, and don't forgets we gotta make Lyla's blaze tonight."

Again, Hank eyed his stupid friend. "Oh, I haven't forgotten."

They worked in silence for the next three hours. Darkness set in, and they finished bottling the moonshine by the dim light of the smoldering fire.

The only task left was bottling Lyla's blaze, and Hank kept a keen eye on his partner. Joey's solo part in the process was to sterilize the bottles. Hank gathered all of the items, carefully measured each ingredient, mixed them by hand, stirred them until the sugar had dissolved, and lastly tended the fire.

Joey carried the bottles to the large tub of boiling water. He dipped each one three times as instructed. Guilt made him feel watched because each time he dared to glance at Hank his partner seemed busy with his own tasks. When all of the bottles were semi-drained, he carried them to Hank.

Hank pulled the first bottle from the wooden box and scolded Joey. "Aren't these supposed to be draining upside down?"

Joey stammered his reply, "Thot they was dry 'nuf."

He took the bottle from Hank's hand and turned it upside down. Both men watched a single trail of clear liquid worm its way down the side of the bottle picking up speed as it rushed toward the neck. Just before the droplets fell to the ground, Joey turned it upright.

"See, hardly no water left."

If Hank had been unaware of Joey's intentions, he would have made him shake out the excess water, but knowing how hard he tried to poison Lyla and how slyly he masked his efforts made Hank's respect leap. He smiled to himself. *Maybe Joey isn't that dumb after all.*

Hank looked toward the sky and whispered, "It's getting late. Come help me seal these with the wax."

Joey jumped to his feet. As this was his first lofty request to help, his chest puffed with pride. He held his first sealed bottle close to Hank's face.

"What do ya think of that?"

Hank smiled, "Looks good, but we gotta finish the rest."

When they were finished, excess drops of red wax littered the ground. Joey beamed with pride as Hank inspected each bottle.

Hank's hands followed each tendril of wax to its end. He carefully inspected each one and smiled at the results.

"They're firming up nice." He turned to find Joey sitting on a stump. He motioned for him to come near. "Which one is the best?"

Joey rubbed his whiskers and proudly picked his best work. "I think this one."

Hank took it in his hands and once again inspected the tendrils. "I believe you are right. This one is a fine job." He extended the bottle to Joey. "You give this one to Chester tonight."

Joey's smile was wide. He marveled at the honor he received. It was then he remembered the arsenic. Suddenly red blotches appeared on his face.

Hank watched the transformation as if Joey's thoughts were audible. "Something wrong?"

"Uh . . . uh . . . nope." Joey hung his head. "I just hope she likes it."

Hank grinned at the double meaning and leaned into his friend. "It'll be our secret." After a sharp slap on Joey's back he said, "Come on. Chester will be waiting."

When the weight of the 'shine cargo burdened the canoe to within a few inches of sinking, the men headed out for Rockery Bay. Hank paddled in silence while Joey held Lyla's bottle careful not to damage the wax. With each stroke, Hank's arm rubbed against the small bag of white wax beads in his shirt pocket.

The new still was a bit farther downstream, adding twenty minutes to their evening ride. Hank's thoughts returned to a conversation he had had many years ago.

He had walked into the speakeasy before its completion. The room smelled of fresh paint and lacquer. An old man stood on the top rung of a tall ladder and had placed the last light bulb in the center chandelier. He yelled down to his young apprentice.

"Hey, Billy, turn it on." The room burst into light.

Lyla clapped, "That is perfect. Thanks, gentlemen. Go ahead and finish up, then come into my office and I'll get you paid." She motioned for Hank. "First, it's your turn."

Hank followed her into her office. Red dresses lined each wall, a rolled rug sat in the center of the floor. Her desk had been pushed against the far wall.

"Sorry for the mess. They just finished polishing the floor."

Hank looked down at his muddy boots. "Sorry, Lyla."

No amount of dirt would dampen Lyla's mood. She waved her hand in the air. "It will clean up. We've got a bit of work to do before next week."

"Opening day?"

"Yeah, it's coming fast." She stared at her half-brother. "Well? Did you bring it?"

"Yep." Hank pulled three small jars from his clothing—one from each shirt pocket and one from his pants. He handed them to her while she placed five glasses on her desk.

She lifted the clear moonshine toward the light and swirled it around in the jar. She watched the liquid settle, removed the lid, and drew in a deep breath of its fragrance. She poured a modest splash into two glasses and extended one to Hank.

"Bottoms up," she winked.

"To the speakeasy."

The chime of the crystal added to the flavor. Lyla nodded with approval and followed the same ritual with a darker bottle.

"Well, that's not quite as potent as the clear 'shine."

"You said make the workin' man's fire a bit weaker and darker in color."

Lyla lifted the glass again to the light. She licked the moisture from her red lips. "Then, I would say you listened well."

Hank nodded but offered no pleasantries.

"Now this," she held up the jar of pink liquor, "is what I really want to taste."

She poured a single glass with a generous portion and savored each sip. "You outdid yourself on this one, Hank." She swallowed the final pinch and extended her hand to her half-brother. "You've got yourself a job."

Shuffling feet at the door interrupted their conversation. Both turned to face Chester.

"This is Chester. He will be my runner. I wanted you two to meet so there would be no problem identifying each other." She motioned for Chester to enter.

"Well, you two shake hands." The men nodded and shook.

Lyla's red dress swished as she strode to the opposite side of the room and opened a closet door. She folded two pieces of paper and handed one to each of the men. She watched as they read their instructions.

"Any questions?"

Their reply was the same, "No."

"Okay. Great. I will not have a single deviation from these plans." She placed her hands on her hips and tapered her eyes. "If the 'shine is not precisely as I say, it will be rejected. Once is acceptable. If it's rejected twice, shame on you.

"I feel I must reiterate this one point—my blaze must have red wax and only pure red wax over the seal. The wax must follow its own path down the edges of the bottle. If one tendril is broken, it will be refused. If the seal is broken, it will be refused. If the wax is discolored, it will be refused."

The men nodded in agreement. They waited in silence for her to continue.

"Do you understand?"

"Yes, Ma'am." Hank spoke first.

"Chester?"

"Yes, Lyla. I understand."

"Good. Then you may go."

Both men turned to leave, but Lyla called for Hank to stay. She spoke in a hushed whisper. "One more thing. If you suspect my blaze to be tampered with in any way, you are to place one of these at the third shortest tendril." She placed a bag of white pea-sized wax drops in his open palm. "Got it?"

Hank searched his instructions for this information but found none. He looked at her puzzled, "But . . ."

"It's not on there, Hank. This is the most secret instruction of all. This is only for us—sister to brother. It could be a matter of life or death." She cupped her hand around his and closed his fist on the bag of wax. "Remember, on the third shortest tendril. Got it?"

"Got it."

Joey's voice from the bow of the boat returned Hank's thoughts to the present. "We're gettin' close, boss. I can see his lights blinking."

"Get the lantern. You still have Lyla's bottle?"

"Yep."

"Have you been careful?"

"Yep." Joey answered with pride, "Careful as a mouse."

"Okay, cuz we don't want her rejecting this one. There's a lot of love in it."

Joey swallowed at the comment. He managed a hoarse, "Yeah." Then he blinked the lantern's light.

They climbed out of the boat in silence. Hank carried a case of the working man's liquor, while Joey carefully handed his prized raspberry blaze to Chester. He held the flashlight close and inspected each tendril as well as the seal.

"Okay," he announced. "Looks good. Nice and red."

Hank added, "Yep, pure red."

A wheeze snuffed his candle.

25

Chester pulled into his driveway. He looked at the blood on his shirt as well as the bloody handprint on his pants. How could he explain this to Sarah?

He opened his car door, stepped out and, standing in the driveway, unbuttoned his shirt. He then rolled the shirt into a tight ball and repeatedly punched it with his fist. He replayed the evening's events in his mind. Why did Lyla cheat him again? And, she pulled a gun on him. Lyla, Oh my God, Lyla! Why would Mickey kill her? What was he going to do now?

He played out every possible scenario. He wondered if he should go to the police. What would he say? He is just as much a criminal as everyone else involved. Sure, he didn't kill anyone, but he transported illegal liquor in his car. He thought about the conversation, the handcuffs, the disappointed look from Sarah, and the shame. No, going to the police was not an option. He just could not do that to his wife.

Suddenly he realized he had been pacing in his driveway for nearly an hour, wringing his bloodstained shirt in his hands and rehashing the same four questions—*What am I going to tell her? Should I come clean? Would she understand? Would she forgive me?*

The neighbor's fence served as a silent sounding board. With each question he pounded his fist into his balled-up shirt. With every answer he pounded it again. Bewildered, he glanced at his hands. They were filthy, black, and bloody—fresh blood. He was startled at first but soon realized his neighbor's fence was old, rusty, and sharp.

Chester wiped his hands on his wadded shirt. That was it! That was his answer! He would tell Sarah he cut himself at the factory. He looked at the distinct handprint on his left leg and then the fresh cuts on his right palm. He smiled. Sarah would be so concerned about his wounds that she wouldn't realize it was the wrong hand.

A lamp in their corner bedroom lit unexpectantly. Chester saw his wife's silhouette move toward the window. Sarah parted the curtain and looked outside. She waved to her husband.

Chester rolled his bleeding hand in his shirt and walked into the kitchen.

"Chester. It's so late." Her not-so-sleepy eyes moved down her husband's dirty clothes and settled on his bloody shirt. She gasped and covered her mouth. "What happened?" She slowly unwrapped his hand. "Oh, Chester! This looks bad. Come over here to the sink. We have to get you cleaned up."

He obeyed her command like a child and stood at the sink with his hands out-stretched, palms up.

"It's nothing, really. It just took a while to stop bleeding."

"I can see that." She shivered at the stains. "I don't think I'll be able to get all of that out."

"It's an old shirt anyway, Sarah. It has seen better days."

For the first time that evening Chester was able to relax. He watched Sarah gently clean his wounds. The sound of the water mixed with its warmth and the scent of soap caused his head to nod.

"Why, Chester Willis, look at you! You are so tired you're going to fall asleep on your feet." She finished washing his hands. "Now take off those filthy pants and go wash up. I'll get some dressing for your hand." She kissed his cheek. "Have I ever told you how much I appreciate your hard work?"

Chester smiled. He loved this woman. "Not today."

She nudged him in the direction of the bathroom. "Now go on, get cleaned up, and then it's off to bed with you."

Chester took his time in the bathroom. The warm water in the soaking tub felt great. He smiled when Sarah checked on him twice.

"Finish up and come to bed. I have some salve ready for your hand."

It took only a few seconds for Chester to fall asleep. Sarah's worry kept her from joining him. She was busy in the kitchen cleaning up the mess. She shook her head at the amount of blood on his shirt but decided to try to save it.

"It would be less expensive to wash it three times than to buy a new one," she laughed to herself.

After scrubbing it the third time with lye soap, she filled her sink with cool water and slid the shirt to the bottom. She glanced at the floor where Chester dropped his pants. His belt jingled as she fumbled to empty his pockets. She laid his penknife, a pocket watch, two pennies, and a pencil stub on the counter and fished in the other pocket. She wheezed when she pulled out a wad of bills wrapped in a rubber band. She turned to listen for the sound of Chester's snores. Satisfied he was sound asleep she unrolled the cash and counted it.

"Twenty-five dollars . . . on a Thursday? It's not payday. I wonder where this came from."

Chester woke up in a cold sweat. He turned to place his arm around Sarah. The bed was empty.

Bright sunlight filled the room even through the drawn curtains. His hands fumbled across his nightstand for his watch. It wasn't there. Slowly the morning fog lifted, and he remembered the previous evening.

He sat up in bed as if released by a spring. His pants? Where were his pants? He retraced his steps trying to recall his actions. Sweat ran down his bare back. He had left them in the kitchen!

Chester threw the covers from his body and pulled on another pair of pants. He opened the curtain and gulped in the air. His pants hung on the clothesline next to his semi-bloody shirt.

"Christ! She hung it out for everyone to see!"

He ran through the kitchen past Sarah and out the back door. He yanked his clothes from the line. Clothespins shot through the air and bounced off the grass. He was breathless when he tossed his damp clothes on the back of the kitchen chair.

Sarah stared at him with wide eyes. Her mouth moved yet spoke not a word. She tilted her head to one side and stood with both hands on her hips.

"Chester! What has gotten into you? Those clothes aren't dry."

"I don't want them hanging out there for the world to see."

"See what? Dirty laundry?"

"No, blood!" Oh no, there he did it. Now Sarah was going to ask questions. And his rum money, where was it?

Sarah lowered her head. "I tried to get it out. I washed it and scrubbed it, but it won't come out."

Chester stared at his wife in disbelief. He almost revealed his biggest secret to her in a fit of panic and she thought he was chastising her laundry ability. He laughed aloud and wrapped his arms around Sarah. "I'm not blaming you. I just . . ." He stopped. He just what? What was he going to say? The corners of his mouth curled in triumph. He lowered his voice and stroked Sarah's hair, "I just don't want our neighbors to worry."

He kissed her forehead. Grabbing his shirt from the chair, he whispered, "Let's just throw this away. It's old anyway."

To be certain the shirt did not make it back to the clothesline, he began to tear it into sections. "Better yet," he grinned, "let's use it as a rag."

Sarah wiped her tears and smiled at her husband. He always knew how to make her feel better.

Chester started to walk toward the bedroom to pull on another shirt until Sarah called for him. "Honey?"

Still smiling, he spun to face her. He watched his wife hold the roll of bills in the air. The smile slid from his face.

"What is this?"

"Money," he stalled.

"I know its money, but what is it for. Payday is a day away."

"I wasn't going to tell you about that." Chester's mind reeled for an excuse.

"Tell me about what?"

"About the twenty-five dollars." He assumed she had already counted it.

"Yes? And?"

He shrugged his shoulders and lowered his head. "Its money someone owed me."

"Who?"

Chester struggled for a name, someone that would make sense. "Does it matter?"

"Chester, who did you loan twenty-five dollars to?"

Again, he lowered his head. He hated lying to Sarah. He told so many lately it was growing difficult to keep them straight.

"Tell me, or I'm going to keep it."

He detected a bit of playfulness in that comment. He smiled at her, confident in another lie. "It was Ray."

"Ray Fluharty?" Her face twisted. "That lazy, no good, rotten excuse for a man! What did he need the money for? To drink, I suppose." Her body shuddered. "Poor Thelma. She always makes excuses for him." Her index finger shook in the air. "Do you know he spends most of his paycheck on booze? Everyone knows about that den of iniquity, that redhead's speakeasy." She spit into the sink. "Something needs to be done with that place, Chester. It's ruining people's lives."

Chester's hands tingled and his jaw ached from the stress of imprisoned motion. His thoughts flashed to the cloakroom while Sarah fussed. She had no idea how right she was.

His candle flame shrank and became smaller and fainter until it cowered to the wick's apex and withered to a puff of smoke.

26

The glow from the match illuminated his face as he lit his third cigarette. He checked the time and tossed the still-glowing second cigarette butt toward a puddle, but before it sizzled out in the cool pool, Officer Little had stepped before him. Skelly jumped.

"Thought no one could sneak up on you guys?" Jack Little hissed through his crooked teeth.

Skelly pulled a long drag from his fresh smoke. "I saw you coming a mile away."

"Really?" Jack eyed him closely. "You always jump when you're expecting someone?"

Skelly stared at the end of his cigarette. Only half of the end caught, leaving the paper to burn erratically. He lit another match and inhaled a second, embellished drag. He eyed the impatient officer.

"I'm surprised you showed."

"Really, why?"

"Didn't take you for the bribing type."

"Who said anything about a bribe? Thought we was just talking?"

"Talking, huh?" Skelly blew a smoke ring in his face. Jack never moved. "So, Officer Little, how many of us are . . . umm . . . talkin'?"

Jack wrinkled his face, "What?"

"Is it just you and me?" Skelly leaned into him. Remnants of his exhale curled in a thin grey haze around Jack's nose. "Or are there others listening?"

"What are you talking about?" Jack's strained voice caused alarm.

"You know how you cops are—always in it for the good of the group."

"I still don't follow."

Skelly squinted at his opponent. "Don't get all defensive now."

He tossed the half-smoked cigarette into the puddle. It briefly sputtered, then died. Both men watched. Finally, Skelly broke the silence.

"Look. I just wanted to talk. You know . . . two men alone in a dark, damp alley, talking about things that bother us, things we'd like to see changed, things that could make a difference. You know?" Skelly nudged Jack's arm. "You know a difference in your town," he waved his arms in the air, "and a difference in mine," he pointed to the north. "You got me?"

Jack smiled, "You sure like to talk in riddles."

"Riddles? I think I'm speaking plain English." He lowered his voice and moved one-half step closer. "I just want to be sure it's just you and me talking here."

Sarcasm threaded Jack's response, "Do you see anyone else?"

Skelly pulled his last cigarette from the pack and lit it. He never made eye contact with Jack. When he placed his pack of matches into his pocket, his fingers clasped the handle of his pistol. He pulled it from his pocket and forced it under Jack's throat tilting his head at an odd angle.

"What the . . ." Jack stopped.

"Shhh," Skelly commanded.

His eyes searched for any movement in the alley. When he found none, he closed his eyes and listened. They were alone. He removed his gun from Jack's throat.

Jack's voice bounced through the alley, "What's that about?"

"Shhh. A man's gotta do what a man's gotta do." He blew a smoke ring in the air. "Don't get defensive, Jack. I just had to be sure."

"Sure of what?"

"Sure we were alone."

Jack rubbed his throat, "Damn."

"You know what they say?"

"Who? And what?" Jack's mixed tones of irritation and frustration were identical.

"An officer will never die alone." Skelly laughed at his horrid joke.

"What are you talking about?"

"Never mind, Little Boy, never mind." Skelly waved his hands in the air. "We've got a lot to discuss."

"It's gonna take all night at this rate."

Skelly dismissed his impatience. He needed to go slow. He needed to be certain this cop won't crack; that he'll follow through with the plan. He needed to be sure Little Boy will obey or the wrath of Vincent will focus on Skelly. He hand-picked this target so he needed to be crystal-clear that this man was solid, or concrete shoes would be Jack's certain fate if Skelly lived to do it.

"Look. It's no secret how you feel about Lyla."

Skelly eyed Jack's response at the verbalization of her name. He watched his neck veins immediately pop as he clenched his jaw and fist. Skelly tried to hide his snide grin. He had only begun to make Jack squirm.

"She embarrassed you." Skelly heard his clenched knuckles crack. "You know what she's doing in there, but you can't catch her." He watched his opponent pound his fist into his hand repeatedly. "She thinks she's smarter than you." Again, Skelly suppressed a smile. "Who does that chubby redhead think she is?"

Jack finally snapped, "What's it to you?"

Skelly ignored the question and continued. "I was there the night of your raid. They have a special signal, you know. Lights go on and off, the band plays louder to cover the sound of disappearing liquor, the door man fakes a stutter to stall your entrance, and then in a matter of seconds all is covered, and in you burst into a room of soda drinkers." Skelly tossed his head and laughed but never took his eyes off his red-faced adversary. "Soda!" His laugh changed to mockery. "Then, she saunters up to you. She makes you wait. She mocks you, treats you like a little boy . . ."

Jack's face colored. His eyes opened wide at the last two words. He lost control. The alley resonated with the colorful cussing that spewed from his hot tongue. When he finished his tantrum, his eyes fell on Skelly's crooked smile.

"What's your point?"

"My point, Officer Little . . ." Skelly carefully chose his words; his derogatory name play had served its purpose. Now that he had Jack's full attention, he needed the officer to buy into his alliance. ". . . is I've uncovered her weakness."

Jack's countenance changed to intrigue. "Go on," he encouraged.

"It's called raspberry blaze."

Skelly began to unfold his carefully orchestrated plan when they heard a loud ring of metal on brick. Their bodies froze, then quietly slid into the shadows. When the haze cleared, Valetta stood in the alley. She paused with crossed arms as the sound of her tapping shoes filled the heavy night air. They heard a huff of disgust and listened to her fading footfalls as she strode away.

Skelly held his finger to his lips and motioned for Jack to follow. They crept through the alley stopping every few feet to listen for the sound of her footsteps. Only when Valetta passed under a street light could they see her silhouette, though they kept a safe distance.

The evening's damp air added to Valetta's sense of fear. She pulled her wrap to cover her face, paying little attention to the uneven surface of the brick sidewalk. One heel caught in a crack, causing her to fall forward.

The men slid back further into the shadows when they heard her cry of surprise and disgust. Holding their breath, they awaited the sound of clicking heels to continue yet heard none. After a few minutes Skelly motioned for them to investigate.

Jack found a shoe, its heel broken. He held the grease-covered pump in front of Skelly's face, then knelt to gather its unbroken mate. The men looked at each other in surprise. Had she discovered they were following her?

They ran to her apartment building. Skelly needed to be certain which room was hers.

"Why exactly are we following her?" Jack whispered.

Skelly muttered, "To be sure which apartment is hers."

"Why?"

"Did you just ask me why?" Skelly shook his head. "We need to be aware of all the players or this plan will not work."

"Plan? Is that what you call this? Come on, Skelly, finish with your plan. I want Lyla almost as much as you, but what that has to do with Valetta I still don't get." Jack's angry tone conveyed that he had had enough for the evening. "I'm tired. I'm wet. You started to explain this plan of yours then we got interrupted by this babe." His hands waved through the air. "Then we lost her?" He lifted her shoes. "Except for these." His words gained speed. "Look, I'm interested. I'm listening. I'll go along with whatever you have planned." His voice grew loud, "And for God's sake, what is raspberry blaze?"

Skelly grinned. It had worked. He had the officer hooked, curious, and irritated—right where he wanted him. He placed his arm around his shoulder and turned to walk back toward the alley.

"Raspberry blaze, my friend, is Lyla's Achilles Heel." Skelly's laugh filled the empty street.

Their candles went dark with the laughter.

27

Hank woke in a cold sweat. Why did he not place a bead of white wax on the end of the third tendril? He knew Joey tainted the blaze, though not with the cyanide, or at least he hoped.

He threw the blanket from his weathered, wrinkled body and ran to his pants crumpled in a heap on the floor. He rummaged through the first empty pocket and felt a brush of panic until his fingers found the slender bottle in the second. He breathed a sigh of relief as he read the partial label aloud.

He pulled the bag of wax drops from the same pocket and held them up to the light that flooded his bedroom. He stared at the moon's position and calculated he had at least two hours before dawn. He pulled on his mud-caked pants and walked out his front door.

The swish of the dry grass beneath his feet left no doubt that rain would be coming before the end of the day. With a roar of his car's engine, he drove toward Salem.

Hank only passed one other vehicle. He pulled in front of a vacant house on Pershing Street and ran toward the speakeasy's fire escape. He was surprised to hear voices in the back alley so he slipped into the cover of an alcove and waited.

Johnny and Chester unloaded the last of the night's run. Hank wanted to question why they were so late, but waited patiently. He knelt to the sidewalk and placed three piles of coins on the brick. His foot rattled a discarded rusty tire iron and snatched it quickly to silence the reverberation. He heard someone approaching and held his breath. He absolutely could not be caught.

He listened as the coins clattered on the sidewalk and smirked when Johnny knelt to retrieve each one. With his fingers wrapped tightly around the tire iron, he lifted it to the extent of his reach. Before Johnny had the chance to stand, Hank struck the back of his head. Hank watched the tire iron fall onto the bricks and used that sound to cover his jump to the fire escape.

He moved over the metal spider without a sound. Years of slinking through the woods to avoid the law gave Hank the feet of an Indian warrior—silent and swift. When he neared the top, he noticed Valetta standing in the alley with her arms crossed. He watched her for only a second until the weighty mist seemed to erase her existence though he heard the sound of her heels signal her departure.

Hank stared at the daunting task of shimmying the pole to the roof though he had done it before and knew it was the only way. He spit on his hands, rubbed them together, and began to climb. His underdeveloped arms felt like wet noodles as he neared the top, but with a last burst of energy, he tossed his body onto the speakeasy's roof and tiptoed toward the trap door.

Surprise lit his face when the trap door opened with ease. The last time he had struggled with it. He smiled at his luck and began his descent. It was not long before the sound of whispers from below made him freeze. A faint light shone through the opening directly below his feet. He held his breath to listen.

"One from lass week, and one from t'night, and this one," the speaker held a bottle in the air, "is the bestest one."

Hank recognized the speaker's voice. It was Joey. Joey then pulled a tall wooden box closer and began unloading its contents. The bottles rattled from his shuffling.

"I don't have no choice. Nope, no choice. Mr. Skelly backed me in a corner." He placed the last bottle on the shelf with a sigh. "Hank's gonna be mad."

Hank's hair stood at attention at the mention of his name. He shook his head in disbelief. He could hold his breath no longer. He slipped down the last few rungs while Joey's rambling continued. He kept his foot on the bottom step and extended his head toward the back of Joey's neck.

"Why would Hank be mad at you, Joey?"

The sound of Hank's hissing voice burned like a trail of fire down Joey's spine. Joey's paste-white face froze, his mouth open though no sound but a faint whimper came from it.

Hank slithered from the ladder and placed his hands on Joey's slumped shoulders.

He squeezed as hard as he could.

"What'cha doing, Joey?"

Neither Joey's expression nor position changed. Hank seized his shoulders and spun his frozen body to face him. His words spewed out like machine gun fire.

Finally, Joey collapsed in a whimper. Remorse filled his whispered response.

"I didn't wanna do it. Mr. Skelly made me." Tears flooded his eyes and coursed down his dirty face, leaving glistening streams that looked like snail slime. "It was the only way we could gets our new still. Can't make no 'shine without a still and can't make no money without 'shine."

Joey wiped his face with his sleeve. He watched Hank's face and hoped he could talk or cry his way out of this mess.

"I didn't know what to do. We was outta time. Mr. Skelly gave me money for all the parts in exchange for only one thing."

Hank was both appalled and proud of what he heard. What surprised him the most was the fact that Joey did this on his own. His angry face softened as his partner rambled on with his confession.

Joey began to sob. "But I lost it. I knew I had it there in the shed." He pointed to his friend. "You saw it too. Thought it was the red dye. Then I couldn't find it. It jus disappeared. I saw a bottle way in the back, layin' on the groun', thought for sure I found it, but it wasn't it . . . only arsenic, not the . . ."

"Cyanide," Hank finished Joey's sentence while proudly displaying the missing bottle.

Joey's face lit with excitement. "Where'd you find it?"

"Who is up there?" Lyla demanded.

Joey once again froze though the overbearing tone in Lyla's voice caused Hank to spring into action. Still on his perch on the bottom rung on the ladder, Hank swung his legs and kicked open the trap door, snapping it off one of its hinges. His feet then connected with Lyla's head sending her body to the floor. His momentum caused his feet to hit a swinging light fixture. Its bulb burst, scattering glass over the floor.

"Now what, Hank?" Joey's desperate whisper filled the dark space.

Hank pulled his lean body back through the opening. He wanted to pound some sense into his stupid friend. Joey sat, oblivious to the fact that he shouldered the responsibility of their predicament.

"What the hell are you doing here anyway?" Hank spit.

"I . . . I followed the runner." His response was as innocent as it was stupid.

"Why are you here?" Hank's annoyed response made Joey cringe.

"I jus' doin' what I's told."

The last thread of patience left Hank. He rushed toward Joey and forced him to the floor. The brief struggle lasted only a few seconds, for Joey surrendered before Hank had even touched him. Besides the sound of their labored breathing, the moan and sound of a sickening snap from somewhere below filled the two with dread. They listened breathlessly as the squeaking of the trap door stopped, its full weight suspended by one weakened hinge.

When silence once again filled the room, Hank relived the past few days, careful to mention every detail—stealing the bottle of poison, watching Joey taint Lyla's blaze, Joey's clever response of passing off the small amount of liquid in the sterilized bottles as water, and then he ended the tale with a description of Joey's pride when he handed Chester the bottle. He made no mention of the absence of the white wax as well as the reason for his appearance but ended with a sinister laugh about Lyla's predicament.

"So, now that you know what I know, I will ask again. If you already put poison in Lyla's blaze, why did you follow Chester?"

"I needed to be sure all the pure bottles were switched. Mr. Skelly said I had to do it quick 'cause Vincent was losing patience." Joey slashed his throat with his finger.

Hank knew the name Vincent Franciasco Sabino. Only a fool showed no respect. Even though most of Vincent's business occurred north of 'shine country, his fingers grew long and tangled in the illegal transport business.

Hank remembered the man who taught him the ins and outs of 'shine making, his uncle Ralph. He was seventy-two when Hank went out on his own. Ralph helped Hank make the copper still, place the pipes for the cold spring water, build his first fire, and even load his truck full of spare parts, just in case he sprung a leak. He was a good old boy with or without the liquor, the best sharpshooter around, and had ears like a rabbit despite his age, but how he ended up hanging upside down with his tongue cut out was attributed to only one man—Vincent Sabino. Ralph mentioned his name once while they were preparing Hank's copper.

"I'll tell ya, Hank. If anything fishy ever happens to me, there is only one guy to look at, Vincent Sabino."

Hank remembered coaxing his uncle for more information, but that was all he said. Short, sweet, and to the point and Hank never forgot it. When he found his uncle's body suspended one foot above his newly placed still with the words "Told you" written in blood, he abandoned the sight and never returned. Vincent was one man that Hank wanted nothing to do with, and here his partner sits confessing that he jumped into bed with him.

"How stupid could you be?" Hank scolded. "Never, never, never go in business with the mob." Hank lowered his voice to a whisper. "You'll just wind up dead."

"That's what I'm telling ya, Hank. I had to do it."

"So why not just tell me? Why all the sneaking around?" Hank shook his head. "We could have built a new still without their money." He leaned into his friend with clenched teeth and hissed, "Now they own us."

"What are we gonna do?"

"What exactly did they tell you to do?"

"Poison Lyla's raspberry blaze."

"Why?"

"They want her dead, says she's gotten too big, makes too much money, flaunts that she don't need them, that a woman can do it better, and that she's cuttin' into their territory."

"So why poison her? Why not just shoot her?"

Joey shrugged. "Wanted it to look like an accident, I reckon."

"So they asked you to do it?"

"Said you wouldn't go along with it." Joey lowered his eyes, "Said you couldn't be bought. Said you proved that years ago." He looked at Hank, "What'd they mean, Hank?"

The vision of Ralph's body flashed before him. "I don't know," was all he could think to say. He sat in silence until in the distance they heard Mickey calling for Lyla.

"Hank?" Joey frantically whispered when a beam from a flashlight below shone through the opening where the trap door dangled.

"Shhh. Don't move."

They sat in the darkness and listened to Mickey's irritated voice. A jingle of keys and shuffling of feet seemed distant. He heard Lyla shout orders, the sound of a soft thud, and then all fell silent.

"Did you do what you came for?" he whispered to Joey.

"Huh?"

"Did you switch out all the blaze?"

"Yep."

"Then let's get out of here before they find us."

The men scampered up the ladder. Hank climbed first with Joey close behind. When they got to the top, the roof was closed. Hank pushed on it, but it would not open.

"It's stuck, Hank. Push harder."

Irritated with the way this night was going, Hank snapped again at Joey. "I'm pushing as hard as I can. I think it's locked."

"How could it be locked? Didn't you come in that way?"

Frustrated, Hank pushed with both hands, stepped up one rung closer, and then tried to push with his back. Tracing the edges with his fingers, he searched for a hidden lock or spring, anything that would release but found nothing.

Sweat covered his face and palms. Again they heard voices from below. This time louder. He was certain one was Lyla.

"Hank! We gotta get out of here!"

"I'm trying!"

Near panic, Hank began to use his whole body to try and force the door free. Though he pushed with his head, shoulders, back, and arms it would not yield.

The voices below rose and fell. It was difficult to tell the number, but at least one was male and one was female. Occasionally a beam of light would shine up the ladder nearly reaching Joey's shoulders. There was little doubt that whoever was below could see Joey's feet and it was only a matter of time before the two met them—either in person or by their bullet.

Joey's burst of terror propelled him past Hank. His hands met the wood with brute force. Yet the hatch remained closed. Joey's hands flailed. Losing his balance, he nearly fell twice. Hank joined in his effort and suddenly, without warning, the door sprang open.

Their entangled bodies burst through the gap. They heard the sound of a gunshot and felt the rush of air from the bullet's near miss.

Joey grasped the pole first and slid toward the fire escape. Just as Hank's hands wrapped around the metal pipe, the shaft door behind them closed on its own.

The men scrambled down the metal fire escape stairs with a loud clamor thinking only of their escape. Once on the ground they scattered, each to his own car. Even their flight on wheels took different routes.

Both candles flared in brightness, faded, then flared again until they burst.

Chandra instinctively moved to clean up the spattered drops of molten wax. Isabell covered her hands to stop Chandra's movement.

"It would be more prudent to wait until it's finished."

Chandra knew she was not referring to the hardening wax.

28

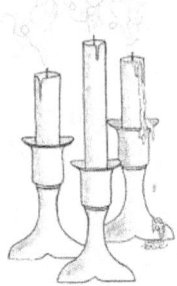

Two candles burst into flame; one flickered as a normal candle should, and the other burned wild and bright orange. Both women held their breath and waited.

Vincent sneered at Skelly, his loss of patience obvious. "I asked you to do this!"

"He demanded to talk to you."

"Why?"

"Says you owe him."

"I owe him?" Vincent's laugh filled the room. "Bring him in."

Skelly ushered the carpenter into the room. Vincent's normal position of lurking in the shadows held a different aura. Skelly obeyed his silent command and slipped out of the room. He closed the heavy wooden door and leaned against it, guarding others from entering. He cradled his shotgun in his arms.

Vincent rose from his chair. He slid his fingers along the edges of his desk, careful to keep his eyes on his guest.

"Where's your respect?" He squinted against the light of the lamp overhead. "Remove your hat."

The oversized brim cast a deep shadow over the man's face. Only his unkempt heavily-bearded chin was visible. He held the unlit stub of a cigar between his teeth. He removed the butt from his mouth and spat on the floor.

Vincent paused, then rushed toward the man and embraced him. "My son, my son! How long has it been?"

"Twelve years?" The man's hands remained at his side.

"You've grown into your own." Vincent pulled on his beard and knocked his hat to the floor. "I knew you would return!"

Vincent walked around his son, patting his back, legs, ribs, and stomach. He eyed Vinchento's attire with great disapproval and filled the room with guttural clamor until settling into a gurgle of joy.

"Is this any way to greet your father?"

The young man surrendered and wrapped his arms around Vincent. "Father."

After a brief moment of backslapping and laughter, Vincent grabbed his shoulders and shook him. "So, I owe you?"

"Sure," contempt laced his tone.

"You left, broke my heart. Your mother cried for weeks . . . and I owe you?'

"Sure," his reply came with certainty.

"You've got a lot of guts to show up here after twelve years," Vincent slapped the back of his head, "and say that."

"You found me. I didn't come on my own." Vinchento's eyes offered only hatred.

"I didn't ask for you to come." His whispered voice left no doubt what was about to unfold. "You requested to be brought."

"I wanted to tell you myself."

Vincent slapped the back of his head. "Always the big man! You limp waste of the Sabino name. Couldn't live with the family business?" Vincent spit in his face. "Coward!" His agitation manifested itself in flailing arms and jagged words.

"You think you're a man?" Vincent scoffed, "A man, Vinchento, would stand and fight, would stand up for himself, for his father, and his mother. A man would show respect, be a good son, one who listened and followed the rules."

He began to laugh. "Instead . . . what do I have?" His laughter turned to aggravated taunts. "I have a son who disappeared when he was needed the most, broke his mother's heart," he leaned into his son, "and her will." He turned his back from him.

"She'll never be the same. Thought you were dead. Begged me to find you, but I refused. I said, "He will return, when he's ready. And here you are. Is this what I deserve? This arrogant disrespect?"

Once again, Vincent turned to face his son.

Vinchento stood firm, unmoved by his father's antics. He had witnessed Vincent lose his temper more times than he could count, most often ending in bloodshed, either immediate or drawn-out by one of his cronies. If honest emotions were summoned, he despised his father. He disapproved of the family business, of his father's attitude toward others, of his lack of conscience and disregard for human life, but mostly for the way Vincent treated his mother.

The last time Vinchento stood in his father's presence, he was fifteen. His parents had returned from a party with his father visibly drunk. The sudden jolt of pounding fists against the front door woke Vinchento from a deep sleep. He rushed to unlock it, but just as he turned the knob, the door flew open with force. The mahogany doorjamb splintered slicing Vinchento's lip and face. He crumpled to the floor.

A shower of blood inundated the entry. His mother knelt beside him using her dress to slow the bleeding while his father gathered fragments of his son's bottom lip from the floor. Both mother and son watched in horror at Vincent's remarks and laughter.

"This feels like jello!" he repeated multiple times with callous cruelty.

Finally, Maria had heard enough. She rushed toward her husband hitting him with a flurry of fists, pounding on his chest, face, head, and hands.

At first, Maria's assault was a mere distraction from the soft, squishy flesh that Vincent held between his fingers, but her last punch brought searing pain in his left eye. His vision hollowed and fell dark. He lifted both hands and shoved his wife.

Maria stumbled over her son's legs, lost balance, and toppled backwards down the hardwood stairs. Her shriek only affected Vinchento.

One by one their three lit candles fizzled until darkness covered them.

29

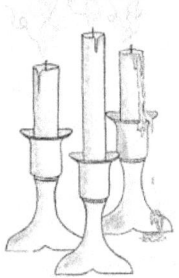

Valetta's hands swung wildly hoping to find the light cord. She forced herself forward a step and cringed at the sticky substance she encountered beneath her foot. A shiver ran down her spine, leaving her legs weak and unstable.

Her second step carried her imagination to horrifying places. The slimy substance soaking her right foot's stocking felt soft and squishy.

Fighting to hold back the grisly images inspired by her imagination, she forced herself to concentrate on finding the light cord—it had to be there somewhere. At last she found it and pulled. Nothing happened. She wrapped it around her fingers and pulled again; still no response. She yanked on the line one last time. It broke. She lost her balance and toppled onto the unseen thing she had tried to avoid.

A soft moan muffled Valetta's scream. Not a normal ouch that hurt moan, but a despondent sigh like expelled air from deep within or something worse . . . from the beyond.

Valetta reacted in fear as anyone would. She jumped from the body she had touched, unable to see in front of her and rolled toward the door. A hard object jabbed her ribs. She reached over to grab it. It was a pistol.

Her panic-inspired imagination drove her over the edge. She thought she saw the unmoving body begin to rise from the floor. An unseen force tossed its clothing. When the body was fully erect, it towered three feet above her. It began to move toward her. Each step became deliberate. Its hands reached out in front of its body as if taunting her. It seemed to call her name.

Valetta opened her mouth to scream, but nothing came out. Terror had paralyzed her voice. The room was supernaturally alive with movement. Unseen coins jingled somewhere in the back. Ice cubes fell into unseen glasses. The sound of soft fabric swished past her ear. Hot fire brushed her face.

In a split second the image before her morphed into a ball of scarves. It spun around her daring her to move. Her fist closed tight around the Derringer's butt. She slid her index finger over its trigger.

The figure erupted into flame and advanced. Valetta fired. Abruptly the room fell silent. Nothing moved. Nothing fell. Only the smoldering flashlight beam flickered.

Valetta's nostrils burned from the acrid odor of spent gunpowder. Her brain demanded her hands cover her face, but instead they collapsed at her sides.

"What happened?" was all Johnny could manage to say.

Mickey pounded Lyla's flashlight once again. It briefly lit, then went dark.

Johnny spat at Mickey in frustration, "Get a light bulb—something! We have to see what's going on here!"

Mickey sighed in response, annoyed that it was not his idea. He disappeared around the corner.

Johnny patted Valetta's cheek. "Talk to me, Lettie. Please talk to me."

A strong smell of gunpowder lingered, underscoring that Valetta was the cause. Johnny pried the pistol from her grip. He whispered softly in her ear, but her incessant ramble continued. He propped her body against the doorframe.

He tried to stand and slipped on the wet floor. He bent down and swirled his fingertips through the dampness and brought his fingers to his nose. It was blood. He set Valetta down and then traced his way through the blood trail. His first physical contact was with the fingertips of the body. He moved his hand up the body's hand to its wrist, and held his breath. Although the room was coal black, he closed his eyes, feeling for a pulse. He felt nothing.

He knew it was Lyla though his heart hollered, "NO!" He moved his hand to her neck, hoping to find a pulse there. But, it was useless. She was gone, shot by Valetta.

Mickey arrived with a light bulb and short ladder. In a moment piercing light illuminated the room. Both men shielded their eyes. Only Valetta remained inert.

They saw Lyla's body lying on her back, surrounded by a pool of blood. Wet footprints marred the floor and fanned out, into a broad pattern. Valetta's dress soaked in Lyla's blood, had drawn waves of red swirls across the floor until settling at her hemline. Johnny searched for a pulse one final time.

"Is . . . she?" Mickey stammered.

"Dead." Johnny hung his head.

"What are we gonna do now, Johnny?"

"We can't call the police, that's for sure."

"Did Valetta . . ." Mickey could not bring himself to form the words. The fact that his love interest had killed Lyla was beyond his comprehension.

Johnny inspected Lyla's body. The bullet had entered her lower jaw, which now hung in sickening strings of torn flesh. Her red dress, pushed above her knees, was saturated in blood. One shoe rested in the far corner of the room, the other still on her foot.

"Look at all the blood!" Mickey's voice trembled.

Johnny traced the blood-covered footprints on the floor. Valetta's bare foot was easily recognized. His were much larger and more pronounced. Another set came toward and moved away from her body and although they were wet, it was not blood. Mickey's sobs interrupted his thoughts.

Mickey struggled to speak. His teeth chattered ripping at the flesh of his swelling tongue.

"What are we gonna do without Lyla?"

"Get a grip, Mickey, we need to think."

"Think about what?"

"About what we need to do."

Mickey stared at the contrast of red—from Lyla's nails, to her dress, to her shoes, her hair . . . her blood. He shook and rubbed his fist.

Johnny looked at him curiously. "What's the matter with your hand?"

Stunned Mickey stared at him with his eyes wide open. He looked down at his hand rubbing the other and quickly dropped them still at his sides, forcing the vision of punching Lyla from his thoughts. His delayed response rose suspicion.

"Huh?"

"Your hand . . . what's wrong with it?"

"Uhhh," he lifted them to show Johnny. "Nothin'." Immediately, his face felt hot.

Valetta whimpered as consciousness returned. Mickey was grateful for the diversion. He watched Valetta cover her down-turned face as she rocked and muttered. Her words were hushed and unrecognizable.

"Johnny! What are we gonna do?" Mickey words burst through guilt.

"I dunno, Mickey."

"We can't go to the police." Mickey's voice sounded desperate.

"I already said that."

"How are we gonna get her out of here?"

"I'm thinking."

"Why did this happen?" Mickey's words escalated to a shriek. He began pacing furiously.

"Mickey, get control of yourself! We have to figure out what we do next." Johnny sat up straight. "Did you lock the front door?"

Mickey's mind raced through the evening's events. He couldn't remember going to the password door. "I think you were . . ." Then he remembered Skelly Canter. He jumped to his feet and ran down the hall.

Johnny turned his attention to Valetta and struggled to comfort her. She laid her head on his shoulder but did not speak. "Please, Lettie. Talk to me. What happened?" He wrapped his arms around her shoulders and rocked his body with hers.

Mickey returned. "The door is locked, Johnny."

"Now, or was it locked before?"

"It was shut tight when I got there." Mickey's eyes shifted avoiding his question.

The door was closed, but not locked. Mickey did not want to expose his irresponsibility to Johnny although he owed Johnny no explanation. He wondered who left it unlocked—Johnny or Valetta or . . . ? Mickey tried to cover his guilt by relaying his story about Skelly. The incessant babbling did not interest Johnny. Mickey stopped in mid-sentence.

"What are you thinking, Johnny?"

"We can't tell anybody. We've got to find out what happened with the gun. We can't go to the police. We can't tell anyone she's dea—." He forced the lump from his throat. "She's gone. We have to put our heads together to protect Valetta."

"It was an accident!" Mickey spoke with certainty.

"I know that! Of course she didn't do it on purpose. But we can't change what happened." Johnny lowered his voice, "I didn't even know she could shoot a gun."

Mickey gulped. He did not know much about Valetta, but he sure liked what he saw. He frowned at his thoughts and tried to recover.

"Do you think we should bury Lyla somewhere?"

"I don't know how we could get her out of here without someone seeing us."

Both men stared at Lyla's gory setting. Not a thing about her appearance looked peaceful. The shinbone that protruded through her skin paled in comparison to the measure of blood that pooled onto the floor. Her splintered lower jaw affected the position of her mouth leaving it oddly gaped and smeared with red lipstick. A thin trail of blood spilled from its corner. Her eyes were fixed in horror.

Johnny turned his face from her. Guilt, anguish, and frustration could not match his level of sorrow. His stomach protested in defiance. He buried his face into his hands.

Annoyingly, Mickey counted silently on his fingers. After the third repetitive motion, he verbalized the options. "Well, we can't bury her. We can't carry her out. We can't leave her here. We can't pretend it didn't happen. And we can't call the police. So what are we going to do with her?" His eyes begged Johnny for an intelligent response.

The sound of Valetta's voice made both men jump. "We have to hide her."

Their candles were hushed to darkness.

30

Friday crowds surpassed most nights by nearly double. The patrons were tired from the week's labor and ready to party. Lyla spent most Friday's in the back shadows, but not this night.

Mickey tried to cover his grief by tipping a bit of his own bottle; Johnny lashed out at the customers, and Valetta spent most of the evening in her dressing room. Their sleepless nights caused exhaustion.

"Hey, Mickey? What's up with you tonight? I need another down here." A man pounded the polished bar.

"I've been asking before you." A second man muscled his way through to the crowd. "Hey, buddy? What's a man gotta do 'round here to get a drink? I've been thirsty all day."

The first man thrust his elbow into the other's rib. "Get in line. I was here first."

"Not on your life, I need a drink." He lifted his waving hand into the air and whistled to Mickey.

Mickey, frantic to keep up with the unruly crowd's demands, poured one shot after another and slid them down the bar. Some slid off the edge and crashed to the floor. Cheers, groans, and gasps erupted simultaneously.

The crowds mixed reaction only added to the agitation of the two bickering men.

"I said, Get in line."

"What are you blabbering about, old man?" He condescendingly lowered his towering body and snickered at his opponent.

"Who's calling who old? Look at you," he cackled. "You can't even stand up straight!"

"I can stand fine. You are the one collapsed on that stool." He continued his maddening wave and whistle. "Hey, buddy . . ."

"I said I was here first. Who do you think you are?"

"A regular."

"Yeah right. I've never seen you here before."

The man moved away from his stool and tried to capture Mickey's attention. "Buddy?"

Followed by the other, he sneered into his ear. "Regular, huh? Guess not or you'd know his name." The old man tilted his head toward the bartender.

His toothless laugh elevated his annoyance. The second man threw the first punch. The old man retorted. Bloody teeth spilled from their mouths. The crowd cheered and surrounded the show.

Johnny watched with placid interest until the confrontation became physical. He smiled at the opportunity. A few quick steps and Johnny was on the outskirts of the circle. He gently tapped on the shoulder of a bystander who turned to face him and instantly moved to the side.

Johnny jumped between the men with his hand halting a punch. Johnny's fist knocked the look of shock from the fighter's face. The man fell to the ground with a thud. Johnny spun to face the second chap who swiftly met the same fate. He pulled both men through the parting crowd; their shoes bumped across the floor.

The patrons exploded into a frenzy of whistles and cheers. The women who stood a bit too close rushed to the powder room to wipe the splattered blood from their faces and clothes; one woman gasped as she pulled a tooth from her hair. The men stiffened their chests and wore the color as if they were the victor.

Mickey remained unmoved by the events of the evening. He glanced at the empty space that for eight years had held Lyla's presence and frowned at the emptiness. He drowned his sorrow uncontested in the clear liquid.

Valetta sat alone in her dressing room. She stared at her mirrored image. It seemed aloof and unreachable. Light pink talc covered her clothes, hair, and vanity stool, leaving her powder jar nearly empty from her incessant puffs. When the cheers from the crowd erupted to its height, two of her co-dancers burst through the door. Valetta remained indifferent.

"Wow, what a fight!" Silvia cheered breathlessly.

"Did you see the blood fly out of that old man's mouth?" Bonnie screeched.

"And his teeth," Silvia added with pride.

"Valetta, you should have seen Johnny in action! He dragged those two men through the ballroom as if they were wet towels." Silvia bent her arm and made a fist pumping up her biceps. "He is so strong!" She sneered toward Valetta and waited for her normal jealous response. Puzzled with no reaction she shrugged her shoulders and left the dressing room.

Bonnie approached her friend and knelt on the floor at her feet. She gently brushed the excess talc from her costume.

"What's wrong, Valetta? You haven't been yourself all night."

Suddenly aware of the powdered mess she had become, she laughed at her reflection. "Look at me! I'm a mess!"

She stood and brushed the powder from her hair and clothes and began to wipe the excess from her face. She looked at herself in the mirror again and laughed. It felt good to be able to use that emotion. She turned to her concerned friend and patted her hand.

"I'm fine. Just a bit distracted, that's all."

Bonnie scanned the mess that surrounded her stool. "A bit?" They both laughed.

"I best get a broom and start cleaning this up or Lyla . . ." Valetta stopped mid-sentence. Horror covered her face. She turned from her friend and vomited.

Apprehensively, Bonnie whispered, "Please, Valetta. Sit down before you fall down. I'll go get some help."

Bonnie raced down the hall and tried to coax the janitor from the bar mess. Her demeanor annoyed Percy. "I'll be there when I'm a finished here, Miss Bonnie. I gots to clean this up first."

"But it's Miss Valetta. She's sick. And there's a big mess on the floor."

Percy patted her hand to calm her. "That mess ain't goin' nowhere. I'll be there when I'm done wif this."

Bonnie crossed her arms and tapped her foot. She watched every stroke of his broom. With his dustpan heaped with glass slivers, she pulled his arm.

"I'm 'a comin'."

When they entered the dressing room, Valetta's body twitched and convulsed on the floor with her hands wrapped around her throat. Percy snatched her from the pool of spew, wrapped his arms around her, and squeezed. Out flew her powder puff. They stared at the pink ball in disbelief.

Bonnie ran down the hall to summon Johnny. Silvia stood beside him stroking his arms, babbling about how strong he was when Bonnie yanked him from the praise.

"It's Valetta. Something's wrong."

He rushed past her and burst through the door. Percy sat on the floor before her with his hands steadying her shaking knees. Valetta slouched in her stool covered in vomit. Her hair hung in damp strings.

Johnny placed his hands under her legs and lifted her from the chair. He carried her down the hall with Percy and Bonnie following closely behind.

Johnny tossed orders over his shoulder. "Percy, go clean up that mess before Lyla sees it." A thick bulge stuck in his throat. He cleared it from his mind and continued, "Bonnie, tell Mickey I'm taking Valetta home."

"But I don't think she should be by herself."

"I said I was taking her home."

"But are you coming back?"

"No, I'm not coming back," he snapped. "That is what I'm trying to tell you."

"But Johnny she swallowed her puff. How do you swallow a puff?"

"Listen, dame. Don't talk." His tone was strained and serious. "Tell Mickey I'm taking Valetta home."

"But . . ."

"He will understand."

"But what about Lyla? When she comes in tonight, she will be furious."

Johnny carried Valetta out the door. Annoyed at the interruption, he spit his response to Bonnie.

"I'll take care of Lyla. You just tell Mickey that he is on his own."

The wick began to fizzle, desperately clinging to its tip. With its final puff of smoke, the fragrance of talc lingered.

31

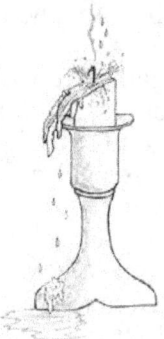

Mickey managed to hold the crowd to the normal issues. With his new solo responsibility, he set his personal white lightning bottle under the counter. He needed to rise to the challenge and drinking was not the answer.

Three times that evening people asked about Lyla's absence and three times Mickey pretended not to hear them. After the last customer fell out the door, Mickey turned the lock with a heavy sigh.

George and the band gathered their instruments and placed them in the music room. They always took special care of Lyla's equipment. After all, had she not purchased each guitar, horn, microphone, or piano, the harmony would have been impossible. Most of the band members did not have enough money to own their equipment except George. He was the only one permitted to bring his brass with him.

George walked up to the bar with his trumpet in his hand. "Hey, Mickey? How 'bout one for the thirsty horn player?"

Mickey smiled at his old friend. "Anything for you, George."

"Anythin'?"

"Yeah, I know what you're asking." Mickey filled a tumbler with three fingers of white lightning and placed it before him. "How's that?"

George picked up the glass and swirled the clear liquid. He watched the liquor slide down the inside of the glass in thin clear strings. "Now looky here at this." George held the glass up to the light and pointed to the tendrils. "Nice fingers."

Mickey smiled again. "Yep, George, that's the good stuff." He filled a shot glass for himself with the same.

"Shore 'nuf, the good stuff."

Mickey patted George's arm. "After the night we had, you deserve it." He winked. "I couldn't have held this wild crowd down by myself, now could I?"

George took a full swallow. "Ahhh," he sighed. He squinted and narrowed his eyes. "What do you think is wrong with Miss Valetta?"

Mickey choked on his shot. "I don't know. She's pretty sick, I guess."

The pair stood in silence both lost in thought. George swirled the spirits around the bottom of his glass and took his last swallow. Mickey rubbed the same spot of his freshly polished bar.

George slammed his tumbler and watched Mickey jump. "Why are you so jumpy?"

"I was just thinking, I guess." His thoughts rolled to Lyla and wondered about the next step.

George eyed him curiously. "You all right, Mickey?"

"Huh? Oh yeah, sure. I'm fine. Just worried about Miss Valetta."

"There sure will be a lot of unhappy men here tomorrow if she don't dance." He watched Mickey shake his head. "Not to mention Miss Lyla. She shore won't be happy either."

Thoughts of the previous night flashed before Mickey. He tried to keep his composure, yet all he could do was clear his throat.

Finally regaining poise he added, "I think Lyla's the one that gave the sickness to Miss Valetta." He fanned his arms around the air. "Otherwise, she would be here, don't you think?"

"Yeah. Where was Miss Lyla tonight?"

"Sick, George. I told ya. She's sick as Valetta."

Paul shuffled into the room and announced Chester's arrival. Mickey groaned at the added responsibility.

"Best I be goin', Mickey." George slapped his friend's arm and winked. "You take care of Miss Lyla's special pink drink, now ya hear?"

Ignoring George's remark, he grabbed the keys. He watched Chester stand in his accustomed position with a bottle of Lyla's raspberry blaze held in the air. Mickey brushed past Chester without giving the bottle any attention and walked down the stairs with George.

Chester stood alone in the empty ballroom. He peered around the corner and listened for any movement. He replayed the scene in the cloakroom and shivered at the memory. His curiosity forced his feet to move down the hall toward the setting. With trembling hands he turned the doorknob and jumped when it opened. He drew in a deep breath and entered the room.

Bright light illuminated the room when he pulled the cord. He found himself staring at an empty floor. An odd odor assailed his nostrils—a mix of liquor and ammonia. The wood floor mimicked the shine on the bar. He fumbled along the back wall for the trigger to open the hidden door to no avail. Chester shook his head again at the memory of Lyla's final moments.

"What are you doing in here?"

Chester jumped at Mickey's accusatory tone. "Looking for my coat," he answered while trying to mask his fear.

"Well?"

"Well what?" Chester threw his hands in the air.

"Did you find it?"

A thick clot of nerves constricted his throat. This emotion was exactly the opposite of what he wished. He just wanted to see how the room looked. He had given into his probing desire and now faced certain discovery. His response was meek and staccato.

"F . . . f . . . find what?"

Mickey's body swooned as much from exhaustion as from the evening's sips. Quickly agitated by this useless conversation, he snapped, "Your coat!"

Remembering his lie he retorted, "Nope. It's not in here."

Chester brushed Mickey's arm as he hurried past him. His only thought was to get out of that room, away from the sordid memory, and put it behind him. He could do nothing else.

Mickey watched Chester curiously as he hurried to gain distance between them. He looked as though he held an argument with himself. Chester then shrugged his shoulders, shook his head, and squeezed the neck of Lyla's blaze. The pink liquid sloshed violently inside the bottle. Bits of wax crumpled beneath Chester's grip and speckled the floor as if marking a path toward the guilty. Mickey followed Chester through the password door and watched him sprint down the steps. Chester left unpaid, clinging to Lyla's bottle. Mickey's expression was one of suspicion.

Finally alone in the speakeasy, Mickey jiggled the contents of his pocket and enjoyed his last shot for the evening, whistling a nameless tune as he polished the bar. He twisted his towel as tightly as he could and then snapped it straight. He chuckled at the sharp snap of the damp rag as he placed it over a hook to dry. When he withdrew his hand, he curiously eyed the red thread he saw wound around his fingers. It was then he remembered the silver key and lock under Lyla's desk. Burrowing his hand into his pocket, he closed his fist around Lyla's keys and smiled.

A feeling of guilt sobered his thoughts. *How could I think of it?* Yet he refused to deny his curiosity. Lyla was gone. As much as he would like it not to be so, he could not change it, and now the red thread taunted him pushing him for answers. He walked to the password door, double-checked the lock, and tiptoed to the door to Lyla's office.

The fragrance of Lyla's perfume still lingered in the room, as a result of her overuse of it. Mickey imagined the perfume changing to tiny life forms and clinging to each piece of fabric in the room—the red dresses neatly hung each on its own hook perfectly pressed, looking as though they had never been worn, the tapestry fabric of her desk chair, the red, navy, and black Persian rug casing her mahogany desk, and even the brocade drapery that curiously framed her closet—all displayed the fragrance fairies. The miniature people that clung to every thread with their minute fingers stared at him, shaking their heads, begging him to leave Lyla alone. Mickey cleared the vision from his mind. He wanted to laugh their little bodies away but felt uncomfortable displaying that emotion in Lyla's office. He slipped past Lyla's chair and gathered himself under her desk.

Mickey fumbled with the cluster of keys. He rattled them into submission, forcing his fingers to grasp the smallest key. His hands felt stiff and oversized, unable to hold the vital object steady. He drew in a deep breath to calm his nerves until his fingers felt normal again.

The key turned easily inside the lock. The wood door sprung open and released the rolled parchment onto the rug. Mickey held the spool in his hands for a few minutes as he argued with himself. With curiosity the victor, he unrolled it and began reading:

I, Anna Lyla Timmons, as being of sound mind and without offspring as heirs, do hereby bequeath all of my personal and professional belongings to be shared as follows:

To my trusted bodyguard and friend, Johnny Pasquel, I leave my guns - the Remington, Smith and Wesson, and Derringer.

To my loyal bartender, Mickey Rollins, I leave my coveted butlers pantry located in my office and all of its contents hidden in the many furtive compartments, and his private liquor stash of which he thinks I am unaware.

Surprise and guilt lit Mickey's face. He straightened his back and once again bumped his head against the desk top. He rubbed the growing tender spot and continued to read.

To my best and I must say favorite dancer, Valetta Hamilton, I leave all of my jewelry —three diamond rings, ruby necklace and earrings, ruby ring, and diamond earrings. Wear them well.

To Chester Willis for a job well done without suspicion or discovery, I award him my car. The best damn Cadillac even if it is red! It will bring laughter to my lips each time I see him behind the wheel.

To the members of the band, I leave each a jug of the best white lightning and the instruments purchased for the patrons viewing. As well as for the best horn player in town, George Whiden, I leave my father's black cameo ring that he admired once many years ago and a bottle of my raspberry blaze if any is left in the house.

To all the loyal patrons of my speakeasy I permit one night (so determined by the two equal partners) to be on the house as celebration of my memory.

Lastly, to my half-brother, Hank Timmons, I leave the contents of my home on 562 Union Avenue, and all the personal contents inside the aforementioned property.

Oh. Did I forget something? The equal partners you ask? To the two equal partners I leave the building located at 378 East State Street, the ongoing business, and all the liquor, furniture, and miscellaneous notions necessary for the continuing of the business. Profits as well as expenses are to be equally shared leaving neither partner in charge of the other. All decisions are to be mutually agreed upon and carried out.

Do you think you two can handle that, Johnny and Mickey?

I, Anna Lyla Timmons, do hereby give my approval for this last will and testament to be carried out in full, unless of course I am murdered by any of the aforementioned.

Speakeasy my friends,

Anna Lyla Timmons

Mickey's flame sizzled doused by his tears.

32

T he lighting and the distinguishing of the multitude of candles made Chandra dizzy. She felt it impossible to keep track. Once again, her thoughts returned to Isabell's explanation of the spirits' staccato revelations. The notion of time and this long, sleepless night became overshadowed by her deep interest in what had happened within the building so many years ago.

Isabell sat motionless in the darkened room, her hands spread over her knees. Her lips moved as though amid a conversation though not a sound left them.

To evoke the memories, Chandra closed her eyes. Upon opening, her surroundings seemed foreign.

Johnny held Valetta as she cried. He stroked her hair and rubbed her back while cradling her body in his arms. Valetta's whimpers sounded pathetic, yet somehow forced. Johnny shook his head to clear the image of Lyla on the floor and Valetta holding a gun. "She is not capable," he thought. Swallowing hard, he dismissed his thought and began to hum.

Valetta held her eyes wide open and never blinked. She stared at the ceiling and moaned.

With each passing minute, Johnny became more concerned. He continued to rock her in his arms.

Not able to hum any longer, he whispered to her, "Talk to me, Lettie. Please, talk to me."

Finally, Valetta began to mutter. She struggled to break free of Johnny's arms but the more she squirmed the closer he held her. Words came in a flurry yet were indistinguishable. After a few minutes of thrashing, she accepted Johnny's care and opened her eyes.

"Where am I?" she asked in a weak, pathetic voice.

"We are in your apartment."

"How did I get here?"

"I carried you." Refusing to mask his pride, Johnny grinned. "It was easy."

Valetta managed a smile. "What happened, Johnny?"

"That," he stroked her hair, "I hoped you could tell me."

She squeezed her eyes tight and shook her head. "I don't know. All I remember is someone standing over me. It was dark and I couldn't see who," she forced a hard squint, "or what it was."

Johnny listened quietly to her story. He wanted to ask questions but decided instead to listen.

"The floor was slippery. I stepped on something soft and squishy." With her eyes closed, her recollection of the night became clear. The memories rolled from her lips. "In my mind I knew what it was. I had tripped over you on the sidewalk earlier, but this felt different. There was blood, a lot of it . . . everywhere, and I couldn't get away from it."

Valetta's hands joined in the dramatic account of the previous evening. "I heard the rattle of metal. The sound of a door slamming shut far above my head. Twice." She continued nodding with her eyes closed. "I heard it twice. Hot breath suffocated me. I coughed and choked. It was too close." Valetta's head shook continually. "The room began to spin. Swirls of wispy fabric surrounded me. I struggled to move away from its searing eyes. The room got hot." She covered her tear-stained face. "I couldn't move. The room spun fast, too fast. I was soaked in blood. Blood!" she screamed.

Their candles blew out together. Chandra watched the smoke rise in parallel fashion slowly inching closer until they met and began to swirl together forming a bold line of smoke. Suddenly as if tossed by an unseen wind, the fumes scattered until they vanished.

A hushed whisper seemed to linger in the room. It was a hiss that refused to be silent. It was then that Chandra noticed a faint glow from the triple-wick candle. Its state remained fixed, neither burning nor fading. How long it had been that way was uncertain but needless to say, Lyla was listening.

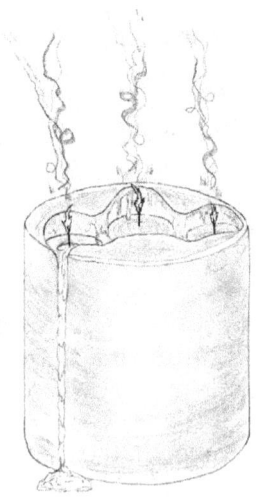

33

Chester fumbled down the double set of the speakeasy's steps. When his feet hit the brick sidewalk, he ran to his car. It wasn't until he crawled behind the wheel that he realized he had a death grip on Lyla's pink blaze. Flakes of red wax dotted his pants and stained his palm an odd shade. He started to move his hand to wipe it on his shirt and thought better of it. He had already ruined one shirt. He dared not think about explaining a second to Sarah.

He mumbled aloud, "What am I gonna do with this?" He stared at the bottle nearly void of all the wax tendrils. "Lyla won't accept . . ." he stopped and hung his head.

When Chester pulled into the driveway of his house, his thoughts had become a tangled ball. He hid the blaze in the bushes by the neighbor's fence and walked into his dark house.

Chester searched his pants for the third time to no avail. They were empty. He forgot to get the run money from Mickey. Remembering how panicked he felt when Mickey caught him in the cloakroom caused chills to run through his body leaving him feeling limp and spent.

How am I gonna explain that to Mickey? I never leave without payment. He crawled into his warm bed beside Sarah, muttering the cyclical lie about overtime that had become second nature.

Guilt had long ago left Chester, despite the consistent mealtime prayers of their housekeeper. He spent so much energy justifying his actions that at times he felt he ran on automatic. He tried to draw deep breaths, but that resulted in a coughing fit. Disgusted, he threw the covers from his body, kissed his wife, and walked into the kitchen.

Alone with his thoughts, Chester tried to deny what he witnessed. Why would Mickey kill Lyla? It simply made no sense. They seemed to have a great relationship. Sure Lyla was impatient, but she had demonstrated that emotion with each employee as a way to embody authority; Mickey was no different from the rest.

The argument Chester overheard seemed less heated than others had. His interpretation of last evening's confrontation frustrated him. He resented the unknown. He recalled their muffled and garbled voices, which only became clear when they escalated. In those moments Lyla simply issued a command, nothing that would warrant her death.

For nearly two hours Chester rehashed the events. He tried to focus on what he knew to be the truth, but his thoughts wandered to the trap door, the ladder, and the roof escape. It seemed oddly curious to him that a hidden exit would actually be an entrance. He wondered how many knew of it. He jumped at the sound of a voice behind him.

"What's the matter, dear? Are you too tired to sleep?"

Chester turned to face his sleepy-eyed wife. He smiled at her concern. He did not deserve her. He stood and wrapped his arms around Sarah.

"I'm fine. Just not tired tonight." He watched Sarah yawn. "But you are, so please, Sarah, go back to bed."

"But . . ."

"No buts. I'll be in soon." He smiled and nudged her back the hall. "I promise."

Sarah shuffled her bare feet and worked her way slowly toward their bedroom. She fell asleep when her head touched her pillow.

Chester's candle faded in silence.

34

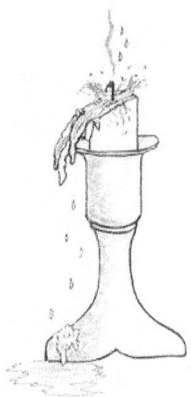

Mickey stared at Lyla's will. His first thought was to destroy it; his second chastised his first. He imagined showing the others and watching in horror at their reactions.

He imagined Johnny to be the first to speak. Overwhelmed with surprise, excitement, dread, and then anger, he would pound his fist on the wall until it yielded. All eyes would fall on the large hole.

In his visualization Johnny fought conflicting emotions. He wanted to scream at Valetta. He knew Johnny wanted to use force to show his authority, yet he watched his friend slide against the wall until he crumpled to the floor in defeat.

Self-pity oozed from Valetta's eyes. She could not have killed Lyla, and if she did, it was an accident. It wasn't her fault! Her hands held her stomach from retching. Why did she insist on hiding her? Why did they listen to her? It only makes them all look guilty.

Valetta imagined herself wearing Lyla's jewelry. She fingered her empty earlobes and pictured the precious earrings there. Her lips curled as she pretended to look in the mirror. She moved her head from side to side, ensuring perfect placement of the earrings. Then her hands moved down her graceful neck until she felt the teardrop ruby at its end. She twisted her hair into a loose bun allowing a few tendrils to skirt across her shoulders. She looked beautiful.

Reality from the heat of piercing eyes forced her hands to hang limp at her sides. Her imagined grandeur faded to a dance hall girl without diamonds, rubies, or pearls. All eyes glared at her forcing a verdict. She hung her head in shame, yet shook her head ruminating innocence.

Mickey's fantasy moved to Chester. He stood with empty hands, his last run unpaid. He watched as his open hands turned to clenched fists.

Mickey tossed him a key. They were to Lyla's red Cadillac.

Chester stared at the odd-shaped silver object. Why would Lyla give him her car? He hated red. Maybe she did it as a way to chide him into eternity. Maybe she wanted to make him the laughing stock of town. Maybe it was her way of ensuring his capture. After all, the police would be looking for a red runner for a car. They would knowingly follow him everywhere and wait for a mistake so they could inspect the vehicle. They would discover his hiding places. They would know his routine. He would spend the rest of his life in prison. And Sarah, he would have to tell Sarah! Chester's shoulders slumped. He opened his hand once again and looked at the key. Then he remembered.

It was a Wednesday, just a few years ago. Sarah came home from the market excitably talking about this beautiful red Cadillac. Sarah described every detail, which surprised Chester because he never thought she paid attention to cars, but obviously she loved this one.

She ran her hands through the air as she imagined the shape of the fenders. She described the interior—the steering wheel, the gauges, gearshift—and she even described the width of the white sidewalls on the tires. He remembered her fingers stretching to five inches wide and he had chuckled silently at her excitement.

Her last mention of the vehicle was about the red dress that hung on a hanger in the back window. His face fell at the mention of the color. It was then he knew the owner of the Cadillac. It was Lyla.

Chester recalled a passing conversation he had overheard about Lyla's purchase of the 1930 Cadillac Sixteen Madame X Sedan Cabriolet. Lyla was elated about every feature the car had to offer but the color; it was green. "Green wouldn't do," she laughed. "So I had it painted the only color it should be – red." Chuckling at her audiences' response, she added, "I know the color red for an automobile is outlawed in many cities, although I'm certain Salem is not one of them. It doesn't matter to me if the color is reserved for fire engines." She scoffed at her own remark. "I simply will own no other color. It had to be red."

Realizing now that Lyla meant for the present to be for Sarah and not for him changed his opinion of the woman. He guessed Lyla had a heart after all.

Chester recalled telling Lyla of Sarah's excitement at his earliest opportunity. He shook his head looking back because he thought she wasn't listening. Her lack of reaction embarrassed Chester. He wished he had left it unsaid. He remembered clearing his throat when he left her room.

When Chester's eyes lifted from the key, Mickey expected him to glare as all others did at Valetta, yet to his surprise Chester's anger seemed focused on him. Mickey recoiled in surprise at his visible clenching teeth.

Mickey shook his head to clear his imagination. He did not like the direction his thoughts were taking him. Hank's face came to his mind. He shook his head again to rid the thought. That man made him feel uneasy. Since Mickey had control of this fantasy, he chose not to have Hank present.

He directed his thoughts toward the band members and watched as their faces lit with excitement at the presentation of their white lightning gifts. Each man held his jug in the air, nodded, took a swig, and then wiped his mouth with his white sleeves. Dressed in their band uniforms of black pants, striped vests, and suspenders, as well as crisp must-be-starched white shirts, they picked up their newly owned instruments and began to play. George's black cameo ring glistened on his finger.

Mickey tapped his foot to the imaginary music and watched his body dance with Valetta across the ballroom floor. For a moment it was only the two of them, dancing and sharing longing glances until a sharp pain rose in his back returning him to the present.

He pulled his crumpled, half-numb body from under Lyla's desk. He gathered his legs to his chest and began to sob.

Soon his sobs turned to a crooked smile as he imagined being half owner of Lyla's club. He pictured another poor sap behind the bar struggling to keep up with the drunkard's demands. He laughed each time a patron became belligerent or a bit too clumsy. A conjured figure a bit larger than Johnny, with a menacing jeer and eyes that ripped through your core, stood along the back wall awaiting his signal from the movement of Mickey's hand. The bouncer slithered through the crowd, grabbed the unruly patron, and tossed him down the double flight of stairs.

Clutched in Mickey's sparkling white teeth was the stub of an expensive cigar. Not many men could afford such a luxury, though in his fantasy, he and Johnny could.

The ballroom was flooded with more people than ever before. The booze ran clear and often, though he gave no thought in his whimsy who would provide the 'shine.

The old band continued to play. Their notes seemed clearer and in perfect unison. Since they now owned their instruments, care of polishing the brass and wood became essential.

And oh, the dancer in his daydream. There stood only one—Valetta. Her movement swayed free in her scanty costume. Mickey watched her every move with interest. She never took her eyes from him; it seemed as though she danced for only him. It was clear in his fantasy that Mickey had won the prize while Johnny busied his attention with a few less desirable women.

Valetta began by shaking her hips forcing the fluff of her fur tail to rattle and flutter. Mickey flushed with desire before her. She pulled one strap from her shoulder and let the thin thread droop over her glistening skin. Playfully she tugged on the other strap. The crowd hung in silence as she toyed with the possibility of a full reveal. Mickey felt the heat rise from his depths. His excitement was obvious. He held out his hand to her. When their fingers touched, she giggled and pressed her scarcely dressed body against him. He skirted her away from the roaring crowd and announced her absence. He slammed the office door closed. He smiled. *Wait! What was that?*

Mickey froze as he listened to the emptiness of the speakeasy. He had been so enthralled with his reverie that he felt unsure if the sound of a slamming door he had heard was real or a fantasy. He held his breath and listened.

Then he heard it. Quiet footsteps, each drawing the perpetrator closer toward Lyla's door. They came slowly, deliberately. They sounded soft, pliable, perhaps the assailant came with bare feet.

Mickey's throat tightened. He swallowed back the urge to cough. He ducked back under Lyla's desk, praying for obscurity. His fingers fumbled with the will as he tried to roll it into its found position. He groped at the red thread. Twice it slithered through his damp fingers. The footsteps continued.

He pulled a string from the rug only to find it attached. He brushed the carpet violently until finally he found the thread wrapped around his finger. In haste, he forced it over his skin. It broke. Panic surrounded him as the shadow stopped outside of the door. The doorknob rattled. Although locked, it gave Mickey no comfort. He shoved the rolled paper into the hidden compartment and locked it with the silver key.

Relieved for barely a second that his secret would be safe, he jumped at the rattling doorknob. Mickey stared at it in disbelief. Its shaking became violent forcing the door to goan from tension.

Mickey wanted to cry out. He wanted to ask who was there, but his lips would not move. He waited and watched, anticipating his worst confrontation. No matter who the visitor his intentions would be difficult to explain.

Just as the door seemed it would burst open, the rattling stopped though the shadow of the feet remained visible.

Mickey's over-held breath caused his head to swoon. His vision faded. Just before he lost consciousness, he thought the door flew open with a loud bang. His head hit the floor.

When Mickey woke, his head buffeted. He tried to piece the moments together while struggling with self-pity for all his recent misfortunes.

Glancing around the room, he found most as it had been. His body lay on the rug just outside of Lyla's desk opening. Her chair sat slightly off to the side. The office door remained closed. All of her red dresses hung untouched on the back wall. Mickey rubbed his face with his hands and felt the roughness of the string wrapped around his fingers.

He stood quietly, careful not to alarm his unexpected, unknown guest. He looked for the shadowed feet that stood on the opposite side of the door. There were none. He sighed.

As he looked around the floor for the other half of the broken string, his hands fumbled in his pocket searching for the cluster of Lyla's keys. He found none. He placed his left hand in his left pocket. He pulled a few coins and to his surprise, the other bit of the red thread.

"Where are the keys?" he whispered.

In a slight panic he thrust both hands in his pockets. Certainly if he kept them hidden long enough he would pull the cluster from one or the other, but both were empty.

His eyes began to search the floor. He crawled under the deck three times, rubbed every thread on the area rug twice, and crawled around Lyla's desk too many times to count. In defeat he searched his pockets once again.

"Where are they?" he asked in a normal voice. He heard a slight thud answer from a distance. He froze in mid step.

Slowly he lowered his foot to the wood floor and crept toward the door. His hand shook as he touched the doorknob. He forced it to turn—one way, then the next. It was locked. He placed his ear against the wood and listened for a second thud. Hearing nothing he walked back toward Lyla's desk somewhat relieved yet still guarded.

The jingle of her keys as they skirted across the wood floor broke his trance. From where he had kicked them he could not imagine, but he smiled when they rested in his palm. He crawled back under Lyla's desk and opened the lock.

With his hand placed under the opening, he expected the rolled paper to fall into it When it didn't, Mickey crawled farther under the desk. Lyla's will held fast, refusing to yield. He wiggled and twisted it, anxious to free it without a wrinkle. Finally, he succeeded. With the final tug, the paper came loose. With it came a small black box.

Next, he did what anyone would do. He shoved his hand into the void and searched each corner for any other hidden treasure but found none. The box was light and felt empty. He shook it and then slowly opened the hinged lid.

A velvet pouch, with its string drawn and knotted, lay neatly folded inside. Mickey wiggled his fingers to loosen the string and became frustrated with the tedious task. Finally, his persistence paid off, and he pulled it open.

Only two of his fingers, though slender for a man, could fit within the top. He felt something soft between them and pulled the contents from the bag. In his palm lay four threads, all red in color- one thick as yarn, the second twisted with white, the third tied in a series of knots, and the fourth was braided. Confused at their purpose, he placed them from whence they came.

He opened the will one last time and reread his fate. He wondered if he should tell the others.

He rested his hand on Lyla's interior doorknob and listened. He paused before opening it as he replayed the evening in his mind. He dismissed the feeling of watchfulness as his imagination and slipped into the ballroom.

He whispered a self-held argument. "Should I tell the others? How would I expla—"

He stopped mid-thought. A lone chair in the ballroom lay on its back. He knelt to pick it up. A shuffling sound from his blind side made him spin. What he saw made him gasp—a second chair faced him, deliberately placed on the top of a round table.

He ran from the room without turning off the lights, without locking the door, and without looking back. He was not alone. His life was worth more than whatever came next.

He ran to rid his mind of Lyla's intentions, her broken body, her blood, and her will. For him, the building once filled with song, life and laughter now held only pain, suffering, death, and danger for all who entered. His thoughts came as a flood and assured him that naught would remain same. He had nothing left. By an odd series of events, Mickey understood. Lyla's speakeasy had reached its pinnacle. It was a fun ride while it lasted. He stuffed his guilt, his involvement, his shortcomings, his secret thoughts, desires, and schemes. He ran as any coward would and never returned.

Mickey's candle though once tall and proud burned to barely a stub. Chandra and Isabell watched the flame intensely burn as it licked the entire circumference forming a pool of molten wax in its core. A bright ball of fire leapt from the wick and transformed into a puff of white smoke. The women understood that Mickey's story had ended—in turmoil, fear, yet mostly tragedy.

35

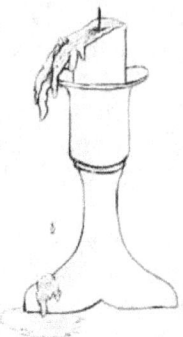

Johnny sprung straight up in bed. He strained to hear of any threat but only heard the sound of Valetta breathing. He patted the space between them searching for her body. She lay on her side with her knees pulled to her chest. Johnny tried to slow his thoughts by focusing on the sound of her soft breathing. Finally, he tossed the sheet from his legs and sat on the edge.

The wood floor felt cool on his bare feet. A slight breeze skirted the fringe of Valetta's silk draperies.

The dim night seemed to warn all light from entering. Johnny walked toward the window. Even the light from the street lamps appeared subdued. Nothing moved. No people wandered the street. He sighed and sat on the floor winding the rug's fringe around and around his fingers. With each tug he moved the corners closer together until the material lay in a ball on the floor. He stood and walked to the edge of Valetta's bed.

The slow rise and fall of Valetta's slumbering chest gave him little comfort. He sighed. He wondered about Lyla's final thoughts. Was she in pain? Did she struggle? Did she cry for help?

As he stood over Valetta, he fought back waves of anger. He tried to focus on their intimate moments together, their quiet evening walks, and the softness of her skin, but each memory ricocheted back to Lyla.

Johnny remembered the first time he knew that Lyla holstered a pistol in her garter. He had worked barely a week as her bodyguard when he experienced their first police raid. The three officers pounded at the door demanding entrance while Paul stammered. Johnny leapt toward the warning switch. He stood in awe at the fluidity of not only of the crowd but of Mickey, Lyla, and the band.

Horns blared a long series of staccato notes while the piano player pounded the keys. Their warning tune resonated through the crowd. In less than one minute, the officers rushed into the room to find a group of people playing cards, dancing, and tapping their toes to the music while sipping sodas.

One officer picked up several glasses to smell the contents. After the fourth sniff, he slammed his fist on top of the table spilling all four drinks over the deck of cards.

"Damn it!" yelled one belligerent participant. "Now look what you've done!" He shook his head in disgust as the four men attempted to wipe the soda from the cards. He nodded his head to the opponent sitting beside him. "What d'you have, Joe?"

"Eight and a six of hearts." He answered exposing his hand.

"What about you?" he asked the man to his right.

He tipped his hand backwards and replied, "Pair of tens."

"Oh, don't even tell me . . ." his disgust grew more agitated as he turned to the last player. "And you?"

The last man threw his cards on the table without revealing his hand. "I don't have nothing."

The first man glared at the fourth. "You were bluffin'?"

The man was silent though his sneer said what his lips didn't.

"Then I would've won!" He turned over his pair of queens. "Oh hell, I would've won!" He pushed his chair back from the table and made a leap toward the officer that caused his loss.

Johnny would be reprimanded later for his slow reaction. Entranced by the scene, his hands hung at his sides as he watched Lyla emerge from the gathering crowd. Without any hesitation she pulled a pistol from her garter and thrust it against the back of the patron's head.

"Simmer down there, Carl. Don't do anything stupid."

The officer's face flushed at Lyla's action. He should've taken better control of the situation. After all, he took an oath to uphold the law and he should not allow a citizen to do the protecting, especially if that citizen ran an illegal drinking establishment. His shoulders sagged at the reality that he now was indebted to Lyla.

"Carl?" Lyla's voice carried a stern reprimand.

"Ye . . . yes, Ma'am?"

"I said simmer down." She pressed her pistol a bit harder. "You probably would've been fooled by Willy's bluff." She tossed her red hair and laughed.

Johnny watched the officer's face burn brighter with each word. He obviously did not enjoy the public humiliation. He turned slowly to face Lyla and Carl. He opened his mouth twice, though said nothing.

Lyla laughed a bit harder and shoved Carl out of the way. She waved her gun in the air and announced to the room. "I'd say these good folks could use an apology for the disruption of their evening."

The room erupted with jeers and whistles. Lyla smiled and leaned toward Officer Little and whispered, "You're welcome."

She pointed toward the door. "Now, get out."

Johnny remembered how defeated the policeman looked. Officer Little shuffled his feet, hunched his shoulders, and lowered his head while being careful not to make eye contact with any bystanders. The other lawmen followed him in silence.

Once they left the building, the lights flickered again. In unison the crowd cheered "All clear!" and Lyla's liquor again flowed.

People danced, sang, drank, fought, and Lyla smiled until her eyes met Johnny's. She motioned to him with her finger.

He remembered the lump in his throat as he neared the red lady. She turned from him and walked toward her office. Each step felt like a lash from his mother. He followed her into the room. She closed the door behind them, muffling the sound of music in the ballroom. The music's beat added to the building tension as Lyla stared at Johnny.

"Bodyguard?"

Although it was a question, Johnny somehow knew not to reply. With his termination of employment eminent, he silently straightened his stance in response.

"Is that what you call yourself?"

He knew not to answer.

"I hired you on recommendations, against my better judgment. Now, I am certain I made a mistake." She paced around the room, lowering her voice with each statement until her voice became barely a whisper. She then slammed her fist on the desk.

Johnny forced himself to stand firm and not jump in surprise. He must have succeeded because he watched Lyla's red lips curl into a smile.

"Now, that's more like it." She walked toward him and patted his shoulder. She headed for the door. Just before she walked out, she tossed a threat over her shoulder, "If it happens again, you won't see daylight."

As Johnny stood in the quiet of Valetta's apartment, the same emotional shame poured over him. He rubbed his thick hair to clear his thoughts.

It had been several years since that incident, and Johnny worked hard to gain Lyla's trust. Within a few weeks from that night, Lyla gifted him with a submachine gun and took him to the outskirts of town for target practice.

Johnny's aim needed little sharpening though he seemed comfortable with each gun she handed to him. Lyla even permitted him to shoot her prized Derringer and her Smith and Wesson revolver. The last gun he fired was her father's Remington.

He rubbed his hands across Valetta's mattress as if caressing the stock of the gun. The engraved hunting scene covered the receiver and ended with a man carrying a trio of dead ducks. The thing that impressed Johnny the most was the stock. Made of walnut burl from a tree on the family property, it gleamed with polish. The odor from the monthly linseed oil rubbing lingered.

"She's a beauty, isn't she?" Lyla asked.

"Boy she sure is. Did he use it much?"

"Oh, quite a bit in his younger years but he just rubbed and cleaned it when he got older." Lyla chuckled and added, "Much like how you are rubbing her now."

Johnny laughed at the realization. He placed it gingerly in Lyla's hand. In one swift move she fired over his head. They both watched a duck fall to the ground.

"And that, my boy, is how it's done."

He smiled at the memory of Lyla's skill. It was difficult to imagine that Valetta could have surprised her and killed her. He replayed the evening's event again in his mind.

He remembered the coins on the sidewalk. He remembered hearing a muffled gun report, at least that is what he thought it was at the time. Vision of the tire iron made him shudder. Then he remembered Valetta tripping over him.

If he had only gone toward the cloakroom instead of Lyla's office, she may still be alive.

"I just assumed you were in your office. That's how it always is. Why were you in the cloakroom? And how did Lettie shoot you?"

He tried to make sense of the situation. He counted all the happenings on his fingers . . .

. . . Broken leg . . .

. . . Mickey left . . .

. . . Flashlight broken . . . two of them?

. . . Wet footprints . . . not blood . . . and hefty . . . definitely a man's . . .

. . . Strong smell of hired man's liquor . . . from where?

. . . Light bulb broken . . . why?

. . . The smell of gunpowder . . .

. . . Coins on the sidewalk . . . a set up?

. . . Tire iron . . . ouch. . . . It still hurts. What a lump . . .

. . . Chester's agitation . . . what's his deal?

. . . Ice and blood on the ballroom floor . . .

. . . Mickey's bowler man . . .

. . . Lyla's gun . . .

. . . The smell of her blood . . .

. . . The open trap door . . . why? What's it for? Why didn't I look?

. . . Shots fired . . . one. . . . No, one pop from a distance . . .

. . . I got struck . . . second shot was Valetta.

He covered his face with his hands. It couldn't have been her. Not his Lettie. It's just not possible.

Johnny stared into the light of the streetlamp for what seemed an eternity. He walked to the edge of the bed and tried to find comfort in Valetta's peaceful sleep, but many nagging questions refused to allow him peace.

He whispered, sobbing, "I failed you, Lyla. When you needed me the most, I failed you." He hung his head and shuffled out of Valetta's front door.

The early morning air brought him no comfort. Uncaring of watchful eyes, he walked through the back alleys. His life was ruined. How could he pretend nothing happened? His mother's warning thumped in his head, "These things have a way of catching up with you, Johnny. Don't bring shame on this family."

He walked up the double flight of stairs. His key entered the lock. After a turn, the door swung open.

Once inside, he slid into the shadows and listened. He heard the faint sound of rattling paper. It seemed to come from Lyla's office.

"Think, Johnny, think," he whispered.

Then, he remembered. Lyla kept a pistol on a ledge above the band's instrument closet. He picked up a chair and placed it on the closest table. Stretching his full length, he managed to barely touch the handle of the gun. He tried to force it toward him with no success. He stood on his tip-toes and succeeded in getting a slightly better grip.

Suddenly, Johnny felt vulnerable—standing alone, on his toes, on a chair, on top of a table. He reached out again and managed to slide the gun close enough to get a good grip on it. Once he had the pistol in his hand, he tried to quietly jump off his precarious perch. But he landed awkwardly, staggered and backed into another chair. The sound of the chair falling to the floor reverberated throughout the room. Johnny panicked and ran to the cloakroom.

His familiarity of the secret closet gave him little comfort as he slid inside. The sound of broken glass crunched beneath his shoes. He held his breath. The lingering smell of hired man's liquor filled his nostrils. His eyes began to tear. Still he remained.

Time seemed suspended in the closeness of that storage room. Alone in the quiet darkness, he began thinking about Lyla's death. Several theories came to mind although many held only nonsense and ridiculous notions.

His thoughts wandered to the wet footprints. Unconsciously, he moved his feet as if walking. The crunch of broken glass jolted his nerves. He stiffened at the realization that the wet tracks of footprints were from the broken bottle. He remembered the smell of spent gunpowder and hired man's liquor—liquor that was stored in this closet. Another thought chilled him. Lyla's killer had hidden in this closet.

He ran through that scenario for the fourth time, convinced of his conclusion. He remembered the damp footprints when he entered the room—how they joined Valetta's, how they stopped at the edge of the pool of Lyla's blood, and mostly how they disappeared as they dried. He squeezed his eyes shut, hoping to recall them more clearly.

His eyes opened and he looked up as a new revelation struck him—the trap door. Lyla's killer had left through the ceiling.

Shifting his weight back and forth, the trap door riveted his thoughts. Where did it lead? And why did Lyla not tell him about it? He thought he knew every inch of this place.

He listened for any noise. He popped open the hinge and cracked open the door. Through the narrow crack, he held his breath and listened again. Confident he was alone he stepped into the room and focused his eyes on the two-foot-wide opening out of reach above his head.

Just then he heard the sound of someone running. He froze in mid-step. He pulled the pistol from his belt, flipped off the safety, and held it steady, aimed at the door.

The hurried footsteps were erratic. He listened as the sound left the ballroom and entered the hall. Johnny braced himself for the confrontation, but instead of coming down the hall toward him, the footfalls raced down the speakeasy steps toward the street.

Johnny ran toward the front window, but by the time he reached it the runner had disappeared around the corner. Johnny did not get a look at the runner's face but thought it to be a man with about the same build as Mickey.

He took only a few steps back toward the cloakroom when he stopped. "It was Mickey!" He yelled, "What the hell is going on?"

Confused, he gathered the ladder from the junk room. Just before leaving, he noticed another flashlight on the floor. He picked it up and pushed the button. It worked.

When he reentered the cloakroom, he leaned the ladder against the wall and aimed the flashlight beam at the opening.

He climbed the ladder for a closer look. His shoulders barely fit through the opening, but he managed to pull his body through the tight space. He crouched on his knees and swung the beam around the room.

On a small shelf on the opposite side sat six bottles of Lyla's pink blaze. A cluster of wooden boxes stood between him and the shelf. He looked inside the slated box and saw three jugs of moonshine. He wrapped his hand around the handle of one box and shook it. It was full and so were the other three. Assuming each box held three jugs, he stared at enough liquor for a week of normal business.

Johnny rubbed his head. He was the one who unloaded the 'shine from Chester's run. He put it away. He stored it in the usual place, either behind or beside the bar for easy access. Who put these here? And how did they get it up here? The beam of the flashlight seemed to lead the way as it illuminated the ladder nearly to the roof.

He stood, placed the flashlight in his shirt, and began to climb the ladder.

When he reached the top, his hands moved over the wood ceiling until his fingers found the seam. He lifted the light closer to the crack and traced the square. It was a foot larger than the one below. He pushed on the center. The door held fast. Again he moved the light around its edges looking for a hinge, a knob, or a latch something that would open it, but saw nothing.

"What the . . . ?" he sighed. "How does this thing open?"

He pushed with all of his strength but the hatch still held fast. He ran his thick fingers around the seam for the third time and found nothing. He placed his hand in the very center and pushed up with the tips of his fingers. A faint click made him smile. Again he pushed on the very center. The hatch swung open and slammed against the roof.

"Hmmm . . ." he grinned. "It takes a soft touch to open it. Go figure."

He crawled out onto the flat roof and stepped onto a section covered in sticky pitch. As he walked across the roof, the soles of his shoes made an odd sucking sound. He walked to the edge and looked down into the back alley.

A loud noise from behind startled him. He spun to face his opponent, reaching for Lyla's pistol. But he was alone on the roof. The hatch had sprung shut on its own.

He pocketed the pistol and walked to the opening and knelt before it. The latch was visible from the outside. He pulled the lever and the door flew up, hitting him in the face and knocking him off his feet.

Blood gushed from his nose. Delicately touching the bridge of his nose, he felt a growing lump. He sighed in disgust. It was broken, again.

He removed his shirt and held it against his nose. He knew the bleeding would eventually stop. The bruise would be difficult to explain. He sighed at the thought and shook his head.

He lifted the flashlight and turned it on. The beam hit the ladder.

He shifted the light to the boxes containing the moonshine jugs. He was startled when he saw the beam illuminate a hand. Johnny stared and, for what seemed an eternity, waited for the hand to move. When it didn't, he cautiously worked his way down the ladder. Upon reaching the floor, he crept to the body. Again, he drew his pistol.

With the body clearly lit by his flashlight, Johnny saw that the man was lying on his stomach. His pinstriped pants and white shirt appeared well cared for, as did his white leather shoes. Johnny remembered only one man who wore white shoes. Johnny kicked the bottom of the man's shoe; no movement or sound transpired.

There was little space between the body, crates, and the back shelf, but Johnny managed to maneuver his way toward the man's head. After hovering over the still body for a few moments, Johnny suspected the man was dead, but felt for a pulse anyway. There was none. He whispered words of disgust at the second dead body and turned the man's head around so he could see the corpse's face. Recognition caused Johnny to drop the head and fall back. It was Paul.

"No wonder he didn't show up for door duty."

Johnny managed to drag Paul's body out from behind the crates. He flipped the dead man around onto his back and began to search for cause of death. He lifted both arms, checked his neck, looked for bullet holes, or anything that could have killed him. Blood was the only missing object. Johnny felt for a pulse again.

"Who would kill Paul? And why?" He rubbed his head, "And how?"

The location of the body did not seem suspicious to him. Maybe Paul had been hiding. Beads of sweat covered his forehead. What if Paul had witnessed the shooting? Johnny shook his head as if to remove the theory.

Once again, Johnny moved the beam of light slowly over Paul's body. A piece of paper protruded out of one pocket in his pants. Johnny reached down and pulled out a slightly crumpled roll of paper tied with a red ribbon. He slid the ribbon off the parchment and began to read:

I, Anna Lyla Timmons, being of sound mind to hereby bequeath all of my worldly possessions to my trusted doorman Paul Henbit in the case of my earthly departure.

Speak easy,

Anna Lyla Timmons

"What?" Johnny's astonished cry echoed through the room.

His candle fizzled, popped, and extinguished with a hiss.

36

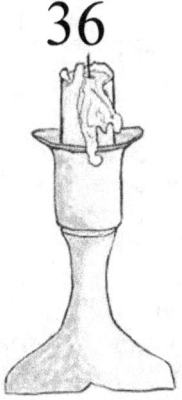

Chester sat in the dimly lit kitchen with his head on the table. Silently he wept over the mess he had made of his life. Lies and dishonesty seemed to be his driving forces although he could not dismiss his love for money. After all it was why he made the moonshine runs and kept his secret life hidden. What good was the money if he worried about spending it? People talk. They accuse first and then prove guilt. Never would he be able to convince anyone he was innocent.

He loved his fast car that the 'shine cash paid for, but Sarah liked Lyla's red Cadillac. No matter what he did, Sarah stood by him, defended him. What would she think of him if she knew the truth? She hated Lyla's speakeasy more than the other four in town because of her first-hand knowledge of the lives it had ruined. She would be devastated if she knew of Chester's involvement.

His thoughts wandered to the prayers of his housekeeper. Each night at the dinner table, she prayed for Chester. She prayed for a change of heart, for his salvation, and the turning of his wicked ways. At times, Chester wondered if she knew. He felt certain she suspected his overtime excuses held nothing but lies.

He rose from the table a broken man. The squeak of the back door reminded him to oil its hinges. He walked to the neighbor's hedgerow and pulled out the undelivered bottle of raspberry blaze. As he poured the pink liquid on the ground, a warm sensation filled him. His tear-stained face looked heavenward.

"Forgive me, Father, for I have sinned. I want to be a better man."

With the bottle empty, he tossed it in his trashcan. The burden of his acts seemed to slide from his shoulders. He felt light, free, and at peace. He crawled in bed beside Sarah and fell fast asleep.

Chester woke refreshed for the first time in ages. He whistled as he dressed for another day at the mill. Wrapping his arms around his wife solidified his decision.

"You're cheerful this morning," Sarah smiled.

"It's a glorious day."

"Why, Chester Willis, what has gotten into you?"

He walked to his wife and took her hand. Soft and sincere he spoke, "The Lord, Sarah. The Lord."

Sarah's mouth hung open. She wrapped her arms around him and cried. With wide-open eyes she listened to Chester's confession, never once losing the smile that covered her face.

Chester told her everything, except Lyla's death. He watched her expressions as he spilled his hand across the kitchen table. When he finished, he took a deep breath.

"Can you ever forgive me?"

Sarah hesitated at the question, not because of her answer but because of her husband's miraculous change. She patted the back of his hand.

"It's a lot to take in, Chester, but I married you for better or worse."

Chester lifted Sarah to her feet and twirled her around the kitchen. He looked at the clock.

"I've gotta get to work. Can we finish this discussion later?" He hesitated, "Over dinner?"

"That would be fine. I'll make a nice roast."

Chester placed his finger over her lips. "No cooking tonight. We are going out to dinner."

Sarah smiled at the invitation. "Oh, dear, that would be great. I'll call Nora and tell her not to come today." The sound of their housekeeper's name made Chester flush. Sarah squeezed his cheeks. "Don't worry. I won't tell her. I won't tell anyone. We need to talk about this a bit more before either of us breathes a word."

He kissed his wife for the tenth time that morning as she handed him his metal lunch pail.

Chester winked, "No overtime for me. I'll be home at three-thirty."

"That's great. Then it will give us a bit of time to talk about what to do with all of this," Sarah hesitated, ". . . blood money."

Chester froze.

No evidence of a lit wick remained—no flame, ember, or smoke. Chandra touched the candle. It felt like ice.

37

By the time Johnny's hand touched Valetta's apartment doorknob, the morning clouds had burst into a show of red, pink and violet. The display left no doubt that it would rain again today.

Johnny walked upstairs to Valetta's bedroom. It seemed to him her body's position had remained unchanged. With his hands resting on the doorframe, he watched her sleep until his nerves had settled. He crawled beside her and wrapped his arms around her.

"Where did you go?" she asked in a quiet voice.

"I thought you were sleeping."

"I was until I heard the front door open." Valetta hesitated, then asked, "What time is it?"

"Early. I think it's around six."

"Where did you go?"

"To the speakeasy."

Valetta rose up on one elbow. Johnny lay on his back facing the ceiling.

"Why?"

"Well, I went there for answers."

"Huh? Answers for what?"

Johnny coughed his response. "To the shooting. Lettie, I knew it wasn't you. I knew it couldn't be. I just had to find out who it was. Although, I still don't . . ."

Now wide-awake, Valetta sat up in her bed. "Johnny, slow down. What are you talking about?"

"I couldn't sleep. So I went to the speakeasy. I tried to retrace everything that happened. I tried to piece it together, you know, but I had too many pieces missing to make any sense. So I went there to think."

"Yeah, and?"

"Well instead of getting answers, I got more questions."

Johnny's nervous rambling made Valetta edgy. Johnny rarely stressed over comments unless accompanied by a flirtatious gesture and then his overprotection reared. The same occurred with Lyla.

"Johnny, calm down. What happened?"

"When I got there, I thought someone was in there. You know, nosing around in Lyla's office so I grabbed the gun that Lyla hid on top of the instrument closet in the back. I was gonna tiptoe to her office and surprise whoever it was, but I backed into a chair and it slammed onto the floor. I thought I was a goner so I ran to the cloakroom."

"The cloakroom!" Valetta shrieked. "Why there?"

"I dunno cause of the hidden closet I guess."

"Hidden closet? What hidden closet?"

"Geez, Lettie, let me tell my story!" Johnny paced around her bedroom. "There's a closet inside the cloakroom with a hidden latch. That's where we store the hired man's liquor. Lyla said it's got to be kept in the dark or it'll taste bad."

"Tastes bad anyway," Valetta offered under her breath.

"So I go in the cloakroom, hit the latch, and hid in the closet. Figured I'd be safe there. But my foot stepped in broken glass."

"Glass?" Valetta hung on every word.

"Yeah, glass. Everywhere. And the smell of the dark liquor was so strong it burned my eyes. And then, I remembered."

"Remembered what?"

Johnny rushed to the edge of the bed and whispered, "Footprints."

"What footprints?" Valetta's request seemed desperate.

"The ones in the cloakroom. The ones all around Lyla's body."

"Johnny, you're scaring me."

He took Valetta's hand. "Look, Lettie. Lyla's killer was hiding in the closet waiting for the right opportunity to escape through the roof.

"The roof? What are you talking about?"

Johnny filled Valetta in on every detail—the ladder, the jugs of shine, Lyla's blaze, the hinged hatch, his broken nose—all but Paul.

Valetta listened to his tale wondering if it was a fabricated story or a dream. She would have dismissed it as either of the two until Johnny opened the curtains. He needed the morning light to reveal his broken nose and the blood on his shirt.

"Oh, Johnny. I'll get some ice." Throwing the covers from her body, she sat up, but before her feet hit the floor, Johnny grabbed her arm.

"It won't help now."

"But . . ."

"Lettie, I'm not finished."

Something in his lowered voice made Valetta pause. She sat on the edge of the bed and waited. No more did she interrupt him until he finished his story. After he revealed the final discovery of Paul's dead body, he placed the will in Valetta's hands.

She could not speak. She felt nauseated. She processed all that Johnny told her. After multiple blank scenarios played out in her mind, she asked one question.

"Who killed Paul?"

What Johnny said next turned Valetta white. The only word she heard was "Mickey."

A puff of air blew out both flames.

38

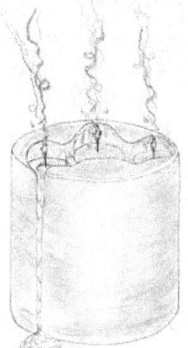

Lyla's candle burst into flame. Her three wicks sputtered and sparked after spending most of the night in a restrained glow. Isabell's face flushed while Chandra squeezed her eyes tight and held her breath. When she opened her eyes, Lyla stood before her.

"I said enter." The constant roll of her hands accentuated Lyla's annoyance.

At first Chandra thought she spoke directly to her, but then a man slid past her. Chandra sighed.

"Did you bring a blank letterhead?"

He shoved his hand deep into a black bag and shuffled several papers until he found a few sheets of blank paper. Scripted in black ink at the top was:

Felix G. Hanna, Esquire
Salem, Ohio

He placed the blank paper on Lyla's desk facing her. On top he laid a fountain pen and a bottle of ink.

Lyla wrinkled her nose as she picked up the worn-out pen. The metal tip sat crooked in the top of the stem and wobbled easily. Littered with teeth marks the used-to-be black handle seemed to house an entire jar of white paste glue and still struggled to cling to the bent writing tip.

"Why this old thing?"

"Tradition," his tone was automatic.

"Tradition?" she scoffed. "For whom?"

"My clients." He looked at his polished nails and played with a jagged edge until it was smooth. After a few minutes he looked up at Lyla and winced at her inactivity. "Is that a problem?"

"No," she snapped, "just odd."

He removed his glasses and began to clean them with his handkerchief. He fogged each lens and polished the smudges from the glass appearing to ignore Lyla's angry stare.

Finally he offered, "Only odd if you don't know how to use it."

"Oh, I know how to use it. I'm just not certain if it's usable," she scoffed.

Felix turned his attention back to his now perfectly manicured nail and looked at Lyla over his lenses. He sighed and acted as if he would retrieve the unused paper.

Lyla's red nails clawed at the empty paper. "Not so fast."

"Then get on with it," he added with his finger rolling in the air.

"Gee, Felix, I swear you are one of the oddest men I know."

"I'm a busy man, Anna. Can we get started, please?"

Lyla leaned over the blank paper, dipped the fountain pen into the ink and began to write. Her penmanship appeared like ornate calligraphy, yet she wrote as fast as her fountain pen would allow. Several drops of black ink dotted the paper leaving a trail from the top to the bottom though the distraction did not stop her intent. She finished with her typical flowing signature under the standard "Speakeasy" sign off. She slid the finished product to her attorney.

He bent over the table, penned his signature as a witness, and blew on his name until it dried. He collected the pen, held it between his teeth until he unraveled a piece of material, wrapped the pen in the stained cloth, and returned it to his bag along with the bottle of black ink. He picked up Lyla's note and read aloud:

I, Anna Lyla Timmons, do hereby leave these instructions as my final request prior to the reading of my will. As you may know several varied copies of my will exist, yet only one holds my true intentions. All others served as decoys, a device used to suit a different yet principal purpose.

A photo is to accompany this letter. In my hand will be the string that is tied around my standing will. I hope that it was not thrown away. A second copy of this picture is kept in the hidden closet in my office. Although I am certain by now, none of you view it as hidden.

The people asked to be present at the reading of my will are:

Mickey Rollins

Johnny Pasquel

Valetta Hamilton

Hank Emmit

Chester Willis

George Whiden, as the band's representative

Make no mistake, only the will wrapped in the thread from the photo carries my true intentions. Use it wisely, my friends.

Speakeasy,

Anna Lyla Timmons

Felix ran his hand over the ink. It smeared in a few places. He frowned.

"Oh good heavens!" Lyla laughed. "Look at your face." Her cackle filled the room. "Who cares if there are a few speckles and smudges? What did you expect after the insistence of using that ridiculous pen?"

Felix glared at her. He didn't care for Lyla. She was too boisterous for his taste. He liked his women more demure and feminine. He sneered but did not recoil. Instead, he fanned the paper through the air until it dried. Satisfied he had all he needed he slipped the letter into an oversized envelope. He stretched his hand out for the photograph.

Lyla placed it in his hand and eyed him curiously as he gawked at it. She held up a sample piece of thin red thread into the air.

"Just in case there are any questions," she waved the string in front of his nose, "this is what it looks like. Be certain. Make no mistake." She leaned into him. "Or I will haunt you."

Felix found little humor in her antics. He glanced at his watch.

"You certainly will keep everyone guessing." He slipped the thread into the envelope. "Now, the only thing left is a copy of your true will."

Lyla placed her hands on her stomach and laughed. "That's the point, Felix. I haven't made up my mind. A copy of each will is in my locked drawer. You know the one?"

Felix nodded. "Under your desk with the little silver key." He rolled his hands for Lyla to continue.

"There are five different wills in there all wrapped with a ribbon. Though mostly red, they vary greatly. I change my mind nearly every day so I shuffle the thin, red string from one to the next. I want to be certain it is wrapped around the right will for my daily mood." She finished her statement with a snap and punctuated her certainty by placing her hands on her hips.

"Lyla, don't you think that is a bit irresponsible? I mean, what if something would happen, and you weren't able to move your strings, and the wrong person benefits from your death?"

"That's the humor in it, Felix. Why should I care? I'll be dead!"

"Well," he straightened his stance, cleared his throat, and fidgeted with his tie. "That is precisely why as your counsel and final voice from the grave, I think you should solidify your wishes and stop playing games with the lives of those you love."

Lyla's face turned a darker shade than her dress, nails, and lipstick. She spit her response to this simple man standing before her. He seemed to shrink with each word.

"Love? I love no one. I have no one. Why does love need to play a part? I am a self-made, self-reliant woman who seized an opportunity when it presented itself. I have what I have because I did it. I saw it! I fought for it! I built it! I created it! It's my baby, my life. No one helped me. No one wiped the tears. No one picked up the broken glass. No one rubbed my aching feet. No one shared my bed."

The walls shook at her rant. She circled her attorney repeatedly slapping his shoulder, arm, back, reserving the final physical blow for the back of his head after her last word.

"It's a business that I built. That I created! No one but me. So why can't this be simply another business decision? Why does everyone assume the word 'will' and 'love' are synonymous? That is the most ridiculous thing I have ever heard!"

Felix winced at the slap on his head. His hat flew across the room and rolled around the floor until finally settling at Lyla's feet.

"Love?" Lyla spit. "Don't ever assume that anything I do is about love." She huffed. "Love is what you say about your hat." She raised her foot and ground the heel of her red pump into its crown.

Felix gasped, though he did not attempt to retrieve his damaged hat. He sighed and walked out the door.

Lyla's face had barely returned to its normal shade before a second knock came on her door.

"Who is it now?" her question was laced with sarcasm.

"It's me."

"Vinchento!" Surprise and horror lit her face. "You shouldn't be here!"

"Don't worry I brought my tools, just in case." He set a wooden box on the floor.

"But what are you doing here?"

"I have seen my mother."

Lyla's blank stare made Vinchento squirm. He lowered his voice "Lyla?"

It seemed as if hours passed before she answered. "I heard you. I was just thinking."

Vinchento heard every creak, snap, and pop the building had to offer. A squirrel scurried across the ceiling, though neither acknowledged it. He waited patiently for Lyla to speak.

"Vinchento?"

"Yes?"

"If anything happens to me, if anything goes wrong, I want you to do me a favor."

"Sure Lyla, anything."

She walked to the back wall of her office and stared at the dresses that always hung there. She ran her hands over each one until finally selecting her favorite. Her smile widened as she turned around. She stroked the dress one last time and offered it to him.

"I want you to give this to Maria. She'll have to wear it."

He took the dress from her. Lying in her hand was a monogrammed white handkerchief with her initials – *ALJ.* "She'll also need this."

Lyla swallowed hard, straightened her shoulders, and lifted her head. "Listen, we have gone over this scenario too often to count, but much could go wrong and probably will. We have tried to think of everything, but just in case something happens to me, Maria will have to take my place."

Vinchento started to speak, but Lyla held up her hand.

"I have spent the day with Felix preparing my will."

"Lyla . . ." Again, he obeyed her hand signal.

"It is a strange feeling you know thinking about your own mortality." Lyla paced around the room while Vinchento's feet remained fixed. "I have bounced back and forth with several different final wishes. I have written so many different wills even I can't find them all."

Her forced laughter brought tears. She used her handkerchief to dab her eyes.

"But then I thought, it doesn't matter. They are just 'things.' Things people kill for, poison for, plot and scheme against. We can't carry it with us. Yes, it makes our lives on this earth easier, more comfortable, but in the end, it doesn't matter. What matters is family." She turned to face Vinchento. "And we are plotting against yours, for what?" She raised her hand for the third time. "Revenge? For your face?"

She walked over to him and gently placed her hand on his cheek. "My dear, dear, Vinchento, you have been like a son to me; one I never had, or deserved. What are we doing?" Her eyes begged for an answer.

"We are doing what is right."

"Right?" she scoffed. "And when 'The Stag' is dead and the business in ruins, who wins? Us? I have all I could ever want right here, yet I'll have to run from it. Hide like a criminal." Her voice slid from boisterous to ashamed. "We plan to do the same to others as they do. It makes us no better. We are monsters as well."

That word flared his temper. "I am not a monster! I watched my father kill an innocent child! For what? For his father's confession! I've witnessed the bloodshed over loyalty, money, women, and booze. I stood by in fear as we drove past burning cars, homes, warehouses, and God help me, even people! We just drove on by as if we were on a Sunday stroll. He has no conscience. He lives and breeds terror. He ruined our family for what?"

Lyla whispered an answer, "Things—power, wealth, status. It makes him immortal."

Vinchento hung his head. "I can't live with that any more."

"Then don't."

He raised his eyes and squinted. He opened his mouth to speak but could not find any.

"Go. Take your mother. Run. Get out of here. And don't ever look back."

Vinchento laughed. "And you think he won't find us?" His cackle grew stronger.

"How many years did you live in secret, right under his nose? If anyone can hide, you can."

He shook his head, "Lyla, do you remember the day you found me? Starving, worn, young, and helpless?"

"You were propped against the outside wall of the church across from my house."

"Exactly. Across from your house!"

Lyla walked over to him. She searched his eyes for truth. "What are you saying?"

"I'm saying I was placed there."

"By whom?"

Suddenly overcome with fear, Lyla began to search for her pistol. Her shoulders relaxed slightly when her hand found its grip. She pulled it from her garter and let her arm hang free.

Aware of her safeguard, Vinchento stood firm. "I mean you no harm."

"Then I don't understand what you're trying to say."

"My father knew all along where I was and who I was with. He knows you, Lyla. I was deliberately placed by that church so you would find me. So you would have pity and take me in. Fast forward a few years . . . my father allowed you to open your club."

"Oh, that's ridiculous!"

"Is it?" His tone softened as he began to tell his story.

"It took me a long time to realize that he knew. It wasn't until the second meeting with my mother that I realized the role I'd been playing all these years. When Mama and I started to plan his death and our escape, that was when we both realized that his reach extends farther than we realized. He has ties in most every large city, and believe it or not, a large following in Salem."

"But I found this building. I planned the club. No one gave me the idea. It was mine."

"Really? And who makes 'shine in your family?"

"I don't see how Hank had . . ."

"And who taught Hank?"

"Uncle Ralph."

"And where is Uncle Ralph today?"

Anger burned in Lyla's eyes. "Wait. So what you're telling me is you are a plant?" She aimed her pistol at Vinchento.

He laughed. "No, what I'm saying is we have been played. That's what I came to tell you. We have to change our plans. And we have to do it quickly. Something is brewing, and I don't like the way it smells."

He hesitated, thinking what to conceal and what to reveal. He took a deep breath and began.

"Officer Little is on our side. Skelly Cantor is a rat. He is planning a hit on you. Soon, I think. Percy has been compromised. Silvia is Skelly's prize. Joey is a goner. Paul has been sampling. Hank is teetering. Lyla, Hank has been . . ."

"Poisoning my blaze."

Vinchento stared at Lyla in disbelief. "You knew?"

"I may not have known your father's plans for my life, but I do know a few things about my brother. One look, one eye twitch, and I know when he is lying. He's not a good poker player. He has a tell." She smiled. "Follow me. I have something to show you."

They left her office for her dressing room. Built between the shared wall was a full-length closet. Lyla removed an oversized panel of wood behind the plethora of red gowns to reveal a multitude of Raspberry Blaze bottles. A tag hung from each one with a date. A few of the tags had a red lipstick X through the date.

"Hank came to visit me on my birthday. Said he wanted to bring me a special bottle of blaze and added, 'Plus I wanted to see the joint'. It tasted awful. He messed with it somehow. I don't think that bottle was tainted because he drank some too, but it made me wary. He passed out and we locked him in the cloakroom. I figured that's when he found the locker and the roof top passageway. He'd be the only one tall enough to get up there without a ladder, at least until he figured out how to lower it from the foot pedal disguised as a loose floorboard.

"Anyway, the next day I looked at all the bottles closely and found this one." She pulled a bottle with an X on it and handed it to Vinchento. "See we had this deal, if he ever thought my blaze had been tampered with, he was to place a bead of white wax on this tendril."

"Yeah, but . . ."

"I know. I know. There's no white, right? It's pure red." Lyla's voice carried pride. "But look at it closely."

They moved their faces closer to the bottle and traced the tendril. A flat impression remained at the bottom.

"Do you see that?" Lyla gloated. "He stuck one on and then thought better of it." She held the bottle up to the light and swirled the pink liquid inside. "It's hard to imagine something so pretty holds something so sinister. I have a few more of them like this, but it seems as though some are missing." She began to count the red X's.

Vinchento's response interrupted her thought. He waved his hand across the loaded shelves and mocked. "But Lyla, look at all this. I thought this was your special drink."

"It is. Just not for me. I don't ever touch the stuff."

"But we've had drinks together."

Lyla winked, "Yep, 'shine and water are the same color."

"Well I'll be," he chuckled. "So why keep it?"

"Oh I figured it would come in handy someday." She lifted the tainted bottle again and removed the tag, "Especially this one." She extended it to him and turned from him before continuing. "If something would happen to me," she held up her hand to silence his objection. "If I don't return home some evening, or anytime of day for that matter, assume I am dead and follow through with what we have discussed." She pointed to the tainted bottle of blaze. "And give this to Maria. She may need it."

Restlessness or anger seemed to build within the melted red wax of Lyla's candle. Chandra noticed the first of two bubbles appear from below and burst when they met the cool air of the surface. She waited for the three wicks to subside to their normal low glow, but the flames burst with contrary brightness. Chandra and Isabell's eyes met, filled with wonderment.

39

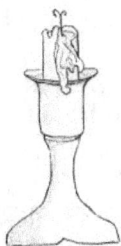

Maria jumped at the Regulator clock's chime. Before the tenth bell she double-checked for her pistol. Twelve years had passed since she last saw it though now she was prepared to use it.

When she opened her back door, the cool breeze did not calm her mood. Her pace quickened. Only when she saw the church did she pause.

She lifted her face, "Father, forgive me."

She touched her head, chest, and each shoulder and drew in a deep breath. Somehow, the Catholic act of crossing herself heightened, instead of reduced, her angst. Pulling a hat from her purse, she placed it over her drawn, dyed hair and slipped into the waiting car.

"Are you ready?" the driver asked kindly.

"As ready as I'll ever be."

The man reached across the seat and patted her leg. The softness of her red dress caught on his rough hands. He frowned at the snag in the chiffon.

"Sorry, Mama."

"It's all right, Vinchento. Today is the only time I will ever wear it."

Maria's eyes followed the pulled fabric to the edge of the tainted bottle of blaze. Its pink liquid sloshed as

Vinchento drove down the winding road. Soon it will be over.

The drive from Liberty to the outskirts of Youngstown passed quickly. Maria watched the streets turn to dirt roads with houses surrounded by green fields of planted crops. She listened to her son as he verbally ran through their checklist. And although she answered each question with a "yes" or a "got it," her mind traveled through her sorry excuse for a life. The only bright spot in her marriage to Vincent sat beside her. She placed her hand on his and squeezed.

"I love you too, Mama," Vinchento answered. "Everything is going to be fine."

She heard his words, but did not believe them. There were too many variables and players. Things may be chaotic. She smiled at his comment nonetheless.

The night Vinchento lost his lip, Maria could not sleep. Vincent had stumbled up the staircase and plopped into bed fully clothed. Normally Maria would help him undress before retiring, but not that night.

Even as a child Vinchento displayed a tender heart. No matter how forcefully his father toyed with him, he did not counter with brutality. Instead Vinchento's response oozed with tentativeness and imprecision. This angered Vincent beyond control, and his advances became more vicious with each passing year. By the time Vinchento turned fifteen, the hope of the first-born Sabino assuming the lead role in the business plummeted and burned in the depths of hell. Vincent turned his attention toward Raffaldi.

Vinchento sought his father's approval subtly. Only Maria noticed. Vincent's brutal opinion refused to acknowledge any worth. "If he doesn't want to be involved in the business to hell with him," became his well-rehearsed response and with each verbalization Maria's resentment grew.

Her tumble down the short flight of stairs had resulted in a broken rib. She writhed in pain though her husband paid no mind. Vinchento with his face disfigured, swelling, and soaked in blood, lifted her and carried her to the downstairs bedroom. Both cried bitter tears.

"You need a doctor," Vinchento whispered.

"Not as much as you," she responded through sobs. "I'll be all right."

"But your beautiful face!" Her cries escalated.

"Shhh. We do not want to wake the monster. Let him sleep it off. Tomorrow morning I'll be gone."

Maria listened carefully. Vinchento cared for his mother throughout the night as she for him, and with dawn's first light he disappeared. She had no idea that he was followed, brutally beaten, and thrown against the wall of a stone church in Salem until their third reunion.

Nine years passed before she next saw Vinchento and another two after that before the second time. When he brushed her arm with the third passing, she made him stop.

It was a sunny Sunday morning. Her new priest had delivered his first message, and she felt uplifted by his words. Vinchento nodded his head as he walked toward his mother. A heavy beard covered his face and the hat brim shadowed his eyes though she recognized him. When he brushed her arm in passing, she seized his. They slipped back into the church to talk.

Fearing discovery, they both entered the confessional. Their hushed conversation continued for an hour. Vinchento told of the night he disappeared, his new life as a carpenter, and his relationship with a woman twice his age.

"I'm so sorry for abandoning you as I did. I can try to justify it all I want, but it was selfish." Vinchento hung his head. "I'm no better than he."

"Don't say that! You are nothing like your father. I don't feel abandoned. I feel blessed. Blessed to have my son alive, sitting with me and talking." She had difficulty speaking through the tears. Her voice trembled. "I knew one day I would see you. My heart leapt the first and second time, but this time I could not let you go. I had to speak with you. I have missed you so."

"And I you. It has been difficult to stay away, but I did it for your safety."

"I know. You are a wise boy . . . man."

"I have been working for a woman in Salem, Mama. She has helped me in so many ways. She gave me a place to stay. She cared for my face. She listened to my story and she gave me hope."

"I'd like to meet her."

"Oh, I would like that, but the time is not right."

"Tell me about her. Is she pretty?"

Vinchento stammered, "In her own way, yes."

"Does she make you happy?"

"Oh yes, Mama, very much."

"She's good to you?"

"Yes."

"Do you have children?"

Vinchento chuckled at her question. "Mama, it's always about children with you."

"Family is important, Vinchento."

"Yes, but my relationship with her is not in that way. She has been a great friend. Nothing more."

"But friends have a way of becoming more."

"Not with us, Mama. It's okay. Be happy for me."

"I am." Maria tried to mask her disappointment. "Tell me more . . . about your life."

"I am busy revamping a building. Lyla is opening a speakeasy."

"Lyla . . . such a pretty name."

"Mama . . ."

Maria listened as her son introduced her to his life. He left unsaid many details yet included all that would make her proud. He explained Lyla's designs for the club—the décor, the chandeliers, the cloakroom, hidden doors, her secretive ways, her half-brother, and the sordid staff. He talked non-stop for fifteen minutes.

He paused and then added, "She reminds me of you, Mama. She's not as . . ." he hesitated searching for the right word, smiled, and continued, ". . . soft, but she has a warm heart. It's a side of her few are allowed to see, but she trusts me." He laughed. "I'm a Sabino and she trusts me."

Maria's eyes opened wide. "It's because you're a Sabino that she trusts you." "I don't follow."

"Your father is not many things, but he is loyal. We can use that to our advantage."

The next ten minutes were spent laying the foundation for their plot. They agreed to meet once a month to form a concrete plan. Neither thought of revenge when they slid into those uncomfortable chairs, yet it became the result of two desperate people craving a life outside of their compressed circle.

Maria's memories faded as Vinchento took his foot from the accelerator. They stopped in front of a cornfield.

Vinchento squeezed his mother's hand for the last time. "Remember to stay hidden until all shots have been fired. Then and only then are you to run from the house. If only a few rounds are heard you must offer the blaze to my father as a congratulatory gift for murdering his eldest son and adversary."

"Vinchen . . ."

"Shhh, Mama. We have been over this too many times. You know what to do," he paused. "With or without me."

Maria shook her head signaling confirmation. She slid behind the steering wheel and watched her son disappear. Soon, she would return to this rendezvous point to either her son or an empty field.

When the taper's smoke cleared, Chandra smiled. The wick was divided.

"Next time it will burn twice as bright." Isabell had also noticed.

40

Hank and Joey made their 'shine and runs in silence. It gave Hank a lot of time to think and gave his cohort time to feel guilty.

After Hank caught Joey above the cloakroom things changed for the worse. Although little trust between the pair ever existed, they did a nice job of concealing it. Now openly worried that each would kill the other, they spent minimal time together and never accepted a drink from one another unless they switched the glasses first, yet Hank proved shrewder.

They waited the following Saturday night after the blaze switch for Chester's arrival. The dark canoe floated in the river until half-past three before they gave up and turned toward home. Joey's voice came first.

"What do you think happened?"

Hank shrugged.

"Think he's dead?"

Hank shrugged again.

"Think he got caught?"

"Could be," Hank's response was automatic.

They rowed for the next ten minutes in silence. Two mason jars rattled near Hank's feet, one cloudy, old and bone dry, the other brand new speckled with moisture droplets. Finally, Hank grabbed the annoyance and filled both to the rim with moonshine. He extended the old jar to Joey.

"No," Joey faltered. "You said . . ."

"Ah, piss on it, Joey. He didn't come for it so I'm drinking it."

"I didn't mean that, Hank. You said no more taking drinks from each other. You know, after you caught me tainting Lyla's blaze."

"Yeah that was pretty stupid of you."

"I tried to 'splain. I was pushed into it by that . . ."

"You could've said no." Visions of Hank's uncle hanging in the tree appeared in his mind.

"And end up dead?"

"Well, either way we're dead, you idiot. If Lyla dies so does our business. Can't make any money, can't eat. Can't eat, you die."

"We can make 'shine for the mob. They wants our goods anyway."

Hank stared at his simple friend. He wanted to scream, 'You are an idiot. Either way you're dead!', but instead he looked at the clear liquid swirling around in both jars and switched jars with Joey. He took a long drink from the old cloudy jar and watched Joey do the same from the new one.

Both men wiped the excess from their lips and said, "Ahh."

"Now, that's the good stuff," Joey added with a wide smile.

After ten minutes the men continued downstream. Hank sat in the back using his oar as a rudder. He knew that after the second bunch of rapids the smooth glide through calm waters would carry them to their homes. Both men enjoyed the restful ride as much as their full jar of 'shine.

Pangs of guilt suddenly hit him. Usually he fought the feeling, but tonight appeared different. Something seemed off, though he couldn't identify what was wrong, he needed his thoughts to come together—to be concrete.

"Concrete." There. That's it. When he was fifteen, he went swimming with a buddy on the outskirts of Bessemer, Pennsylvania. The drive to the quarry seemed a long one, but after the first jump in the deep, cool water, the boys forgot all about their illegal drive north.

The hot summer air that year hung like a thick veil. No matter where you stood, sun or shade, your body felt as if it were melting.

They pulled off a back road to an open dirt parking area. They were surprised to find themselves the only ones there. They stripped to their dingy undershorts and ran to the edge of the cliff. The calm water waited just ten feet below.

His buddy jumped first. The water churned into a white pool of invitation upon his buddy's impact and before his friend's head came up for air, Hank's feet had left the ground. He nearly landed on top of his friend.

Rumored to be over fifty feet deep, the boys held a contest to see who could touch the bottom. To be certain to keep each other honest, they descended together.

After several attempts they swam to the only viable resting place—a fifty-foot sandstone fragment that poked above the water's surface. Its top, smooth from a magnitude of use, invited the boys to rest.

"Are you ready for one more try?" Hank's friend tested.

Without hesitation he said, "Sure."

His buddy moved into position to jump. Hank whistled to get his attention.

"Hey, idiot! We can't jump from here!" Hank warned.

"Why not?"

"You wanna get killed?"

"Huh?"

"Did you see the huge pile of rocks under this one?"

"Nope," he answered without reservation.

"Well, they are jagged and sticking up everywhere. We will have to wait to dive until we are away from the rocks."

"Okay. Whatever."

They worked their way off the rocks and slithered into the cold water. Only the first two feet held any warmth.

Beyond that the water felt like ice. Though it was refreshing, it astounded them. Both surfaced at the same time.

"That's freezing!"

"Feels like winter!"

"Okay," Hank's friend challenged, "one more deep breath and let's go as far as we can."

"You're on."

They took three deep breaths together and slipped into the deep. Soon their bodies felt light as a feather. They moved down with little effort. Hank was the first to tug on his friend's arm to signal he was going to go up. His friend ignored him and continued to descend.

Hank's lungs burned. He released a bit of air to alleviate some pressure. It helped, and he joined his friend for a few more strokes toward the bottom.

The low light left little growth for foliage. Hank watched his friend gather a fist of silt from the quarry bottom. The race was over. His friend won.

Hank turned toward the surface without reaching the bottom. With little air left, he swam into a pair of arms. Panicked, he struggled to free himself from the dead man whose feet were imbedded in a block of cement.

Hank struggled to break the surface. His arms felt like lead, and his legs denied his command for movement. He released a bubble of air, but it did not help. The light above him grew brighter with each stroke although he felt death was certain. When his hands burst through the water's surface, he nearly collapsed with relief. He felt light-headed, certain he would pass out. He floated on his back until his hands found the rock and waited for his friend to come to the top. He never did.

Hank's neighbor filled his head with tales of the Westies, the Irish mob, and convinced him they were the culprits, but uncle Ralph told a different story. He explained all about the Sabino family in Youngstown, though he left out the part that he knew them personally. It would be several years until Hank would hear the rest of the story.

"Hank?" Joey's voice broke the spell and Hank for once felt gratitude for the distraction.

"What?"

"What do you think happened to Chester?"

"Who knows, Joey. Could be a million things."

"Yeah, but what's your gut say?"

Hank had a gift; one that most members of his mother's family shared. Some may have called it intuition, but the family referred to it as "The Know." It was an odd calming sense that coupled with a bit of reason or deduction was usually correct. Hank was especially good at it.

"My gut," he lied, "says all is well. Got a flat tire. That's what I'm feeling."

"A flat tire?" Joey questioned. "A runner that don't know how to change a flat?"

"Oh, he knows how to change one for sure. He just missin' his tire iron."

Hank's candle sputtered. Its yellow flame burst into a brighter, bolder shade, and spit sparks until it settled to a constant orange torch.

Hank watched Mickey keep busy stocking the bar for business. He slipped off the chair twice, but Mickey walked him back to the bar each time he tried to sneak away. When Mickey dropped a glass, he saw his opportunity.

Disappearing around the corner and tiptoeing down the hall, he crept out of the ballroom unnoticed. He opened the door to Lyla's office, walked around her desk and nestled into her wingback.

Boredom or overuse of moonshine made Hank edgy. He shuffled papers around her desk and began to pick them up and read them. A bottle of simulated pink blaze lay on his lap.

The first paper he read was a list of supplies needed. That did not interest him so he crumpled it up and tried to toss it into her waste can. He missed. Without looking at the next paper, he wadded it into a tighter ball. Raising both hands high in the air he aimed again at the basket. Again he missed.

One by one, the papers disappeared from the desk and reappeared across the room as paper balls. Some made their target, but most lay sporadically around the floor. Weary of the game, he walked to the waste can and gathered his mess.

One of the wads lay half-open. Hank pressed the paper to flatten it on Lyla's desk. His eyes opened wide as he read:

I, Anna Lyla Timmons, being of sound mind, do hereby bequeath all of my worldly possessions as well as my club and all its assets to my friend and bartender, Mickey Rollins.

Speak easy,

Anna Lyla Timmons

Hank's body recoiled as if stuck with an arrow. He rushed to unfurl each paper ball. He found a grocery list, appointments, a long record of telephone calls, miscellaneous doodles, and then he gasped. The document in his hand read:

I, Anna Lyla Timmons, being of sound mind and spirit, do hereby bequeath all of my worldly possessions including my club and all of its assets and inventory to be equally split as equal triple partners leaving no one in command or charge of another making all decisions in a gentlemanly manner to the following three men:

Mickey Rollins

Johnny Pasquel

Hank Emmit

Play nice boys.

Speak easy,

Anna Lyla Timmons

Hank covered his mouth. He felt nauseated. The last thing in the world he wanted was another partnership. He had enough grief being in the 'shine business with his derelict friend Joey. He shredded the letter and crumpled each minute piece. He crunched the shards into a tight ball and hurled it across the room into the trashcan. The first will met the same fate.

He rummaged Lyla's desk in search of blank paper to cover his sins. He opened each drawer in near panic until he found a stack of loose paper in her bottom drawer. Only the top piece of paper had any writing. It read:

To the only member of my family as I use that term loosely, Hank Emmit,

I, Anna Lyla Timmons,

Being of sound mind do hereby bequeath all of my business and personal possessions including the real estate of 378 East State Street, Salem, Ohio, its business assets as well as the entire inventory.

Do our Daddy proud, Hank.

Speak easy

Anna Lyla Timmons

A menacing smile covered Hank's face. This one he liked. He folded the paper and placed it in his pocket. He heard Mickey calling for him. He snatched a few blank papers and placed them in Lyla's trash can. He picked up the bottle of pink blaze and walked out of her office. He had just positioned his body in the hallway as if he had passed out when Mickey rounded the corner.

"What are you doing?"

Hank mumbled.

"We need to get you back where you were before Lyla sees you."

He helped Hank to his feet and placed his arm around his waist. Hank stood several inches taller than Mickey, but his lanky frame made maneuvering his body an easy task. Mickey placed him on the barstool.

"What were you doing back there anyhow?" Mickey did not wait for an answer. He thought Hank was too drunk to speak. "Now sit here and wait for Lyla. She should be here any minute."

"Hank! Stop rocking the boat!"

Hank shook his head trying to bring his thoughts back to the present. He sat with his oar dangling in the water. His old mason jar sat at his feet half full of moonshine. Joey's jar rolled on its side in the bottom of the canoe. Not a drop was left in it.

Joey stood in the center of the canoe and tried to walk toward Hank. He toddled over the middle seat and fell smashing his head against the side. The canoe pitched violently. Hank lost his oar in the water and grabbed the gunwales, certain the canoe was about to capsize. After several sways it settled into calm waters and continued to drift down the stream.

Hank lifted his moonshine jar and took a big swig. When he wiped his mouth with his sleeve, he noticed a ring of moisture around his front shirt pocket. Inside, the once full bottle recently reduced to barely an inch had broken in the near capsizing. He sneered as he pulled several pieces of broken brown glass from his pocket. The pungent smell of bitter almonds made him cringe. He held his hand over the edge of the boat and watched each shard of glass plop into the water. He was about to feel sorry for himself when Joey's mumblings became clear.

"Hank?"

"Yeah?"

"I feel sick."

Hank smiled and tossed the last chunk of the broken bottle in the river. The half-missing label flapped in the water until finally separating itself from the brown glass and floated to the surface. The letters c-y-a-n-i brought a deranged smirk to Hank's face.

One of the taper's flame disappeared. Its spent wick lay before them cut off from the rest. The other smoldered in defiance.

41

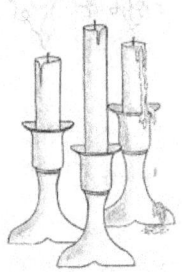

Skelly opened his car door. He refused to toss his cigarette butt; it tasted like success to him. He spent weeks fine-tuning his plan—bribing the door man, wooing Silvia, agitating Mickey, following Valetta, and his biggest trophy—persuading Officer Little. He could not help but smile. He stood on the back steps of his apartment savoring each deadly puff until the last spark went dark. He tossed the spent end into the hedge.

He walked into his dark apartment remembering Vincent's lessons. His exaggerated second step bypassed a blank sheet of tissue placed near the threshold. His daily ritual performed before he walked out of the door had captured many unwanted footprints. Tonight, the paper lay as crisp as when it was placed.

As a final safety net he hid multiple guns—a Winchester 1907, Remington Model 8, Browning A5, along with various whippets on both floors, as well as his trusty Super 38 deeply tucked into his front pocket. His fingers molded into the handle. It felt like home.

He walked through the kitchen in silence mentally checking for anything misplaced. He stopped at a spent shell case lying on the fringe of his Persian rug. Instinctively, he knelt to pick it up. He did not recognize it.

Then he heard the distinctive click of a pistol's hammer being cocked behind him. He raised his hands as he slowly turned around.

"You're late."

"Says who?" Skelly lowered his hand moving closer to his pocket.

"Where have you been?"

"What's it to you?" Skelly struggled to recognize the voice.

"Everything."

"Everything, huh?" Skelly's hand made it to his pocket.

"Don't even think about it, Slick."

"Who are you?"

"Don't you recognize me?"

"If I did would I ask who you are?"

"Sarcasm, Slick, will buy a nice pair of heavy shoes. Now, get your hand off your pistol grip, or I'll remove it for you."

Skelly took his hand out of his pocket and rolled his open, empty hand for the man to see. "I'm clean."

"Really?"

"Yeah, really." Skelly rolled his hand again making a few steps toward his buffet—the closest hiding place.

The man tossed the bullet clips of all the hidden firearms at Skelly's feet. "Now, can we just talk?"

Skelly's eyes never moved. He stared at the shadowed body propped in the far corner of his living room.

"Where'd you get the money, Skelly?"

"Money?" He struggled to conceal the surprise. "What money?"

A flurry of bills flew through the air. It seemed to take hours before each piece of paper settled to its resting spot.

Skelly swallowed his fear. "I've never seen that before."

"That's what they all say."

"Who says?"

"The Takers."

Skelly held his breath. With that accusation thrown in his face, he found it difficult to live up to his nickname. He thought about the first time he heard that phrase.

He was with Vincent and four others hiding in the Westie's warehouse on the south side. It was the first time that Skelly realized no matter how nervous he was, his hand never shook. On this night had he not relieved himself a few minutes ago his case of nerves would have resulted in a serious embarrasment.

Finally, the door swung open and instead of the expected Irish mob king entering, it was one of their own and a cop. No one moved, including Vincent. They witnessed the entire conversation—the plan, the diversion, the money exchanged—all without as much as a single twitch. Their celebratory collaboration drink ended before they took their first sip. Two shots resonated. Two bodies slithered to the floor. Two glasses exploded into wet splinters. Six men left the building in silence.

"A Taker? How's that?"

"Where were you, Slick?"

"What's it to you?"

"In a meeting, huh?"

Suddenly Skelly knew where this was going. "Yeah, sure."

"With who, Slick?"

"Yeah, yeah . . . blah, blah. I was talking to Officer Little. What's the problem?"

"You were talking to a cop?"

"Yeah. He's eating out of the palm of my hand."

"Is that so?"

"Yeah. Got him right where we need him."

"And where's that?"

"Look." Skelly moved his hand again toward his pocket still unsure of his visitor. "We've got the same interests in mind."

"Go on."

"We have the same target, just different streets to take. You got me?"

"Yeah, I'm following."

"I just needed to make the suggestion that our way was best. And he needed to go down our street. The view is clearer."

"With a better end?"

"Yeah, I think so. We both get what we want."

"How do you know what he wants?"

"Because he told me."

A sinister laugh rolled from his lips, "And you believed him?"

Skelly hesitated. Of course he believed him. He called the shots. He pursued Jack Little. Skelly had orchestrated the entire demise although at a much slower pace than Vincent's expectations.

"What's that supposed to mean?"

"What if you were played?"

"I'm not."

"And how do you know?"

"Because I approached him!"

"Really?"

"I showed him the way."

"And what if he showed you?"

"Showed me what?"

"Ah, c'mon, Slick, are you really that stupid? We've been dancing this waltz for ten minutes now, and you still haven't figured it out?"

"And what's that?" Skelly squeezed his pistol grip.

"She's dead! And you had nothing to do with it!"

Skelly's hand slipped from his pistol. "That's not possible. I've got everything planned out. Everything is ready to go. Tomorrow is the night."

"Too late, Slick. You've been had. Played. Suckered."

"By whom?"

Vinchento laughed and moved from the shadows. "Me."

Two shots rang out. One made its target. The other missed.

Silvia shot out of bed to her feet. Her nightgown clung to her slender, damp body. She brushed her sweat-soaked hair from her face and looked out of the window. Her quickened pulse made her hands numb. She placed her hand on her chest and forced deep breaths. Something was wrong. She knew it.

Both Silvia and Skelly's candles fell from their holders spilling their wax to an intertwined pool. Only Vinchento's remained lit.

42

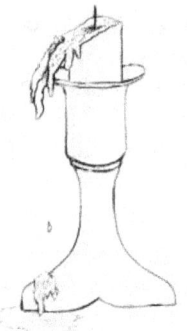

Chester sat proudly in the church pew beside Sarah. He gave no credence to the long disapproving stares from the other members. Surrounded by clusters of huddled conversations, Chester paid no mind to the congregation's stares as they guessed at what unknown holiday had brought about his appearance. Even the pastor choked on his opening remarks when his eyes fell on Chester.

Each glance, whisper or stutter made him sit a bit taller in the seat. Sarah held his hand for support, though Chester felt it unnecessary. Warmth from the Holy Spirit enveloped him. His voice became louder and stronger as he sang each hymn and soon his heart felt as if it would burst.

Overwhelmed by his feelings, Chester felt like a child on Christmas morning. He stared at the sermon title "To Whom It May Concern" and wiggled in his seat until the time came.

His fist slid into his pocket and surrounded a roll of his rumrunner money. He remembered the scene a few days earlier when he unveiled his secret.

When he returned from the mill, Sarah sat at the kitchen table dressed for an evening out as promised. Chester burst through the door, lifted her off the chair, and twirled her body through the kitchen. They laughed together.

"Before I bathe, I want to show you something."

He took Sarah's hand and led her into the bedroom. He knelt by the side of the mattress and pulled the sheets from the corner. Without hesitation he removed each bundle.

Sarah gasped at the amount of neatly wrapped money. Each time Chester fished his hand into the mattress, he retrieved at least two more rolls of cash until the money nearly covered their throw rug.

"There's still some in there, but I can't reach it." He laughed at the look on Sarah's face. "What?"

"I never expected this much." Her words were staccato. "How . . . much . . . do you think . . . is here?"

"I don't know." Chester shrugged his shoulders.

"Well let's see," he counted on his fingers. "I started in the summer of '21. . . I made at least five runs a week . . . at thirty-five dollars a run . . ." He continued to add the amount on his fingers. "That's one-hundred seventy-five dollars for a normal week. And there were a few months where I had an extra run or two."

He looked at his wife, his face covered with embarrassment. "Of course, I did pay for my new car."

Sarah jumped. "I thought you borrowed that money?"

"I . . . I . . ." he hung his head. "I paid cash for it."

"Chester Willis," Sarah scolded with her hand planted firmly on her hips, "How many lies have you told me?"

"Hundreds," he answered quickly though the speed of response did not hide his shame.

"So what did you do with the money that you supposedly used to make the car payments with?"

Chester pointed to the diamond cross that hung around Sarah's neck. He watched as she lifted her hand to cover it.

"Oh, Chester. How could you?" Sarah slid to the floor.

"Sarah," he took her hand. "This is not easy for me to tell you. I am ashamed of what I have done. I have lied so many times that I couldn't keep them straight. I had it justified in my mind that I was doing this for our future, for a better life, and instead I fear I only broke your heart."

He slid close to Sarah. His eyes flooded.

"I am so very sorry. I never meant to hurt you. I hated lying to you, but I kept getting in deeper and deeper and didn't know how to stop."

"So what made you?"

Hard lumps filled Chester's throat. Waves of nausea brought beads of nervous sweat to his forehead. He opened his mouth to speak but only produced a small squeak. He watched his wife eye him curiously. He had been so clever in concealing his lies in the past that this new reaction became a curiosity to him. He wiped the gathering moisture from his face while he forced to swallow the mass.

He tried to silence his head. *Just one last lie. I can't tell her about Lyla. I just can't!*

"I dunno," he muddled.

Sarah looked at her husband with deep reservation. She suspected he held something back from her, but she did not want to make him squirm.

She sat on the floor with a rug full of money between them and felt uncertain of her next move. Part of her wanted to take the money and toss it in the air. Another part wanted to scold him for his involvement, but ultimately the part that won wrapped her arms around Chester scattering the cash across the floor.

"I forgive you."

Guilt rushed from his body though not without giving a final twinge of pain. He winced and then dismissed the thought of Lyla's dead body.

"I don't deserve you."

Sarah smiled but kept her response silent. Instead, she focused on the obvious dilemma before them.

"What should we do with all of this money?"

"Well, I have an idea but want to hear your thoughts first."

Chester's thoughts returned to the present as Sarah handed him the collection plate. Stern warnings came without words just by a look. Chester pulled his hand from his pocket with three night's run money rolled together. He placed it in the gold salver and handed it to the usher without looking up. He did not want to see the man's reaction. Giving up the first of much to come came easily; facing public knowledge for his wrongdoing would be insufferable.

As members surrendered their tithes and offering, Chester became more relaxed. His gifts felt more like a cleansing for his dark deeds. He whispered a prayer of thanksgiving when the members in the last pew gave the plate to the usher, and the man walked passed Chester without a question. He settled in his seat, comfortable in church for the first time in his life.

The preacher walked solemnly to the pulpit. "Will you bow your heads in unified prayer?"

The silent reverence of the church made Chester smile. Only Sarah's smile appeared wider.

"Heavenly Father, we are grateful today for your bounty. We praise you in all things—good or bad, joy or sorrow, and sickness or health, but especially today, Father, we thank you for our ability to hear and see that which has been given to us as Your good and perfect gifts. Take our offerings, large or small, and bless them for the advancement of Your kingdom, Oh Lord. In Christ's name, Amen."

The final word of the prayer came with two unison voices—the preacher and Chester's. Sarah patted the back of her husband's hand as a sign of approval. They held hands for the duration of the sermon.

Coupled with the sermon title were several scripture verses. The first he quoted came from Psalm 130:3, *If you, O Lord, kept a record of sins, O Lord, who could stand?* The second reading came from Romans 7:18, *I know that nothing good lives in me, that is, my sinful nature.* The following verse rendered more guilt: Romans 6:23, *For the wages of sin is death.* Chester wrestled to sit still during that reading, and so did Sarah. He squeezed her hand a bit tighter hoping something good would follow that warning.

Then the pastor flipped to the final verse. He invited all who held their Bible to open it to Hebrews 7:27.

Chester looked at Sarah. She held up her empty hands. She forgot her Bible at home. Chester reached for the pew Bible and handed it to Sarah. He did not have a clue where to find Hebrews. Sarah flipped through its crisp pages quickly.

"Let us read together," the pastor suggested. *"Unlike the other high priests, He does not need to offer sacrifices day after day, first for his own sins, and then for the sins of the people. He sacrificed for their sins once for all when he offered himself."*

Chester listened intently as the pastor explained each verse in detail. He heard the story of salvation just about every holiday that he went to church, but today the words made sense. He sat mesmerized as the pastor explained the simplicity of asking for salvation. His sermon's summary, however, held the largest impact.

"It's like writing a letter," the pastor theorized. "If you are uncertain who to send it to, you address it as this: "To whom it may concern." It is a fully acceptable practice. If your letter ends up on the desk of a secretary or the president, it will be read. The unnamed, semi-anonymous heading is overlooked . . . ignored . . . and disregarded. It is the content of the letter that is important, not to whom it is addressed.

"Our lives are like that to Christ. The heading, our beginning, what is at the top of the letter does not matter. What interests Him is the content—your heart. He is asking for that today. He wants to let you know that your sins were forgiven the day he died for you. He is standing before you with a clean slate. The extended gift is yours. Will you take it? Will you trust Him? Will you accept the simple fact that He loves you? He died for you. He wants to have a relationship with you. Moreover, if you look at the signature at the bottom, He signed it in His blood. He forgave you."

Chester rose from the pew and walked forward before the preacher began the altar call. Gasps rose in each pew as he walked the center aisle. His feet felt light. His body felt as if it floated toward the front. By the time Chester knelt at the front of the church, the pastor greeted him and called for any other to join him. Sarah knelt beside him.

Chester's candle flickered until it faded to barely a glowing ember. Chandra heard a soft male voice sing the final stanza of "I have been forgiven" just as the spark turned to ash.

43

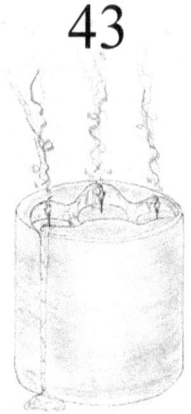

In the stillness of a Sunday night, Lyla sat in her office. She fumbled with a multitude of threads. Choosing five of her favorites, she placed the rest inside a velvet pouch. After folding the soft fabric to the perfect size, she placed it inside a box. The snap of the spring hinge made her jump.

On her lap lay a cluster of keys. She fingered each one slowly as if thinking about their purpose until she stopped at the littlest one. Despite what she told her attorney, her last will and testament held the utmost importance. Yes, she played a little game on some of her employees, but that was nothing more than an outward show of her awkward sense of humor. Her true intent made her melancholy.

She crawled under her desk. Not an easy task for a large woman, but she managed to squeeze toward the back to open her prized compartment. Her hand fell on two rolled papers. She placed them on the floor and fished for the rest. She frowned.

"There should be five. Where are the rest?" she spoke to only herself, not softly or whispered for she felt confident she was alone.

She retraced her actions and then remembered she had left Hank's will in her drawer. Mickey had interrupted her before she could finish and she never returned to the task. That was a week ago last Friday, her birthday, which happened to be the same day as her surprise visit from Hank.

Shock covered her face when only a multitude of blank papers stared back at her. She wondered if she accidentally discarded it. She stood and walked over to the wastebasket. It was empty.

"Well, of course it's empty," she spoke in her normal gruff voice. "Paul empties it every night before he leaves."

Her thoughts slipped to the beauty of the speakeasy operations. On a run night Mickey and Johnny escorted the last of the intoxicated guests to the door. Paul stood guard until every person left. With the door secured, Paul picked up the trash from all the containers, all but the one behind the bar. Responsibility fell on Mickey for that one. After his payment Paul gathered the trash and left with the band members. Usually Percy, the night janitor, waited until then to mop the floors. He followed Lyla's strict rules about the water without fail.

There were three ways to drink at Lyla's club. First were the tokens, mostly given as gifts or for services rendered, although at times Lyla passed them out to a few good or derelict customers as an appreciation for their patronage or as a sympathy "sorry for your back luck" voucher. The second and third way to taste the 'shine carried the weight of the profit.

The patron gained access only after Paul accepted his knock on the mouth speak door. Once inside the three-foot-by-three-foot entry, the customer stared at another door with two holes and a slit carved into it. The client would not gain access until Paul accepted a second series of knocks. At that time the consumers made a choice—pay the five-dollar entry fee and drink a bottle, or pay a single dollar and shell out fifty cents per drink.

The lesser of the two paid the five-dollar entry fee. They received a red mark on their hand and a bottle through the round hole in the door. If the customers found themselves still coherent with an empty bottle, they could once again choose—pay for each drink or buy another bottle. All opened bottles, whether full, half-full or nearly-empty stayed within the walls of the speakeasy. That liquor was poured into the "Last Call" jug.

The second group outnumbered the former. With those patrons a single dollar gained entry. Without a red mark on their hand, Mickey knew they had to pay for each drink by either a token or coins.

Mickey's moneybox was bolted behind the bar. Not that Lyla mistrusted him in as much as she wanted to deny accessibility to the clients. A simple slit in the top of the box allowed the money to go in but not come out.

A second check and balance for Mickey's honesty came from the glasses. Each crate housed five stacks of twenty glasses. Mickey marked each broken glass and compared it to the ones used for the evening. Unless the night held innumerable incidents that created chaos, the two numbers coincided close enough for Lyla's satisfaction. She expected pilferage from Mickey as long as it was minimal. He made her plenty of money.

Lyla, with Johnny at her side, carried the money into the office each night. Once she closed the door, Johnny stood guard outside. Depending on the number of clients and their method of payment it took a while to finish, but Johnny never left her door.

Lyla separated the tokens first and placed them in a metal box. Next, she pulled out all of the singles, and then began to separate the rest of the denominations. Usually, the daily cash flow fell between the parameter of two to four hundred, but occasionally a poor drunken soul mistook a large bill for a lesser value. Those mistakes Lyla kept for herself.

Each employee visited Lyla's office at the end of the night for his or her day's wage. She insisted they count their pay only once in her presence. If they attempted to count it a second time, they received a stern warning; upon the third they were fired. No questions asked. Lyla then would walk out of her office, shaking her head, reiterating her famous line, "You can't trust someone who can't trust."

After all were paid, trash removed, Mickey's clean up and glass count, Johnny's guarding, floors mopped, insruments packed, dancers changed, and money counted, Chester came to the door. By that time only Lyla, Mickey, Johnny, and occasionally Valetta remained. Mostly Johnny, though occasionally Mickey if Lyla was still counting money, listened for the proper response and permitted Chester's passage. Chester tossed his car keys to Johnny, and both men walked out the door.

With the evening settled, moonshine stashed, hired man's liquor locked up, and Lyla's blaze inspected in her office, Chester received his payment and his car keys. The successful night would result in a late morning rise and for the day to begin all over again with the exception of Sundays, the speakeasy's dark night. Rarely did anything happen on that day but rest for all and paperwork for Lyla.

After looking in several hiding spots for the missing three wills, Lyla threw her hands in the air. She rarely misplaced a thing and she grew furious. She left her dressing room, slammed the door, and bumped straight into Vinchento's chest.

"Oh my! You scared the daylight out of me."

Doubled over laughing, he caught his breath. He chided, "You should've seen your face."

"It wouldn't have been so funny if I would have shot you," she finally offered a smile. "How did you get in?"

"How do you think?" He shook his finger in her face. "Lyla, you've gotta lock that trap door. It's too easy to get in here."

"Aww, come on. Only you and I know about that, remember?"

"Until today."

Lyla's smile turned to a scowl. "Who did you tell?"

"My father."

Lyla listened as Vinchento told of his visit. He left nothing unsaid, especially his feelings.

215

"I'll tell you Lyla, finally seeing him again face to face made me nauseated. I found it difficult to share the same air. I wanted to kill him!"

"Vinchento," her voice was calm. "He will be gone soon enough. He's old and has too many enemies."

"True. Some with the same blood."

"Calm yourself." She motioned for him to follow her. "Let's go have a drink and decide what we can do about it."

Lyla's candle began to flare. A constant gurgle resonated within the molten wax. Some of the air raced to the top and burst like thermal mud pots. Chandra made no mention of the change. Isabell's eyes remained closed.

44

One by one, each candle burst into flame. Chaotic, angry light flooded Chandra's apartment. She held her breath. The story neared its end. She could feel it and sensed barely enough night remained to tell all. A quiet hush filled her ears. The wick's radiance warmed her face though it did not feel calming. She closed her eyes and tried to breathe.

Sticky sweat covered Chester's face. The load tonight was twice the norm, and Lyla's blaze was missing. Nearly finished with the unloading process, he was hot, tired and late. He looked at his watch. It was nearly three thirty in the morning. He rolled his eyes at yet another lie he would have tell Sarah.

"I have one more jug in the trunk, Johnny."

Johnny grunted a reply. "Go see Lyla and get paid. I'll follow you back down and get it."

Chester walked back to Lyla's office and rapped on the half-closed door.

Lyla met him at the door. Her eyes searched his empty hands, but before she spoke he offered, "They said it wasn't ready." He watched her body language slip to annoyance. "They said they would bring it to you in person."

She offered no response, just a huff of disgust and a silent hand jesture for Chester to follow her.

Chester walked into Lyla's office. His rehearsed speech about the missing ten dollars was difficult to start. After stammering for the words, he blurted his thought.

"Lyla, I was short ten bucks."

Clutching his pay in her hands, she sneered at his comment. "What did you say?"

Her red hair fell into her eyes.

Chester stuck out his chest. "I said I was short ten bucks."

"Are you accusing me of cheating you?"

Chester face turned white. "I . . . I'm just saying I was short ten bucks."

"And who always gives you the money?"

"You do, Lyla."

"So if I always give you the money, then I cheated you?"

Chester felt Johnny's presence behind him though he dared not turn around. "This is not what I wanted to happen," he thought.

Lyla drummed her long, red fingernails on her desk. Each finger tapped Chester's thirty-five dollars challenging him to advance. Her other hand slowly lifted her skirt searching for her pistol.

Johnny butted his chest against Chester's back. "Do you want me to . . . ?"

Lyla waved off his question with a nod of her head. Her hand found her gun and in a split-second drew it from her garter.

Chester held up his hand in defeat. "I don't want . . . trouble."

"Too late now, Chester." She gritted her teeth.

"Now, Lyla, calm down. I just thought you should know. I just noticed I was ten dollars short. I thought it was a mistake. I didn't think you cheated me." He lowered his arms. "I wasn't accusing you of anything." He attempted a laugh though it sounded like nervous stutter. "I just wanted to tell you . . . thought it was a simple mistake. I'm sorry."

Lyla eyed Chester and returned her pistol to her garter. She crumpled his money in her hand and stepped toward him. She held his pay tightly to his chest. "Go on . . . count it if you must." She shook her head. "Mother always said not to trust a shifty man." She turned from him and tossed, "And I guess she was right." She could not resist adding her final thought, "You can't trust someone who can't trust."

Chester took his money and left with Johnny following close behind. Johnny jingled the speakeasy keys for reassurance and closed the door. The door bounced and sprung ajar unnoticed. A wide strip of tape covered the latch and strike plate.

Chester rushed to his car and opened the trunk for the last jug. His rusty tire iron wedged the container against the hidden compartment. He pulled on the hunk of metal until it suddenly sprang free, out of Chester's hand, and hurled through the air into the shadows nearby. It slammed into something soft and fell to the ground.

"Geez," Johnny mocked.

"I'm telling you. She shorted me ten bucks!"

"Go home, Chester. Did it ever occur to you that it may be a test?"

Hank stood hidden in the nearby shadows holding his bruised hip. The tire iron lay at his feet. He watched Chester slip into his Ford coupe, and drive away.

Johnny sauntered up the sidewalk. Each step brought him closer to Hank. Nervous that the shadows could only hide him for a bit longer, he knelt, picked up the tire iron, and lifted it above his head. When Johnny kicked and scattered the coins, Hank seized the opportunity and brought the tire iron down on Joynny's head. Johnny fell like a rock.

Quickly, Hank jumped up, grabbed the bottom rung of the fire escape and began to climb.

Once on the roof he heard two men talking below in the alley. He peered over the edge and shrugged. He did not recognize either of them and remained thankful that his ascent was unnoticed.

Sarah woke to a loud knock on her front door. She opened it to see her best friend's tear-stained face.

"What's wrong, Thelma," she blurted with concern.

"It's Ray, Sarah." Thelma's eyes looked down. "He's passed out downtown. I can't move him." Recoiling with shame and self-pity Thelma added, "I need your help, Sarah. I could only ask you, because I know you won't judge me . . ." She sighed, ". . . or him."

"Oh, Thelma . . ." Sarah began.

Thelma covered Sarah's lips with a finger, "But I love him, Sarah. I love him."

Pained by the embarrassment on Thelma's face Sarah whispered, "Okay, then. Let's go."

Ray Fluharty sat awkwardly on the ground across the street from Lyla's club. He appeared dead.

Thelma knelt beside her husband. "Ray?"

A trail of slime trickled from the corner of his mouth. His eyes, opened barely a crack, stared into the empty street. He tried to speak but only uttered slurred mumbles.

"Let's go home, Ray."

Chester drove a few blocks and parked his Ford in an unused alley. He crushed his half-smoked cigarette into the brick sidewalk, exhaled, and ran back quietly to the speakeasy. Anxious to avoid another confrontation, he scurried one block past Johnny to Broadway Avenue. He hurried around the corner to the wooden door that led upstairs.

He stopped at the landing halfway up the narrow staircase and listened. He heard voices. They were shouting. Several minutes passed as he carried on his silent battle—stay or go. He closed his fist around his shorted pay. Leaving was not an option. He drew in a deep breath and walked the second half of the staircase.

He recognized Lyla's voice as well as Mickey's. Although it was difficult to tell, it seemed there were at least two additional people, perhaps three.

When he reached the top of the staircase, the speakeasy door was ajar. Surprised by the lack of security and ignoring the alarms that rang in his head, he slowly swung the door open and slipped into the adjacent cloakroom.

Chester's throat tightened and beads of sweat gathered and slid down his forehead. The salt burned his eyes. His heart seemed to catch in his throat. He held his breath as the speakers came closer.

Panicked over the fear of certain exposure and rising suspicions with his unannounced return, he slid farther into the room and pressed his body against the back wall. Nervously his hands felt the panels for any place to hide. His belt loop caught on the hidden switch and released it. A veiled door sprung ajar. He fully opened it and slid into the safety of darkness.

Thelma and Sarah struggled to lift Ray's two-hundred-twenty-seven pounds of dead weight. They nearly had him to his feet when Sarah noticed Chester walking into the speakeasy door. She dropped Ray on the sidewalk.

"Sarah?' questioned Thelma.

Sarah tried to shake the vision from her mind. Chester was at the mill working overtime. He never smelled like liquor when he came home. Convinced that her eyes had failed her and finally hearing Thelma's cries for help, she slipped her hand under Ray's arm and helped him to his feet again.

Sarah whispered to her friend, "I'm sorry. I lost my grip." She felt no guilt at the lie.

Ray stumbled twice while the women struggled to walk him toward Thelma's car. Finally, with their arms aching from the weight, they forced him into the back seat. Sarah lifted his feet inside and closed the door.

Though her friend showered Sarah with praise, it was the look of Thelma's relief that brought a smile. She placed her arm around Thelma's shoulders and squeezed.

"Thelma, it's nothing you wouldn't do for me. Now, get that man home and fill him with some good strong black coffee."

She watched Thelma's car pull away from the curb. A movement at the periphery of her vision caused her to turn. A man stood at the bottom door of the speakeasy. Sarah slid around the corner of the building and out of sight and waited.

She counted to fifty and peered back around the corner. She watched the speakeasy's door close. Certain that Chester was inside, her heart burned with betrayal. She ran across the street to the door.

Mickey hit the ballroom light switch and watched the lights flicker out. The click of his heels echoed down the hallway as he walked to Lyla's room. The door was ajar.

He knocked as he entered, "Miss Lyla?"

The door swung open. Her dressing room was a bit disheveled but not unusually so. He checked her office next. The only thing missing was Lyla.

"Lyla?" he questioned louder. "Hmmm." He shrugged his shoulders and walked out of her room.

After a few steps down the hall, he began to yell her name. His voice echoed through the building. He checked each room leaving the obvious for last.

When he opened the cloakroom door, darkness greeted him. With his first step his shoe crunched broken glass. Remnants of a light bulb swung from the ceiling.

"Lyla?" he whispered. "Are you in here?"

He heard a faint moan. Suddenly somebody from behind struck Mickey, causing him to fall to the floor and hit his head against the doorjamb.

Paul hovered over the unconscious Mickey. This was the second time he knocked Mickey out cold. He wondered from where his strength had come. His head felt woozy as he staggered to the foot pedal. He stepped on the edge of the loose floorboard and waited for the ladder to descend. It only slid part way.

Although it hung low enough for his reach, Paul struggled to lift his weight. Finally, he made the second and third rung. His lungs felt heavy as if filled with water. He struggled for air. He thought if he could only reach the shelves where he stashed a few bottles of Lyla's blaze, each branded with a red X in lipstick, he would feel better, rested, and be able to breathe. He walked behind the crates of moonshine and collapsed.

Hank waited. The voices on the street below him faded. After listening to only the rhythmic sound of the falling rain, he opened the hatch and quietly descended. He froze when he heard a voice he recognized. He listened closely as Joey carried on a whispered conversation with himself.

"One from lass week, and one from t'night, and this one," Joey held a bottle in the air, "is the bestest one."

He then slid a tall wooden box closer and began to unload its contents. The bottles rattled from his shuffling.

"I don't have no choice. Nope, no choice. Mr. Skelly backed me in a corner." He placed the last bottle on the shelf with a sigh. "Hank's gonna be mad."

Hank's hair stood at attention at the mention of his name. He shook his head in disbelief at the words. He could hold his breath no longer. He slipped down the last few rungs while Joey's rambling continued. He kept his foot on the bottom step and extended his head toward the back of Joey's neck.

"Why would Hank be mad at you, Joey?"

The sound of Hank's hissing voice burned like a trail of fire down Joey's spine. Joey's paste-white face froze with his mouth open though no sound but a faint whimper came from it.

Hank slithered from the ladder and placed his hands on Joey's slumped shoulders. He squeezed as hard as he could.

"What 'cha doing, Joey?"

Neither Joey's expression nor position changed. Hank seized his shoulders and spun his frozen body to face him. His words spewed out like machine gun fire.

Finally, Joey collapsed in a whimper. Remorse filled his whispered response.

"I didn't wanna do it. Mr. Skelly made me." Tears flooded his eyes and coursed down his dirty face, leaving glistening streams that looks like snail slime. "It was the only way we could gets our new still. Can't make no 'shine without a still and can't make no money without 'shine."

Joey wiped his face with his sleeve. He watched Hank's face contort and hoped he could talk or cry his way out of this mess.

"I didn't know what to do. We was outta time. Mr. Skelly gave me money for all the parts in exchange for only one thing."

Hank was both appalled and proud of what he heard. What surprised him the most was the fact that Joey did this on his own. His angry face softened as his partner rambled on with his confession.

Joey began to sob. "But I lost it. I knew I had it there in the shed." He pointed to his friend. "You saw it too. Thought it was the red dye. Then I couldn't find it. It jus' disappeared. I saw a bottle away in the back, layin' on the groun', thought for sure I found it, but it wasn't it . . . only arsenic, not the . . ."

"Cyanide," Hank finished Joey's sentence while proudly displaying the missing brown bottle.

Joey's face lit with excitement. "Where'd you find it?" His question bounced around the room.

"Who is up there?" Lyla demanded.

Joey once again froze, though the over-bearing tone in Lyla's voice caused Hank to spring into action. Still on his perch on the bottom run on the ladder, Hank swung his legs and kicked open the trap door, snapping it off one of its hinges. His feet then connected with Lyla's head sending her body to the floor with a loud thud. His momentum caused his feet to hit a swinging light fixture. Its bulb burst scattering glass over the floor. Hank struggled to pull his body back through the opening.

"Now what, Hank?" Joey's desperate whisper filled the dark space.

"Shhh. Listen." He waved his hand in the air. "Shut off that light!" They crouched in silent darkness and waited.

Lyla awoke, finding herself lying on the floor, arms and legs entangled. Gingerly touching the side of her head, she felt a growing lump near her temple. Though dizzy from the blow that had knocked her out, she managed to stand upright. Her hands moved through the darkness searching for the light cord. She huffed in disgust when, after pulling it, the light didn't go on.

"Get me a flashlight!"

She repeatedly screamed until Mickey heard her. He struggled to reach his knees. He wanted to choke her to silence. His head pounded and her incessant rant jumbled his thoughts. Mickey groaned.

"Mickey! Didn't you just change this?" she nagged.

Mickey staggered down the hall toward the ballroom. Fixated on rage and frustration, he ransacked his bar shelves until he found another flashlight. He tottered toward the cloakroom swinging the flashlight, covered in sweat.

Lyla fumbled through the dark room muttering obscenities about incompetence. She complained about Mickey, Johnny, and had an especially lengthy fit about Chester. She shuffled her feet across the floor toward the back wall while she finished her tense solo conversation. She heard Mickey's clumsy approach before she saw his flashlight beam.

Mickey was breathless and still lightheaded when he entered the room. "I forgot where I put the other one. I had one but I dropped it when . . ."

"Just give me the damned thing! I don't want excuses. I just need to see!"

Mickey brought up the flashlight, its beam illuminating her face. She painfully flinched from the blinding light. He smirked.

"What are you doing?" she angrily screamed, grabbing the flashlight.

She stumbled backwards, causing the flashlight to fall out of her hand. It hit the floor, and went out.

In the darkness her screech chilled the air. "Now, look what you've done! I can't see a thing. Get another light, Mickey!"

"But Miss Lyla, I only had two and they're both . . . busted." His pathetic tone sounded defeat.

"What?" her tone reached an octave higher. "Then go get another one!"

Mickey rolled over in his mind where he could find a third flashlight. Lyla's continued ranting grated. He hated it when she chided him like he was a misbehaving schoolboy. His head pounded. He felt faint. He tried to concentrate, but couldn't.

He snapped. He clenched his fist and lashed out in the dark. The blow knocked her to the floor.

"Miss Lyla!" Mickey gasped, suddenly alert. "Oh my God!"

Garbled sounds spilled from her lips. Then a shrill howl pierced the air. Lyla clasped both hands around her left leg. She felt her dress become moist. Waves of queasiness raced through her. Her fingers touched a protruding bone.

Mickey asked in a hesitant whisper, "Miss Lyla? Are you all right?" He held his breath awaiting a reply.

"Oh my God, Mickey!" Her strained voice neared panic. "My leg's broke!"

Mickey gasped, filled with regret.

"I can't move. Turn on the light!"

"But . . . I can't. The flashlig . . ."

"Don't talk. Just listen!" If he were closer, she would have punched him. She gritted her teeth and hissed, "Go to my office. Under my desk . . . on the floor is another flashlight. Grab it and bring it back." Her tone softened slightly, "Hurry, Mickey. I'm bleeding."

Hank and Joey sat in the darkness above Lyla and listened to Mickey's voice flood with irritation. A jingle of keys and shuffling feet seemed distant. He heard Lyla shout orders, the sound of a soft thud, and then all fell silent, as silent as Paul's dead body laying a few feet from them.

Chester covered his mouth in the hidden closet. He strained to hear. The sudden silence baffled him though he remained.

"Did you do what you came for?" Hank whispered to Joey.

"Huh?"

"Did you switch out all of the blaze?"

"Yep."

"Then let's get out of here before they find us."

The men scampered up the ladder. Hank climbed first with Joey close behind. When they got to the top, the roof hatch was closed. Hank pushed on it, but it would not open.

"It's stuck, Hank. Push harder."

Irritated with the way this night was going, Hank snapped again at Joey. "I'm pushing as hard as I can. I think it's locked."

"How could it be locked? Didn't you come that way?"

Frustrated, he pushed with both hands, stepped up one rung closer, and then tried to push with his back. He pounded on the wood until the echo seemed deafening. Tracing the edges with his fingers, he searched for a hidden lock or spring, anything that would release but found nothing.

A loud crack reverberated throughout the small shaft. The flawed hinge gave way, releasing the weight of the trap door. It crashed to the cloakroom floor below. Its impact rattled their ladder.

Sweat covered his face and palms. Again they heard voices from below. This time louder, closer. He was certain one was Lyla.

"Hank! We gotta get out of here!"

"I'm trying!"

Near panic, Hank began to use his whole body to force the door open. Though he pushed with his head, shoulders, back and arms, it would not yield.

The voices below rose and fell in pitch. It was difficult to tell the number, but at least one male and one was female. Occasionally a beam of light would shine up the ladder nearly reaching Joey's shoulders. There was little doubt that whoever was below could see Joey's feet, and it was only a matter of time before the two met them—either in person or by their bullet.

Joey's burst of terror propelled him past Hank. The blaze in the bag slung over his shoulder nearly knocked Hank from the ladder. Joey's hands met the wood with brute force. Yet the hatch remained closed. Joey's hands flailed. He lost his balance and nearly fell twice. Hank joined in his effort and suddenly without warning the door sprang open.

Their entangled bodies burst through the gap. They heard the sound of a gunshot and felt the rush of air from the bullet's near miss.

Joey threw the bag of bottles to the ground, grasped the pole, and slid toward the fire escape. As Hank's hands wrapped around the metal pipe, the shaft door snapped shut behind him.

The men scrambled down the metal fire escape stairs with a loud clamor thinking only of their escape. Once on the ground, they scattered, each to his own car. Even their flight on wheels took different routes. The bag that once held Lyla's bottles lay wet and torn in the alley. Glass, wax, and raspberry blaze littered the ground.

Mickey sprinted down the hall into the ballroom. He jumped over the bar his black heels dragging across its polished surface. He plunged a bar towel into the glacial water and filled it with as many ice chunks as he could find, and then snatched a second dry towel.

He raced around the end of the bar and tripped. His wet rag slapped his cheeks as the frozen chunks skirted across the floor. When he pulled the towel from his face, he found his nose pressed against a wet shoe. The cackle of mockery startled him.

"Have a nice trip?" the voice taunted through the glowing embers of his cigarette.

Mickey chased the skating ice around his knees. The laughter continued. He closed his fist around the largest piece and hurled it at his target.

The man dodged the projectile. "Got any more?"

Mickey stood with his hand positioned for a second catapult. He recognized the man by his outdated bowler. "What are you doing in here?"

"I came for a drink."

"You were told never to come here again." Mickey forced the strain from his voice and lowered his pitch. "And besides," his eyes narrowed, "we're closed."

"Nope, the door's wide open." He lit a second cigarette with the butt of his first. "Didn't even have to say the password."

Mickey got up, grabbed the man's collar and pulled him from the stool. The man laughed at his futile attempt.

"So you're gonna throw me out . . . without the big guy?"

His cackle taunted Mickey. Impulsively Mickey threw a punch. A distinct loud crack left no mistake. Mickey watched the blood gush from the man's broken nose.

Skelly snatched the wet towel from Mickey's hands and wiped his face. Smoke curled up from the floor where his just-lit cigarette had landed. Skelly crushed it with his heel.

"Christ's sake. I just wanted a drink!" came his muffled response.

"It's long past hours. You know this. What the hell are you doing here?" His hurried, jumbled words caused delay. He felt nervous and needed to return to Lyla with her flashlight, and this idiot kept him from it.

With rising annoyance, Mickey shoved Skelly and shouted, "Get out of here!"

Skelly staggered with his first step but quickly regained his balance. He pulled the cloth from his face and threw it at Mickey. Deep red blotches covered the bartender's white shirt and speckled his cheek.

Mickey pointed toward the door, "I said get out!'

"I'm going . . . I'm going," Skelly stammered as he disappeared from the ballroom.

Mickey hurried to reclaim the melting ice. He kicked the bloody bar towel across the floor and pulled a third one from a shelf. He heard a loud bang and spun toward the door expecting to see his uninvited guest reappearing.

No one was there. Dismissing it as an echo, he finished gathering his makeshift compress and ran down the hall to Lyla's dressing room.

He fumbled with the keys at her door. "C'mon . . . c'mon. One of these has to open it." He tried several until one worked.

A sense of reverence filled him when he entered her room. Although invited to enter several times, this was the first without a guard. This room whispered of secret deals and broken laws. Many hushed meetings were held behind this locked door.

His mind wandered to the keys. It was a curious bunch—two silver ones, three gold, one rusty brown, and one of tiny silver. He held the small key close to his eyes. A crooked smile covered his face.

"What are you doing, Mickey?" he chastised himself. "Get her flashlight."

Lyla's oversized chair was nestled in the center of her desk. He forced it to the side while he dropped to his knees. "It's supposed to be under her desk," he mumbled to himself. With his face pressed against the wool rug, he shoved his arm under the right side drawers. He swept the underside, hand skimming the carpet, but felt nothing.

"Must be over here," he whispered as he shimmied to the left side drawers. Again, he fumbled for the flashlight. He felt its metal base and pulled it to him. Thinking about the other two broken ones, he flipped the switch to be certain it worked. The lens remained dark.

"Ah, come on!" he yelled in frustration. He slammed the side of the flashlight against the center drawer of Lyla's desk to no avail. "Come on!"

Guilt from his lengthy delay caused him to sweat heavily. He fumbled with the switch multiple times. He shook the flashlight one last time, screaming obscenities at it. Finally the batteries and circuit connected. The bulb, dim at first, slowly became brighter.

Thrilled that it worked he abruptly sat up and slammed his head against the underside of Lyla's desk drawer. Wincing in pain, he noticed the light illuminated a keyhole in the backside of the center drawer. With his head pounding and his shirt soaked with sweat, he just sat there staring at the keyhole.

Suddenly the image of that odd little silver key popped into his head. It would open the lock! His fingers fumbled in his pocket until they found it.

He inserted the key into the escutcheon and turned it. The lock snapped open. A single sheet of paper rolled up document style and wrapped with a red thread dropped to the floor. Beside it also fell a black box.

Overwhelming curiosity seized Mickey's attention. He forgot about Lyla. He forgot she was bleeding. He wanted to read the note.

He slid the thread from the paper and began to unroll it. A shot rang out in the distance. "Oh, my God! Lyla! What the hell am I doing?" He struggled to replace the string around the paper. His wet hand trembled. He shoved the two items back into their furtive space and locked it.

He slid from under Lyla's desk clutching her flashlight. He did not bother to close her door. He had been gone too long. Lyla needed him and he had forgotten about her. He ran to the cloakroom with the flashlight in his hand unaware that the red thread wound through his fingers.

Sarah's hands trembled, making it difficult to turn the doorknob, but anger goaded her on. Once inside she slipped off her heels and ran up the double flight of stairs. When she arrived at the top, the door was open wide. She heard two men arguing from the dimly lit ballroom. Certain neither voice was Chester's she tiptoed down the opposite hall and backed into what she thought was a dark closet. She slipped on the floor and fell onto Lyla.

"Mickey, what the hell are you doing? Give me the flashlight. I want it now!"

Sarah, paralyzed with fear, did not respond. She took one step backwards and felt something hard, cold, and metal under her bare foot. She knelt to pick it up thinking it must be the flashlight of Lyla's incessant rant, but it was a pistol.

"I'm not playing games, Mickey. This isn't funny. Give me the light!" She struggled to stand. Her head hurt. "The light, now!"

Lyla's dress and shoes were soaked in her own blood making it difficult to maneuver. The thought of the protruding bone made her nauseated. The room spun.

"I said, give me that damned flashlight, Mickey!"

Lyla's hand lashed out. Sarah froze at the contact. The pistol fired.

Sarah raced down the long staircase and out the speakeasy. The sound of her feet added to her angst. She ran to her car, shoeless and horrified, and fumbled with the door handle unable to open it. She screamed until her hands obeyed. Once in the car she sped toward home.

Chester could only imagine what was occurring scarcely ten feet from his hiding place. He placed his ear against the door, held his breath and listened. He lifted his hand to wipe the sweat from his brow when he heard a loud crack. Jammed in the tight quarters, his elbow rattled some glass beside him. Without warning a bottle smashed at his feet. He covered his mouth to silence himself. He rolled his eyes in the dark as if their movement would aid in his hearing, though he heard no sound.

Lyla had barely managed to stand upright when the bullet whizzed past her head. Unable to sustain her weight on one leg, she collapsed onto the fallen trap door. Wedged in a fixed position, the broken latch pierced her lung. Immediately, she gasped from the pain. Warm blood gushed from her wound.

Overcome with need to flee after the sudden silence, Chester popped the door open. He gasped at the outline of Lyla's body. Between the foul odor of his shoes soaked with the hired man's moonshine and Lyla's body, he covered his mouth to suppress nausea.

Several feet separated them, yet Chester refused to move toward her. With his eyesight well adjusted to the darkness, he saw the flashlight lying on the floor a few inches from her hand. He went to pick it up and shook it. It didn't light up. He tapped it against his hand and was startled by the sudden brightness of the beam.

Chester knelt beside Lyla and placed his hand on her chest. Its rise and fall was shallow.

"Lyla," he whispered. "Can you hear me?" She remained unresponsive.

Chester looked around the room. Only he and Lyla remained. He replayed all he had heard and tried to make sense of it. Their argument was short and no more heated than any other time that Lyla chose to chastise an employee. He didn't know Mickey well, but his impression of their relationship was one of trust. He shook his head at his questions.

Again, he leaned into Lyla. "Why did Mickey do this to you?" He tapped the side of her cheek, yet she refused to respond. "Lyla, can you hear me?" he pleaded.

Chester was not a religious man, but he muttered a prayer for Lyla. He pushed the missing ten dollars from his thoughts. He only felt concern for his employer. After all, without her money Chester would not enjoy his current financial position.

He glanced around the growing pool of blood and recoiled before it touched his shoes. "Lyla . . ." He patted her face. "Please wake up."

Chester placed his hand behind her head and brushed her red hair from her eyes. He watched as her eyes fluttered. Filled with hope, he spoke in his normal voice, "She's awake! Lyla, can you hear me?"

Her neck and arms began to twitch. Her eyes snapped open and closed. Her red lips parted and trembled, but no words came.

Chester spoke softly to her. "Be still, Lyla. Don't try to speak. Save your strength. Help is coming." His voice quivered as he spoke.

Again, he lifted his eyes in prayer. It was then he noticed the hole in the ceiling. The flashlight's beam was focused on a partially lowered ladder. He strained his eyes to see and moved his hand from Lyla's head. He stared at his blood-soaked palm in disbelief. When his eyes returned to Lyla's face, he saw that her now unseeing eyes were fixed on him. A wide stream of blood trickled from the corner of her mouth. He stood up in a panic.

Valetta rubbed her twisted ankle. She struggled to stand and finally decided to pull herself up using the object that tripped her. It was warm and soft to the touch. She screamed at the thought of a large dead animal. Johnny moaned.

"Johnny!" Her voice was strained. "Are you okay?"

He answered her with a series of grunts. Slowly he pulled his sore body into a sitting position.

Valetta was more impatient than concerned. Again, she repeated her question. "Are you okay?" Realizing the answer was not coming soon, she redirected her thoughts. "What happened?" she asked softly, trying to mask her irritation.

Johnny rubbed the back of his head. He shook his head and shrugged his shoulders. His fist squeezed the coins.

"I found some money on the sidewalk." His words were slow and deliberate. "I . . . I guess I kicked them or something." He opened his hand to be sure he was remembering correctly. "I bent down to pick them up, and someone hit me over the head." His eyes accused Valetta.

Immediately, she was enraged. She knew that look. It came too often.

She shrieked, "Don't look at me! I had my own problems tonight." She eyed him suspiciously. "But I guess you don't care about that!"

Realizing that she was supposed to wait for him in her dressing room, he became irritated. His eyes narrowed.

"Why are you out here?" He hesitated for only a moment and added, "Weren't you to wait for me inside?"

Valetta knew Johnny well. For the most part, he had a calm personality. Only if provoked or confronted with a demonstration of her independence did he display anything different. She smirked in the darkness. She knew how to handle him.

"Baby." She stroked his shoulder. "You know how impatient I get." She moved her fingers to twirl his thick black hair. "After the night I had, I just needed some air. I waited for you, but you never came." She lowered her eyes. "I had no idea you had been assaulted or I wouldn't have left."

"Left?"

"That's what I have been trying to tell you. I started to walk home alone, but . . ." she looked in all directions and moved close to his ear, ". . . someone followed me."

Protectively Johnny jumped to his feet. "Where is he?"

"There were two of them. They had my shoes."

"What? Your shoes?" He slid back to the sidewalk and rubbed his head.

Valetta spilled each detail of her walk home. She loved the drama and built it to a mounting climax. ". . . and that's when I found you." Proud of her tale with a few extra details she waited for his response. When none came, she was disappointed. "Johnny? Are you okay?"

His head, slumped over, nearly touched the sidewalk. He tried to recall the events. Suddenly he remembered the sound of the muffled pop that came from inside the speakeasy. He jumped to his feet and ran toward the staircase yelling, "Lyla!"

Johnny took the speakeasy stairs three at a time. His sweaty palms slid across the walls of the second set of stairs. When he reached the top, he burst through the half-opened door. He yelled Lyla's name though no response came.

Valetta yelled from the bottom, "Wait for me!" She knew he replied but could not hear what he said— something about looking this way. Disgusted, exhausted, and flat out irritated she shuffled her feet and kicked a pair of women's shoes.

As she began to hobble up the long staircase, she sighed at the sight of her dress, her missing and torn stockings, sore ankle, and barefoot appearance. Again, she sighed. She loved those shoes.

It was an eerie feeling to be inside the speakeasy this late at night. She was usually snuggled in her bed by now after spending the walk home warding off Johnny's advances.

Valetta's pink-lacquered fingertips caressed the password door and pushed it open without hindrance. She walked quietly down the hall toward the cloakroom. A rising anxiety kept her voice from calling Johnny's name. When she came to the cloakroom, she found the door ajar. A dim beam of light lit the back wall.

Chester listened to the sound of footsteps as they advanced. He heard Johnny's voice shout Lyla's name. In a panic he jumped up, grabbed the bottom rung of the suspended ladder and pulled himself up. His feet disappeared out of sight just as Valetta entered the cloakroom.

He held his breath as he fumbled up each rung. His thoughts raced. Why did he leave? He didn't do anything. He just wanted to talk to Lyla. He wanted to ask why she shorted him ten dollars. Why would she do that?

He remembered her rant. His body raged with anger. He had done nothing wrong. It was Hank's fault that he didn't have her special bottle, not his. Was that why she shorted him?

Chester's climb was halted when his head hit the flat surface of the trap door. Running his hand over it, he found a seam and traced it with a finger. It felt small, yet big enough to push through.

He heard another loud sound followed by a woman's scream. Then he heard the sound of multiple feet shuffling below him. Another man's voice joined that of Johnny's. Their tone rose and cadence quickened. He used that distraction to his advantage and pushed gently against the trap door, opening it.

The cool night air was a welcome change from that of the stifling shaft. He crept out of the opening and stood on the roof. In the distance he saw a tall man limping away in the opposite direction. He strained his eyes to focus but lost sight of him in the growing darkness. The hatch swung shut muffling the shouts below.

When Valetta stepped inside, her nostrils were assailed with an odd smell that permeated the cloakroom. It smelled damp, slightly musky or burnt, and mingled with the unmistakable fragrance of the hired man's liquor. It made Valetta queasy. She fumbled for the light cord.

Her bare foot stepped in a pool of goo. She suppressed a scream. She detested wet, slimy things. She took one step forward but refused to place her weight on the soft object beneath her foot. She whimpered as she shivered remembering a similar feeling on the sidewalk earlier that evening. She whispered Johnny's name.

Johnny ran into the ballroom. Puddles of water mixed with chunks of ice littered the floor. He slipped twice and fell. His arm rested on a bloody towel. He stood in a panic, but for reasons unknown he felt uncomfortable shouting Lyla's name again.

He held his breath and pressed his body against the wall. With his arms outstretched he slithered around the doorframe and into the hall. A light from Lyla's open door lit the corridor. Each step moved him closer. Her dressing room was quiet.

Valetta struggled to find the light cord. She forced herself forward a step and cringed at the sticky substance she encountered beneath one foot. A shiver ran down her back, leaving her legs weak and unstable.

Her second step carried her imagination to horrifying places. The slimy substance soaking her right foot's stocking felt soft and squishy.

Fighting to hold back the grisly images inspired by her imagination, she forced herself to concentrate on finding the light cord—it had to be there somewhere. At last she found it and pulled. Nothing happened. She wrapped it around her fingers and pulled again; still no response. She yanked on the line one last time. It broke.

She lost her balance and toppled onto the unseen thing she had tried to avoid.

A soft moan cut off Valetta's scream. Not a normal ouch that hurt moan, but a despondent sigh like spent expelled air from deep within, or worse . . . from the beyond.

She reacted in blind fear as anyone would. She jumped from the body she had touched and rolled toward the door. A hard object jabbed her ribs. She reached over to grab it. It was a pistol.

Her panic-inspired imagination drove her over the edge. She thought she saw the unmoving body begin to rise from the floor. An unseen force tossed its clothing. When the body was fully erect, it towered three feet above her. It began to move toward her. Each step became deliberate. Its hands reached out in front of its body as if taunting her. It seemed to call her name.

Valetta opened her mouth to scream, but nothing came out. Terror had paralyzed her voice. The room was supernaturally alive with movement. Unseen coins jingled somewhere in the back. Ice cubes fell into unseen glasses. The sound of soft fabric swished past her ear. Hot fire brushed her face.

In a split second the image before her morphed into a ball of scarves. It spun around her daring her to move. Her fist closed tight around the Derringer's butt. She slid her index finger over its trigger.

The figure erupted into flame and advanced. Valetta fired. Abruptly the room fell silent. Nothing moved. Nothing fell. Only the smoldering flashlight beam flickered.

Valetta's nostrils burned from the acrid odor of spent gunpowder. Her brain demanded her hands cover her face, but instead they collapsed at her sides.

Johnny stood silently outside of Lyla's open office door. He jumped when he heard the sound of a hard thud. Fear of the unknown stopped him in mid motion. He wished for a gun. Lyla had a gun; in fact, she had two—one in her desk and one in her garter. How could he get his hands on either of them? Lyla was missing and someone was in her office.

He placed his hand on the oak door and drew in a deep breath. Poised for a fight he took one step into the empty room and listened. It was silent. He relaxed his shoulders and took another step.

His body jumped at the sound of a gunshot. He spun and ran toward it. With each stride Johnny felt as if he moved backwards. The shot's report reverberated inside his head. His rapid pace struggled to match his heart rate. He pleaded for Valetta's safety, for Lyla's safety, and for this nightmare to end.

The sight of the cloakroom gave him little comfort. He heard Valetta's murmurs long before he reached the door. His feet slid past the opening as he tried to stop, desperately grabbing at the oak frame to slow his motion.

The sound of hurried footsteps made Johnny turn. A dim light bounced off the polished floor as it moved closer to him. Mickey appeared breathless, bloody, and wet, carrying a useless flashlight.

"What happened?" was all Johnny could manage to say.

Mickey pounded Lyla's flashlight once again. It briefly lit, then went dark.

Johnny spat at Mickey in frustration, "Get a light bulb—something! We have to see what's going on here!"

Mickey sighed in response, annoyed that it was not his idea. He disappeared around the corner.

Johnny patted Valetta's cheek. "Talk to me, Lettie. Please talk to me."

A strong smell of gunpowder lingered, underscoring that Valetta was the cause. Johnny pried the pistol from her grip. He whispered softly in her ear, but her incessant ramble continued. He propped her body against the doorframe.

He tried to stand and slipped on the wet floor. He bent down and swirled his fingertips through the dampness and brought his fingers to his nose. It was blood. He set Valetta down and then traced his way through the blood trail. His first physical contact was with the fingertips of the body. He moved his hand up the body's hand to its wrist, and held his breath. Although the room was coal black, he closed his eyes, feeling for a pulse. He felt nothing.

He knew it was Lyla though his heart hollered, "NO!" He moved his hand to her neck, hoping to find a pulse there. But, it was useless. She was gone, shot by Valetta.

Mickey arrived with a light bulb and short ladder. In a moment piercing light illuminated the room. Both men shielded their eyes. Only Valetta remained inert.

They saw Lyla's body lying on her back, surrounded by a pool of blood. Wet footprints marred the floor and fanned out, into a broad pattern. Valetta's dress soaked in Lyla's blood, had drawn waves of red swirls across the floor until settling at her hemline. Johnny searched for a pulse one final time.

"Is . . . she?" Mickey stammered.

"Dead." Johnny hung his head.

"What are we gonna do now, Johnny?"

"We can't tell anybody. We've got to find out what happened. We can't go to the police. We can't tell anyone she's dea . . ." He forced the lump from his throat. "She's gone. We have to put our heads together to protect Valetta."

"It was an accident!" Mickey spoke with certainty.

"I know that! Of course she didn't do it on purpose. But we can't change what happened." Johnny lowered his voice, "I didn't even know she could shoot a gun."

Mickey gulped. There was a lot about Valetta that he didn't know, but he sure liked what he saw. He frowned at his thoughts and tried to recover.

"Do you think we should bury her somewhere?"

"I don't know how we could get her out of here without someone seeing us."

Both men stared at Lyla's gory corpse, the shinbone that protruded through her skin, the mass of blood that had pooled on the floor, her splintered lower jaw. A thin trail of blood spilled from its corner. Lyla's eyes were frozen in horror.

Johnny turned his face from her. Guilt, anguish, and frustration could not match his level of sorrow. His stomach rebelled. He buried his face in his hands.

Annoyingly, Mickey counted silently on his fingers. After the third repetitive motion, he verbalized the options. "Well, we can't bury her. We can't carry her out. We can't leave her here. We can't pretend it didn't happen. And we can't call the police. So what are we going to do with her?" His eyes begged Johnny for an intelligent response.

The sound of Valetta's voice made both men jump. "We have to hide her."

The hiss of Lyla's candle manifested her voice. "So, hide me they did."

Mickey and Johnny picked up Lyla's bloody, broken body and carried her to her dressing room. Only Johnny and Paul knew of the false wall behind the sea of red dresses and Mickey was amazed at the amount of raspberry blaze.

"Wow! Look at the stock pile!"

Johnny chastised Mickey's comment with only a look. He hung his head. "Lyla didn't drink."

"But . . ." Mickey pointed to the bottles. "So why this?"

"Who knows. Insurance policy?"

"Didn't help, did it?" Mickey shrugged and shoved his hands deep into his pocket. He wound a narrow red thread around his fingers. He joined Johnny and stared at the floor.

"Things are not always as they seem!"

As Lyla's final warning echoed through the room, the melted wax began to gurgle. Soon bubbling like molten lava, its rolling red core burned deep within until her anger forced the wax to explode. A frenzied crimson gush splattered the cluster of candles, building with every drop, until it hardened into a smothering veil. Distain garroted their wicks to silence.

45

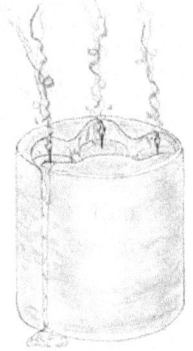

Chandra and Isabell stared at the candle in disbelief. Bits of red wax littered the table, their hands, clothes, and several fragments splattered across the wall. Most of the white tapers before them had been reduced to stubs. Only a few remained with their wicks barely burned, yet all dripped of red wax that smothered their wicks and extinguished their flames.

The women sat in silence for what appeared to be an eternity waiting for another candle to flame to life. Then the faint hint of sunlight crept in the front window and broke the night's spell. Isabell's whisper sliced the stillness.

"I believe all has been spoken. There is no more to be told." Isabell's slow rising from the chair showed her age as she winced from the stiffness of a long night spent sitting in a chair.

Chandra helped her to the front door and down the long staircase. When they opened the oak paneled door at the bottom, the sunrise breathed promise of a new day.

"I'm at a loss for words, Isabell."

"It's been a long night, dear." Isabell patted Chandra's hand. "It's time now for all things to be brought into the light."

Chandra smiled at her double meaning. "I guess we both know what my next step should be."

Isabell's gray eyes revealed she was deep in thought. This task had been exhausting, and her face confirmed the enormity.

"I should walk you home. You're tired."

"It's been a tough one—hard to listen, difficult to imagine—but, it needed to be told." She smiled at Chandra and touched her palm to her cheek. "The torch has been passed to you, my dear. My part is over. I believe what lies before you may be daunting." She grasped both of Chandra's hands. "Promise me you will not do this alone."

Chandra squeezed her hands and whispered, "I promise."

"It took much courage for all to come forward. Their restless spirits could no longer wait. Lyla would no longer remain hidden. Her story must be finished." Isabell patted Chandra's hand and smiled.

Chandra stood silently, at the threshhold, watching the morning shadows begin to fade as Isabell toddled down the sidewalk. She looked up at the third floor windows and relived her night. A delivery truck rushing to beat the shifting yellow traffic light interrupted her thoughts.

"Hmmm . . . red," she thought. "That color will never seem the same."

She listened to the sound of her feet as they shuffled quietly up the same set of stairs that Valetta had climbed carrying her Number One, that Chester walked up for his pay, that Mickey had skipped to the top on Tuesday evenings, and Johnny rushed to climb when he heard the shot, but especially the stairs that led toward the place of Lyla's death. Chandra swallowed back the growing lump in her throat.

After preparing the coffee pot with her morning beverage, she entered her over-sized bathroom, the only finished room in her apartment. The large floor tile ran at an angle and stopped at her shower's entrance. She turned on the jets and held her hand under the water until it was warm.

She showered and washed her hair in record time. The hot water brought her little comfort. With her hair and body wrapped in towels, she tiptoed to her cell phone. It was 6:40 a.m. The contractor should arrive within the hour so she rushed to dress and prepare for the day. The sputter of the coffee pot interrupted her thoughts. She walked into the kitchen and poured an over-sized cup of coffee and sat at the kitchen table.

Subconsciously, she fingered the multitude of hardened red dots scattered across the surface of her table while she stared at the kitchen wall peppered with red wax. She shuddered at the peculiar image. She lifted her smart phone and snapped a picture. The splattered wax on the wall loosely outlined the shape of a plump woman wearing an ankle-length dress. Chandra dismissed the image as a figment of her imagination, yet her mind saw nothing else at every glance at the wall or her phone.

A series of deliberate knocks on her front door brought her to the present. She jumped to her feet, ran down the long staircase, and opened the door to see the bewildered face of her contractor.

He shook his head, "The electrician is finally coming today with your door bell. I told him he couldn't leave until it was working."

"I'm sorry. Have you been here long?"

"About five minutes." He gathered his hand tools and started up the stairs. "I thought you weren't home."

For the final time the pair discussed the new kitchen layout—cabinets, counter, appliances, doors, trim, and flooring.

Chandra cleared her throat. "I think you were right."

Her contractor turned to her, "Oh?"

"I believe that wall needs to come down after all."

He looked at the kitchen wall splattered with red wax and smiled. "I knew if you thought about it long enough it would make better sense."

"You were right. It will open up the room. It won't feel so," she cleared her throat, "closed in."

"Okay. We should tear it out today then. It's going to be difficult the next few weeks managing without your kitchen."

"Oh, I'm prepared for it." Chandra laughed, "Actually I am looking forward to eating out." She took a few steps back. "I'll get out of your way and let you take that wall down."

He made no remarks of Lyla's waxed outline on the wall as he quickly unpacked his tools. His two employees also prepared for work without words. The first blow of the sledgehammer opened a hole in the image's heart. Chandra hid her face. She could not bear to watch.

The sound of demolition filled her apartment. Bangs, creaks and crashes punctuated the disappearing kitchen wall. It helped to drown her thoughts of the previous evening as she watched the dust particles flutter through the ray of sunlight spilling in the front window.

In a moment all fell silent. After a series of gasps, one worker asked, "What in the world is *that*?"

The men stood still, peering into a hole in the plaster. One worker picked up a sledgehammer to broaden the hole.

The contractor shouted, "Hold up!" He waved the other men out of the way. "Let me see."

After peering into the opening, he turned toward Chandra. "Chandra! You need to see this." Chandra looked into the opening and saw a human skeleton. She immediately knew who it was.

Somehow staring at Lyla's skeleton affected her differently than she expected. She had come to know this woman as a feisty, vibrant, strong-willed, self-made lady and seeing her reduced to dust-covered bones moved her to tears.

She had promised Isabell not to do this alone. She kept her word. In a struggle between secrecy and the desire to share her bizarre evening, she struggled to regain control. The men watched her curiously.

Finally, she forced the words to come, "I need to call the police."

The youngest and most-intrigued of the three spoke first. "Who do you think it is?"

"How should we know?" snapped the second carpenter.

The youngest one moved closer to the opening. "Looks like he's been dead a long time."

"It's a she," Chandra whispered.

"How do you know it's a she?"

Chandra answered, "She's wearing a red dress."

Chandra spoke with such certainty the men did not question the possibility that fragments of fabric were once a dress. The closet's inside corner served as Lyla's prop. A diamond and ruby earring glistened on the fabric of what used to be her lap. Red pumps appeared tossed in the setting. The position of her head left a sense of loving placement.

Finally the contractor spoke, "This gives me the creeps." He turned to Chandra. "We need to call the police."

She knew the woman's identity as well as how she died, but how could she explain? The experts should uncover that information. She stared at her phone. A gentle hand patted her shoulder.

"I'll make the call." His tone was hushed.

She watched the other two men huddle around their boss as he spoke on his cell phone. After a series of hand gestures, stifled words, and a few affirmations, she looked away and knelt on the debris-littered floor at Lyla's feet.

Overwhelmed with sorrow, Chandra felt it wrong for Lyla to spend the past eighty years hidden in a closet. She wondered how the smell of decomposition went unnoticed, how they explained her disappearance, how they handled their guilt, and then the answer came—that was why they came to her.

With many of the interior walls removed prior to her renovation, Chandra insisted that particular kitchen wall remain. She spent the past several weeks trying to convince her contractor. Raised-wood panels covered the backside of the wall, and after the evening's events, Chandra realized they belonged to Lyla's office. The urgency for the many participants to reveal their stories became clear. Without the evening spent with Isabell and allowing the group to clear their conscience that wall would have remained today, and Lyla's body would have remained hidden, unable to rest.

The police department, coroner, and forensic photographer arrived within thirty minutes. It did not take long for a small crowd and two television crews to arrive. A local reporter from *The Salem News* was the only press permitted inside the building.

Chandra watched with interest as the journalists' cameras flashed, recording the removal of Lyla's remains. Much of the discussion centered on her broken shin until the examiner placed the final piece on the stretcher. A sheet covered the skeleton from peering eyes.

"What is this?" The examiner's excitement attracted everyone's attention. He pulled a stained envelope from the floor once covered by Lyla's body. The group of people pushed closer for a better look. Pieces of the paper floated to the floor from the crumbling envelope that held four photographs.

Chandra stood behind one of the officers. Her gasp could not be contained and all turned to look at her.

The chief looked at her curiously, "Do you know this woman?"

She tried to force words from her lips but the words felt like sand in her mouth. After a few stammers she cleared her throat and held out her hand.

"May I see them, please?"

The officer handed her the photographs. In the first Lyla sat behind her office desk. She wore a red hat, bright red lipstick and nail polish, and the bodice of her dress was heavily beaded. An all-knowing smile covered her face, and the sparkle in her eye made Chandra smile.

The second print revealed the interior of the ballroom. Lyla, dressed in red, appeared small in the oversized room. She stood in the doorway with her hand in the air.

The third photograph was somewhat blurred though the bar of the speakeasy was clear. The glasses that hung above sparkled like crystal, yet the man who stood behind it appeared as a smear. It was Mickey. Seated at the bar was a broad-shouldered man. His turned head hid his face. A thin, beautiful woman stood beside him with her gloved hand placed on his shoulder. Her body poised like a star for the camera. It was Valetta standing beside Johnny.

The final picture made Chandra's stare in disbelief. It was a close-up of Lyla's face. Her hair and make-up were finished to perfection. Each facial wrinkle accentuated her playful smirk and wink. Her open palm and puckered red lips mimicked a blown kiss. A thin, red thread lay coiled in her palm.

Chandra swallowed the welling sensation of tears. She understood its meaning. She whispered to the chief as she placed the photographs in his hand.

"These photos are of Anna Lyla Timmons, the owner of this building's speakeasy during Prohibition."

He stammered for a moment. "How . . . do you know her?"

"Oh, I don't really. I have heard stories of this place when it was a speakeasy, full of life, crowds, and laughter . . ." Her thoughts trailed off with her words.

"Is she a relative?"

Chandra laughed, "I wish, but no. I've heard about her, how she started this place, how she only wore red . . ." She looked at the picture of the kiss, "But I've never seen any photographs of her."

The chief looked toward the gurney and pointed. "Do you think that's her?"

"Yes, I do." Chandra responded without hesitation.

"Why do you think that?" asked the reporter while scribbling in his notebook.

"Because of this." Chandra tapped her finger on the close up of Lyla's earring.

She gathered the bag of evidence and placed it near the photograph. The forensic photographer moved in for a closer shot. The reporter quickly followed.

"I believe you're right," chuckled the chief. "Guess it didn't take long to solve this mystery." He turned to the coroner, "Now we just need a cause of death."

Chandra bit her lip forcing silence. She watched the group leave together from the top landing. The chief of police was the last to leave.

"Thank you for your help, Ms. Minch."

"You're welcome."

"Will you be comfortable staying here?"

Somewhat surprised by the question, she chuckled. "Not a problem. This kind of thing doesn't spook me at all." She smiled and added, "Chief?"

"Yes?"

"Will you keep me in the loop? About the cause of death?"

He shook his head and tipped his hat. "I certainly will."

46

With thoughts of her tumultuous night and predicable morning swirling around her, she picked up her cell phone and dialed Brad. With assurance of her decision, her voice was exact.

"Brad?"

"Hey. What's up? Crazy storm, wasn't it?"

"Productive, I'd say." She hesitated at Brad's silent response. "I uncovered a name."

"What?"

"A name . . . for the restaurant."

"Oh, I'm sorry. It's early and I haven't had my coffee. My neurons aren't firing yet."

She disregarded his humor and looked at the time. It was nearly noon. "I'm serious. I found a name." She waited.

"Are you gonna tell me?"

"Before I say it, it's nonnegotiable."

"Oh?"

"Anyway, you'll agree. It is perfect." She felt she had caused him enough anxiety. His coffee pot gurgled in the background. After his final sigh of impatience she whispered, "speakeasy."

"Speakeasy? As in an old time club Speakeasy?"

"Yes. And I know exactly how I want the bar to look."

"Since when did you become a designer?"

She ignored his sarcasm. "Just listen; it will be perfect!"

Hours prior to the grand opening of speakeasy, Chandra and Brad rushed to finish the busy work. They reminisced about Brad convincing Chandra to look at the property and laughed together.

Chandra began to recant her first tour of 378 East State Street in Salem, Ohio. . . .

The real estate agent, Kathy Hendricks, flipped on the lights, one after and another. When the décor sprung to life, Chandra gasped. A wall of stone on the left elevated a fountain area. A fish and crane burst into action with the final switch. Water spouted into two kidney-shaped pools. Hanging on the wall above were two more fountains that joined the ballet. The blended sound of falling water was artful.

Their heels clicked on the flagstone as they walked into the garden shed. Kathy turned on the single light bulb by a tug on the dangling string.

"Typical light you'd find in a shed, don't you think?"

Chandra smiled; no need for a verbal reply. Her face showed it all.

They continued through the garden area graced with a flagstone patio, several birdhouses sat on top of weathered porch posts, iron garden fences at the beginning and the end complete with their own gates, cocoa shells on the floor for mulch, and even the ceiling tiles were painted sky blue. Trees that had once been living canopied the room with wired leaves.

"In the spring and summer," Kathy explained, "the trees had green leaves wired to their branches which became orange, yellow and red in the autumn. But the winter," she sighed with her eyes wide, "that was enchanting. The owner covered the fountains with what appeared to be snow and ice. Quilt batting lined each tree branch that gave the appearance of fresh snow. Music echoed the emotions built in this place. It was a fun garden store. Everyone misses it."

They continued through the antique iron gate that ended the garden and walked onto the veranda. The original wooden floors gleamed with over one hundred years of wear and imperfections. A wide wooden staircase led to the second floor, but their tour continued into a different part of the building; the second floor would have to wait.

After the tour of the veranda, they entered a room mimicking the front parlor of a stately house. The wool carpet boasted of mauve and purple irises centered within a greenery border, antique fireplace, and bookshelves. The ceiling, billowed in floral fabric and gathered in the center by a satin rosette, enhanced the fabric swags that lined the perimeter. The etched light fixtures lit the four corners while the chandelier that dripped from the rosette displayed a choice of electric or candlelight. Its centered mouth-blown vase's near invisible suspension accented its roses and ivy as art.

They exited through a back door and walked down another flagstone path. Multiple building facades, each painted a different color, served as additional window displays. Brass house numbers attached to the doors or mailboxes added to the alley ambiance. The path led them to the outside back entrance. A large warehouse dock door opened into the back alley and served as a second entrance adjacent to one of the city's public parking areas.

The non-public area had two stockrooms; one large enough for a commercial kitchen with wide access to the basement, the other smaller in size but large enough for food storage. Kathy gave Chandra a folder outlining specifications for changing this once retail shop into a restaurant. Chandra slid it under her arm.

They continued to the second floor. Kathy quickly pointed out the size to be a perfect studio or an additional retail shop. It had a powder room as well as its own storage room. The front over-sized windows faced East State Street. Cars moved quickly and foot traffic was heavy. Again, Chandra smiled.

To the left of the front street-level door was an antique wooden door that led to the third floor. The door opened easily, but its hinges creaked from little use. After climbing seventeen steps, they stood on a small landing. The sign on the glass door, *Salem Photography*, showed the alternative entrance to the second floor studio.

Kathy tapped on the glass, "This would be useful for off-hour access to the studio."

After eighteen more steps, they walked into the third-floor doorway. Kathy turned to Chandra before they continued their tour.

"Now, I have to warn you. This is rough. No one has done anything up here for at least forty years. It used to be an apartment. You'll see what is left of it. Most of the partitions and suspended ceiling have been removed."

They walked into the main room. Pieces of the ceiling littered the floor. Faded wallpaper hung in strips. A claw-foot cast iron tub sat in the middle of the room. Scattered newspaper lay in party-favor fashion as torn bits of *The Salem News* stared back at Chandra.

"Wow! You weren't kidding. This floor is a wreck!"

Kathy thumbed through her folder. "Now the previous owner replaced the roof four years ago. I know it looks bad, but it's all old damage. They also have signed a guarantee which would protect you if something unforeseen shows its ugly face."

"What about turning it into an apartment?"

"I gathered all of the information you would need to make an educated decision. It is in that folder." She pointed to the one under Chandra's arm.

Chandra inspected the papers. Her eyes scanned the information, but her mind was too excited to focus.

"As you can see," Kathy continued. "This third floor spans two buildings. As it stands right now, you share this floor with your neighbor. You may choose to either divide it or purchase it from them. But, if you purchase it, along comes all of the roof responsibility."

"I understand." Chandra said. Her busy mind mapped out the floor plans for her apartment.

Brad Cotton, a chef friend of Chandra's, emailed the listing to her. He admired this building ever since the Olde English Garden Company opened. Often in years past, he enjoyed his lunch in the garden surrounded by its peaceful atmosphere. Although Brad knew he could not afford this project on his own, he hoped with Chandra's help it could become a reality. When the garden shop closed, and a realtor posted a "For Sale" sign in the window, Brad contacted Chandra immediately. He was thrilled when she made plans to drive from Pittsburgh the following weekend.

Chandra's emotions enveloped her as she stood in the center of the room. She knew it could work. As long as she had her computer, she could work from home. She liked the idea of a renter for the studio on the second floor and a restaurant on the main floor. Her thoughts returned to Kathy in mid conversation.

". . . list of other properties . . ."

Chandra cut her off, "I don't think that will be necessary. I feel strangely centered with this one." She walked over to a mass of old doors stacked neatly in a corner.

They spun to greet the sound of shuffling feet. An elderly woman smiled at their reaction. Without asking, the answer came.

"Those doors are from this building. This used to be an old speakeasy during prohibition." Chandra's mouth hung open.

The woman pointed to the oversized baseboard. "See how the baseboard goes up here," her finger pointed to the opposing walls while she continued, "and there? Those were the two stages, one for the band and one for the dancers." She pointed back to the stack of doors. "Those doors were placed anywhere the patrons entered or retrieved their bottle. See, they have bottle holes carved in them. They needed replacement often." She held her hand to her mouth as she whispered, "Because of overuse."

"How cool is that?" Chandra's voice rose. Her mind raced with questions of the old speakeasy that she did not stop to consider her uninvited guest.

The woman continued in a trance-like voice. "Salem actually had many speakeasies. Who knows how many there actually were. Some say five. I don't know. I've only talked to the people from this one."

Chandra paused, deep in thought about Isabell while Brad eyed her curiously. He knew parts of the story, but this was the first time he heard it from the beginning.

Chandra stared at the bar area that used to be the cash wrap area of Olde English Garden Company unaware that her story had ended. She stood lost in thoughts of Lyla, Raspberry Blaze, Valetta, Johnny, Mickey and the others. Her smile was wide.

She remembered the speakeasy photo found under Lyla's body. During the recent restaurant's renovation, they had recreated the speakeasy perfectly. Glasses hung above the polished wood bar just as they had in the 30s. The glass cabinets on the back wall mimicked those before. Chandra even took special care in explaining to the contractor how to make the liquor "disappear" as it did in raids of the past.

The center wall cabinet was lined with clear bottles filled with pink liquid, their tops covered in red wax. The photo of Lyla blowing a kiss holding Mickey's thin red thread sat amidst her simulated blaze. Only one bottle seated to the right of her photo was original. Chandra discovered it in the ceiling above what used to be the cloakroom. The wax was brittle to touch, though not near as toxic as the moonshine inside. She guessed it to be one of the ones switched by Joey and Hank the night of Lyla's accident.

Accident—yes it was. Officer Little, grandson to the original, called Chandra nearly four weeks after the discovery of Lyla's body with the news. He explained that the bullet wound in Lyla's jaw was post mortem. Lyla's cause of death was a puncture wound in her back that pierced her lungs. A small remnant of the hinge lodged in her ribcage left identification difficult but eventually successful. She asked for a copy of the photos after the close of the investigation.

Old crates filled with glasses surrounded large empty jugs. The pendants behind the bar mimicked the originals. Ice filled two large zinc tubs. A stack of Prohibition tokens filled a slender canister and vintage towels hung from brass rods. The only thing missing behind the bar was Mickey.

Although the grand opening would not include The Pussycats, the barmaids were dressed in similar, yet more modest Prohibition attire. Chandra smiled at their costumes—black skirts with fringe, garters and stockings, striped fitted shirts, and a black, beaded headband finished with a pair of kitten ears.

When the musicians began to practice, Chandra and Brad toasted to the photo of Lyla. Although some of the other players' endings remained a mystery, her story was complete. Anna Lyla Timmons could finally rest, and she could rest at the speakeasy.

With the last settling of the linen tablecloths, Chandra placed a single red candle in the center of each table. A low voltage spotlight accented its color. The speakeasy was finally ready.

A knock came to the front door. Chandra looked at her watch. It read 5:20 p.m.

Chandra yelled, "We open at six."

The knock persisted. Chandra opened the door. It was Isabell.

"Come in, Isabell. How are you?"

Ignoring her question she leaned into Chandra and whispered, "I had another visitor."

"Oh?"

"It was Vinchento."

"Vinchento? I wondered what happened to him. He never finished his story."

"Well, he gave me this." Isabell placed a yellowed newspaper in Chandra's hand. "He wanted you to have it."

"Thank you." She glanced at the headline: "The Stag" Mob Boss Found Dead. August 12, 1933. She read the first few paragraphs with her mouth open.

According to local authorities, mob boss, Vincent Franciasco Sabino, nicknamed "The Stag," was found dead in a warehouse south of Youngstown on Saturday, August 12, 1933, along with his son, Raffaldi Francis Sabino, and four other members of the Sabino crime family. Sources say according to an unnamed eyewitness a red-haired woman dressed in a red hat and dress was seen leaving the scene in a new-model Cadillac of the same color immediately after multiple shots were heard. The police are searching for this mysterious woman and have several leads including a monogrammed handkerchief apparently left as a calling card. All evidence points to a city south of Youngstown where the possible suspect's home and business are located. Wife of The Stag, Maria Rosa Mariucci-Sabino, was questioned and released to grieve her loss, with the only surviving son, Vinchento Mariucci Sabino.

Chandra stopped reading and extended her hand, "Please, Isabell, come in and have a seat. This is amazing!"

She patted her hand. "Thank you, dear, but I really must go. You are sure to have a busy night on your hands." She giggled. "I pray mine is just the opposite."

Chandra held up the newspaper. "Perhaps this is the final piece. Maybe now they will allow you to rest."

"We shall see, my dear. We shall see. Only time will tell."

Isabell walked out of the front door. Chandra smiled at the growing line outside. She left the door unlocked.

"We're ready. Right, gang?" she tossed to the crew.

In unison the staff replied, "Yes!"

Sound of the "eses" filled the room. Chandra dismissed the thought as well as the prickling on the back of her neck. That feeling had been too familiar in the long evening with Isabell and after reading Vinchento's newspaper article, she felt the suggestive notion begin to stir.

She lit the last of the table's red candles and watched the surly light burn. From behind her a cool breeze wafted the flames. They flickered with a soft glow until suddenly they burned bright orange. Hearing the sound of shuffling feet, she spun around to see who was approaching. It was Mickey.

The End ?

Karen Biery is an artist and writer who has spent the majority of her life in the creative realm. She began her career in retail management with small entrepreneurs, grew through one of America's leading corporations, and ultimately designed her own retail environment Olde English Garden Company in Salem, Ohio. She attended Kent State University for creative writing and studied watercolors under the instruction of Tom McNickle. She blends these skills to design the cover and interior illustrations. She lives in northeast Ohio with her husband, Jeff.